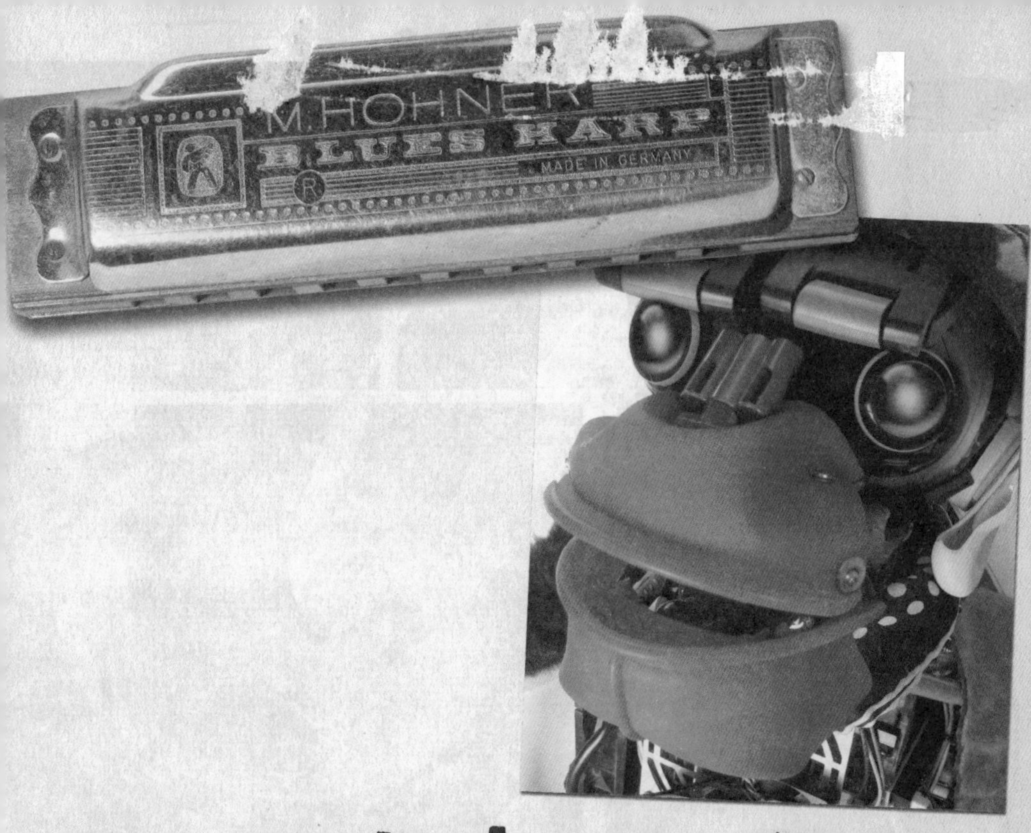

CAPTAIN 'ACE' CRANKSHAW

GUITARIST EXTRAORDINAIRE/ FRETBOARD NINJA

IF FOUND, PLEASE RETURN THIS NOTEBOOK TO:

THE MILL, [illegible] LANE,
GRAVESEND, KENT, ENGLAND,
U.K., PLANET EARTH,
SOLAR SYSTEM

(first right after Alpha Centauri, then
straight on for 4.37 ligh[illegible]

AGE: 14

SKILLS: Guitar – Harmonica [illegible]

NOTABLE ACHIEVEMENTS IN L[illegible]AR:

Owner of Britain's only privately funded space programme

AMBITION :

To play a stadium gig with my band using a
40,000 Watt P.A. system

This is a work of fiction. Names, characters, places and incidents either are the product of the author's imagination or, if real, are used fictitiously. All statements, activities, stunts, descriptions, information and material of any other kind contained herein are included for entertainment purposes only and should not be relied on for accuracy or replicated as they may result in injury. • First published 2010 by Walker Books Ltd, 87 Vauxhall Walk, London SE11 5HJ • 1 2 3 4 5 6 7 8 9 10 • Text and illustrations © 2010 Joshua Mowll • The right of Joshua Mowll to be identified as author and illustrator of this work has been asserted by him in accordance with the Copyright, Designs and Patents Act 1988 • This book has been typeset in Godlike • Printed and bound in China • All rights reserved. No part of this book may be reproduced, transmitted or stored in an information retrieval system in any form or by any means, graphic, electronic or mechanical, including photocopying, taping and recording, without prior written permission from the publisher. • British Library Cataloguing in Publication Data: a catalogue record for this book is available from the British Library • ISBN 978-1-4063-0937-9 • www.walker.co.uk

The GREAT SPACE RACE

BY JOSHUA MOWLL

WALKER BOOKS

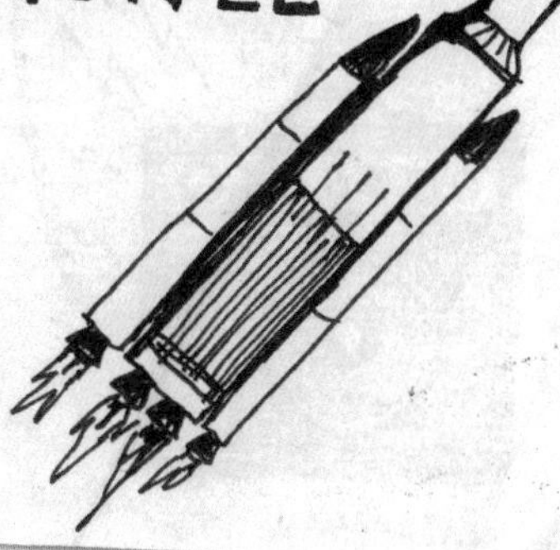

4
UFO TOUR BUS
TOP SPEED — 100,000 X THE SPEED OF LIGHT
'LOBSTER FACE'
ALIEN ROCK GOD
8 EYES
ENORMOUS HEAD
LOBSTER CLAWS
SHADES
OVERSIZED GENETICALLY ENHANCED LEFT ARM WITH 5 HANDS
INTERGALACTIC ROCK SALUTE
PREPARE TO ROCK EARTHLINGS
BLUE BEARD
• THE FASTEST GUITARIST IN THE GALAXY
• CAN PLAY 5 SOLOS AT THE SAME TIME
• ONE DAY ALL ROCK STARS WILL LOOK LIKE THIS*
• GLOWING 5 NECK 30-STRING 'LES PAUL' STYLE GUITAR
THE LOUDEST AMPLIFIER IN THE GALAXY
20 MEGAWATTS
SMELLY CLAW FEET
* DAD SAYS SOME OF THEM LOOK LIKE THIS ALREADY

It's good to have a plan. It doesn't have to be a secret one like mine, but take it from me – always have a plan. Especially when everything is going wrong ... really, severely, wrong, wrong, wrong. Or if you have a dad like mine.

The Secret Plan had first begun to form when Dad received the letter summoning him to court for non-payment of bills. My sister had reckoned if the worst came to the worst we could be booted out of our house (an old water mill) for good. Seriously. Things had actually got that bad.

I'm fourteen and my name's Eric. Eric Crankshaw. But my friends call me Ace. Thank God. I guess I didn't draw the shortest straw, though. After me, my mum and dad had quadruplets. They must have run out of ideas for names or something, because the boys all just got named after days of the week – Monday, Tuesday, Wednesday and Thursday. We call them the Quads – possibly the noisiest nine-year-olds in all Britain. All bad haircuts, grubby hands and snotty nostrils. And always borrowing my stuff and never bringing it back. You get the idea.

Then there's my big sister, Shufty, better known as the General. At sixteen, she thinks she's in charge of us. Lots more on her later.

The bloke who is *meant* to be in charge is the uncrowned King of the Crankshaws, the man without a plan, the undisputed

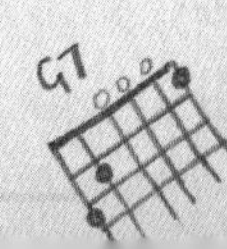

WHAT WAS DAD THINKING WHEN HE SIGNED US UP FOR A GIG AS RUBBISH AS THI
WHAT CAN I SAY? WE PLAY SONGS YOU'VE NEVER HEARD OF FOR 2 HOURS IN THE FREEZING C

master of financial disaster ... in other words, Dad – Arthur Crankshaw. He's an inventor. He used to be a successful pop singer, but he gave that up years ago to invent stuff. Like a jet-engine-powered barbecue. (Yeah, you read it right.) He didn't make any money from his ideas, so we were flat broke. No money whatsoever.

And Mum, of course. No one ever forgets her. She got really ill and now she's no longer with us – R.I.P. It was her dying wish that we all play a musical instrument. She'd been a professional musician herself. Dad's not great at keeping promises, but he did stay true to this one and, to cut a long story short, that's how our family band got started with the utterly rubbish name of Crank Up The Volume (Dad's idea).

£5 - ADMIT 1
OAPs TEA DANCE ON ICE
WITH THE MUSIC OF
CRANK UP THE VOLUME
FEATURING ARTHUR CRANKSHAW & HIS UNUSUAL VIOLIN
* 2 HOURS OF OLD SKOOL MUSIC
* FREE TEA AND CAKE
* MEDICAL ASSISTANCE AVAILABLE
NOTE TO CUSTOMERS: NO WALKING FRAMES ON ICE
C
CONCESSION

So it was the night before Dad was due in court. I was up in my room gazing at the stars through my telescope. I focused it on the constellation of Orion and listened to my brothers and sister practising. They were over at our barn working out a new number for our next music gig.

The rehearsal wasn't going well. Monday had broken into a superbly complex four-minute drum solo, and I could hear Shufty yelling at him to shut up. Situation normal on Planet Crankshaw.

Funny how your brain comes up with schemes when you're worried. At first the Secret Plan had seemed a stupid idea. Crazy. A random connection of stuff flying round in my head. And lots of stuff flies round in my head. Like, are there alien rock bands out there in our galaxy playing huge stadium gigs? Or is there really a time portal built by the US government in the Nevada desert capable of zapping you instantly to anywhere in the galaxy? (This is my mate Jake's theory, and he's got some pretty good evidence for it, believe me.)

Little by little, though, the Secret Plan began to shape into something more solid. Then, with a bit more thought about who might help me out with the tricky bits, it was suddenly complete. A plan! And I couldn't see how I hadn't thought of it before. It was simple! Obvious! In fact, why hadn't anyone else come up with it? It would sort out all our cash problems easily. Yes, the Secret Plan was born like a galactic star.

I glanced down into the garden, where Dad was tinkering with the jet engine on his barbecue design. Yep – instead of going over the court-case paperwork, he was hammering a throttle lever into place with a sledgehammer. Great.

Was it really going to be down to me and the Secret Plan to save the Crankshaw family? Was I the only hope left? Really?

I faced the facts. If the court hearing went wrong the next day – known in the family as Judgement Day – my plan really was the only option left, whether I liked it or not.

Not good. Not good at all.

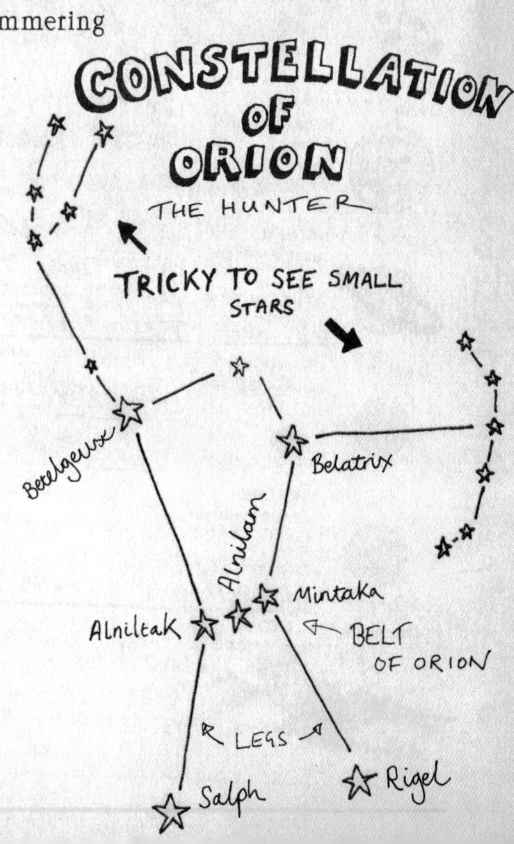

(8)

PUPIL'S NAME ~~CAPTAIN~~ ERIC ~~ACE~~ CRANKSHAW ~~STAR PILOT 1ST CLASS EARTH DEFENCE~~

SEE HEADTEACHER AT 9.30 TOMORROW TO EXPLAIN THIS.

READ THE QUESTION – YOU WEREN'T ASKED TO COLOUR THESE IN.

Our Solar System in the year 9000AD X This is lamentable drivel.

Please describe some of the **notable features** of these planets and objects in our Solar System *(3 marks each)*

SCIENCE FACT NOT SCIENCE FICTION. PLEASE.

Question 7.1: **MERCURY**
Notable features: LOCATION OF PRISON COLONY ALPHA 23 – HOUSING DANGEROUS ALIEN MERCENARIES, ROGUE ANDROIDS, AND SHAPE SHIFTERS. HOT AS PITTA BREAD JUST OUT OF THE TOASTER X

Question 7.2: **VENUS**
Notable features: SURFACE TEMP. OF 400°C ✓ SO REMAINS TOTALLY USELESS TO LIVE ON. EARTH-SIZED, ✓ BUT ATMOSPHERE 90 TIMES AS DENSE ✓. ALL IN ALL, A BIT LIKE JAKE'S BEDROOM AFTER A 'FART-OFF' X AGAINST HIS BROTHER

Question 7.3: **EARTH**
Notable features: EARTHLINGS HAVE PERFECTED THE ART OF PLAYING ROCK GUITAR AND CREATING VIDEO GAMES. FEW OTHER TECHNOLOGICAL ACHIEVEMENTS FROM A GALACTIC POINT OF VIEW. INHABITANTS PRETTY MUCH BOILED THEMSEL[VES] TO EXTINCTION WITH GREENHOUSE GASES IN THE 21ST CENTURY. PLANET NOW RUN[S] AN INTERGALACTIC ROCK SCHOOL. MAIN EXPORTS TO SPACE – GUITARS, HAIR GEL AND BU[...]

Question 7.4: **MARS**
Notable features: IN THE YEAR 2087 A.D. NASA DISCOVERED THE SUBSTANCE 'CORAX BETA 17' X TWO MILES BENEATH THE SURFACE. THIS ST[UFF] ENABLES SPACESHIPS TO TRAVEL FASTER THAN THE SPEED OF LIGHT X. ONCE WE GOT OUR HANDS ON IT OTHER ALIENS TOOK US SERIOUSLY. X

Question 7.5: **ASTEROID BELT**
Notable features: A BUNCH OF ROCKS ✓. GOOD TO FLY THROUGH IF YOU ARE TRYING TO ESCAPE ENEMY FIGHTERS LOCKED-ON TO YOUR ~~EXHU~~ EXHAUST PORTS

Question 7.6: **JUPITER**
Notable features: JUPITER HAS A HUGE, HUGE RED ZIT ✓ X WHICH STILL HASN'T BURST. I USE IT AS A TARGET WHEN I TEST FIR[E] MY LASER WEAPONS AFTER THEY'VE BEEN IN FOR A SERVI[CE]

Question 7.7: **SATURN**
Notable features: THE 23 MOONS ✓ OF SATURN ARE USED AS BASES BY OUR EARTH DEFENCE FORCE FIGHTER SQUADRONS TO PATROL THE OUTER PLANETS. ONCE I RETIRE I'M GOING TO SET MYSELF UP HERE TRADING HANDMADE GUITARS TO OTHER STAR SYSTEMS. I PLAN TO OPEN A SECOND SHOP OFF THE BELT X OF ORION WHERE THERE IS A LOT OF PASSING TRADE

Question 7.8: **URANUS**
Notable features: GREAT NAME FOR A ROCK BAND X

Question 7.9: **NEPTUNE**
Notable features: KNOWN ✓ BY US SPACE PILOTS AS 'THE GIANT FART PLANET' X COZ OF THE METHANE ✓ IN ITS ATMOSPERE (THAT'S WHY IT LOOKS BLUE). ALIEN OUT[POST] DISCOVERED LAST YEAR ON TRITON (ONE OF ITS MOONS). WE ATTACKED AT DAWN WITH 25 SHIPS AND COOKED THE PLACE WITH LASERS X

Question 7.10: **PLUTO**
Notable features: SO DULL THEY DOWNGRADED IT TO ~~A~~ DWARF PLANET ✓ STA[TUS]. LAST STOP TO FILL UP ON CORAX FUEL BEFORE THE BIG WIDE YONDER OF OUTER SPACE. DUE TO ITS REMOTE LOCATION IT'S LATELY BECOME A HANG OUT FOR SMUGGLER[S]. AS ROUGH AS A BADGER'S BACKSIDE X

I was in the kitchen playing my guitar – my mind wandering between our rather boring solar system and the much more exciting Ice Planet of Hoth – waiting for Dad to come home. Shufty was yelling at the Quads, who were making *neeeaaaarrr* sounds (motorbikes, I think) and racing each other round the table. The din was incredible.

Finally, I saw Dad's Land Rover lurching up the drive.

He was back.

So this was it. Judgement Day. The motorbikes saw him too and cut their engines. The room fell into an uneasy silence.

Dad strolled into the kitchen whistling a sea shanty. His whistling trailed off as he saw all of us staring at him. His eyes flicked from one questioning face to the next. He carefully dropped his car keys in the bowl, but still said nothing. He had a guilty look about him, I reckoned.

No-one dared say a word.

Dad's mouth opened as if he was about to speak, but he paused, scowling, as if he was trying to remember something complicated.

Eventually he uttered these immortal words. "Errrr ... yeah. Ummhh ... errrrrr ... any grub left?"

Was that all he had to say?

After all those sleepless nights of worry, the anxious build-up for

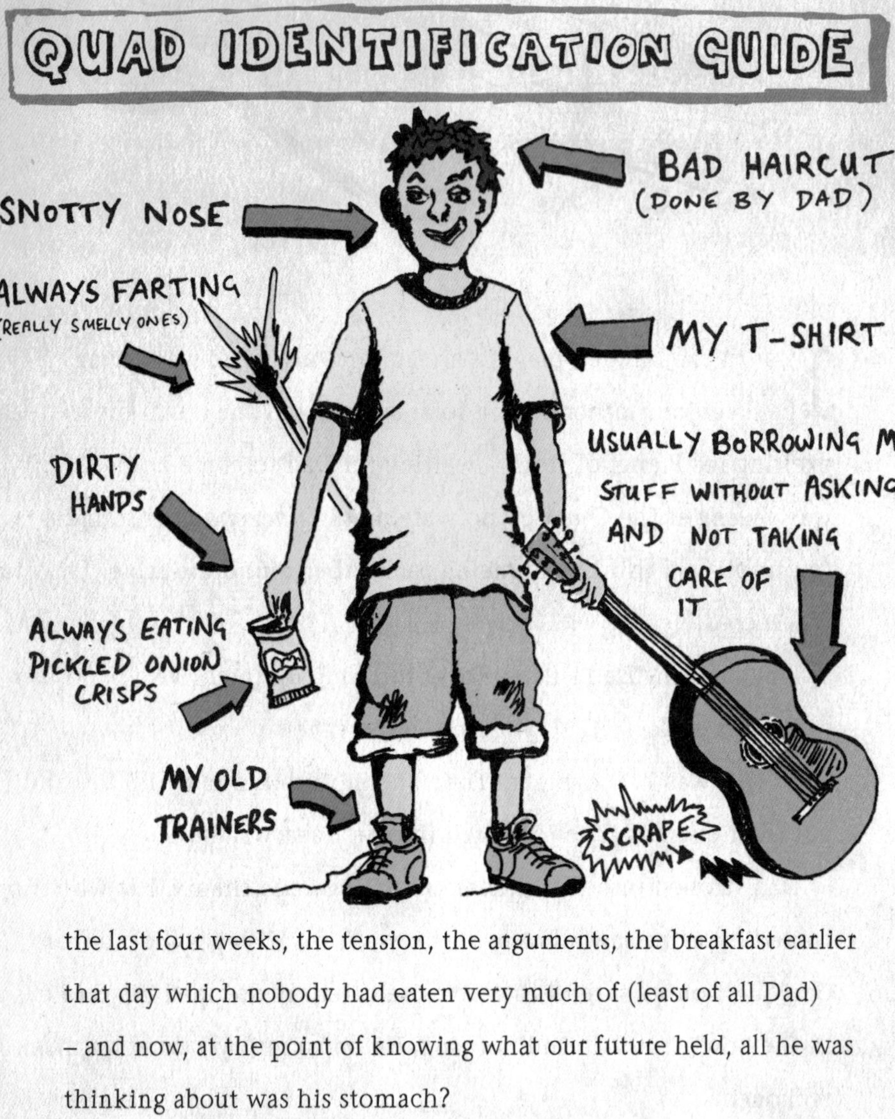

QUAD IDENTIFICATION GUIDE

BAD HAIRCUT (DONE BY DAD)
SNOTTY NOSE
ALWAYS FARTING (REALLY SMELLY ONES)
MY T-SHIRT
USUALLY BORROWING MY STUFF WITHOUT ASKING – AND NOT TAKING CARE OF IT
DIRTY HANDS
ALWAYS EATING PICKLED ONION CRISPS
MY OLD TRAINERS
SCRAPE

the last four weeks, the tension, the arguments, the breakfast earlier that day which nobody had eaten very much of (least of all Dad) – and now, at the point of knowing what our future held, all he was thinking about was his stomach?

"What are you all looking at me like that for?" he said.

Shufty finally cracked. "The court hearing finished at twelve o'clock! It's nearly two-thirty now. Where have you been?"

"Oh, here and there, Shufts," said the old man, shovelling the remains of my cheese-and-pickle sandwich into his mouth with a muffled "Cheers, Ace". "I popped over to the Mermaid Shopping Centre on my way back."

For a second I forgot the court hearing. "You haven't got any money. What were you buying at the shopping centre?"

"Oh no, I, err ... I wasn't buying anything, Ace. They want us to play a gig next week. Two hours for a hundred quid. All in. Not bad, hey? I also had to pick up some stainless-steel bolts for the barbecue. I'm planning to run some engine tests on it later—"

"Stop!" yelled Shufty. "Before you get into all that barbecue drivel or ... or ... or the Mermaid Centre, just tell us what happened. Are they going to boot us out of the house or not?"

"Oh ... err ... that stuff," he replied, as if he'd forgotten. "No worries."

No worries? Two months of misery, forty-five letters from the bank, eighteen final demands from the gas and water companies had all been boiled down to two words – *no worries*? I somehow doubted it.

Shufty was thinking the same thing. "No worries? No worries? What's that meant to mean?"

"It's all under control. Now," he coughed again, changing the subject, "once I've had a cup of tea, I'm going to max out the barbecue on full afterburner. See what she can really do."

He didn't seem to be taking Judgement Day half as seriously as we were.

"What did the judge actually say, Dad?" asked Shufty.

"Oh ... err ... she gave us two months to get some cash together. Or was it three...? Well, anyway, I explained I was inventing a very promising barbecue idea—"

"You told the judge that heap-of-junk barbecue out there was worth something?" yelled Shufty. "You're barking mad. If they've given you time to sort this mess out, you need to get a proper job, and fast!"

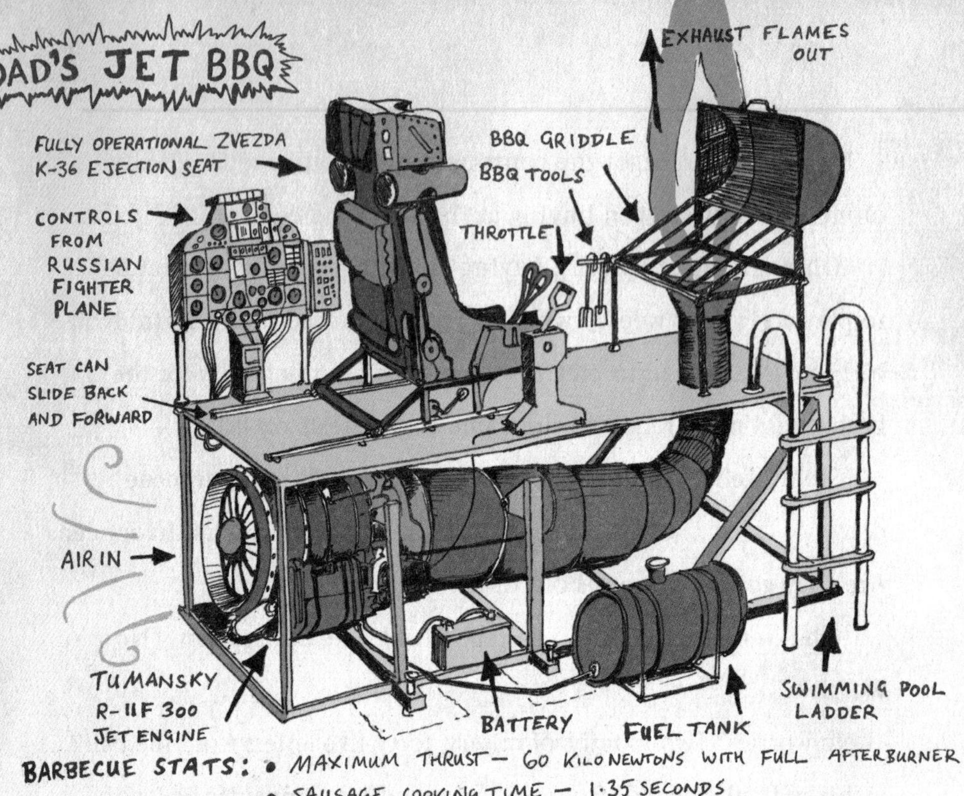

"Dad *has* a proper job," said Monday.

"He's an *inventor*," added Wednesday.

Dad winked at Wednesday. "Exactly. Look, Shufty, that heap-of-junk barbecue, as you call it, is powered by a jet engine which used to propel a Soviet fighter plane through the air at 1,800 miles an hour. That's three times the speed of sound. I'm harnessing all that power to produce the most advanced barbecue on the planet. It's going to be fast food ... *extra*-fast food."

"Dad," sighed Shufty. "Please. There is nothing left in the bank. That pile of bills over there needs to be paid, and pronto. You might think you're an inventor, but you haven't earned a penny since you sold everything you made that was half decent to Zack Zircon FOUR YEARS AGO! If Mum was still alive she'd tell you exactly what I'm telling you."

Now perhaps I should explain here that Dad had in fact rustled up not one, but two superb inventions in the barn a few years back. He liked to use these as his trump card whenever Shufty said he was rubbish at inventing.

The first invention was the Brain-o-Matic 3000. This allowed him to copy the brain function of a living monkey. Now I want to point out straight away that the original monkey was never hurt during this process. The monkey in question belongs to my Grandpa Crankshaw and is still very much alive and well and living in Bognor Regis. The machine was designed only to copy stuff, so it didn't suck the monkey's thoughts out, or wipe its brain, or anything nasty. (Dad's too much of a softie to hurt animals, so rest easy, nature-lovers.)

The second invention was Barry, the old man's first attempt to create an artificially intelligent monkey toy. This was the clever bit. He designed software to control Barry using the data collected from the monkey by the Brain-o-Matic 3000.

There was no denying it. He'd created the best toy ever. A cute robot monkey capable of thinking for itself. "Every kid'll want one of these for Christmas," Dad had declared when he switched Barry on for the first time. He was right. Barry was an instant hit with the Quads, who loved him to bits (literally to bits, sometimes, coz Bazza was quite fragile).

Dad built a second, more reliable, prototype called Eve. The multibillionaire Zack Zircon leapt on the idea after reading about Eve on the internet. Dad sold the whole idea to Zircon for pennies in a totally rubbish deal. Zircon had renamed the invention the ZircoBot, and Dad's part in the invention was very quickly forgotten.

CONSTELLATION OF CASSIOPEIA →

LOCATION – GROUND FLOOR OF THE BARN
DAD'S INVENTIONS
1 "BRAIN-O-MATIC 3000"
THIS INVENTION WAS DESIGNED TO COPY ALL THE INFORMATION INSIDE A BRAIN. SENSORS STUCK TO THE INSIDE OF A 1960s HAIRDRYER DETECTED MEMORIES AND STUFF, THEN CONVERTED THEM INTO DIGITAL DATA. SOLD TO ZIRCON FOR £500
BUNCH OF WIRES
BRAIN WAVE SENSORS
HAIR DRYER UNIT

2
THE COMPUTER SET-UP
THE DATA FROM THE BRAIN-O-MATIC WAS SAVED ONTO 10 MASSIVE COMPUTER HARD DRIVES. DAD THEN WROTE SOME SOFTWARE SO THAT THE DATA COULD BE USED TO CONTROL A ROBOT MONKEY TOY'S ARTIFICIAL BRAIN
COMPUTERS STILL FOR SALE-OFFERS OVER £800
4
OTHER STUFF
FOR SALE (OFFERS INVITED)
• USELESS AMPHIBIOUS CAR
• MOST OF A SUPERMARINE SPITFIRE
• THE 19TH HOLE GOLF CART - HAS BUILT-IN REFRIGERATOR FOR DRINKS
BARRY + EVE
3
ROBOT COWBOY MONKEY TOYS
DAD DOWNLOADED HIS NEW SOFTWARE ONTO THE HARD DRIVES OF HIS TWO PROTOTYPES CALLED BARRY AND EVE. EVE ALWAYS WORKED BETTER THAN BARRY, SO WAS SOLD TO ZIRCON
EVE + SOFTWARE SOLD TO ZIRCON FOR £500
COWBOY BARRY
COWGIRL EVE

ZircoBots had sold in their millions and made Zircon even richer than he already was. If Dad hadn't signed such a give-away deal, a percentage of all that money would've been ours. But, unfortunately, we'd never seen a penny of the ZircoBot fortune.

Something didn't quite ring true to me about the court case. "You must have given the judge more than the barbecue idea to go on? They deal in evidence. Hard facts."

"Ah," Dad grinned. I could tell what he was about to say before he said it. So could everyone else in the room. "I told them about Barry and the Brain-o-Matic 3000. And if Barry worked, why not the barbecue?"

"Ahhhhhhhhhhhhhhhhhhhhhhhhhhhh!" yelled Shufty.

Barry was sitting on the chair next to me, grinning and twirling his ears.

There was a knock on the door, followed seconds later by someone booting the thing so hard that the handle and lock exploded, splintering off a sizeable chunk of the door frame.

"Get back, kids!" yelled Dad, grabbing for a chair. "Phone the police!"

"Like, hello?" said Shufty. "We can't. We've been cut off. Remember?"

"Well then. Errrrr ... take cover!" ordered Dad. The Quads were the only ones who bothered. They crawled under the table and emerged on the other side, peeping over the table top with wide, frightened eyes.

A bodybuilding thug with Celtic tattoos ringing his tree-trunk-sized biceps strolled in, and smirked at us. He was clutching a

clipboard with a wad of papers pegged to it. Four more men loomed up behind him. "Knock, knock," he growled. "Are you Arthur Crankshaw?"

"Possibly," gulped Dad. "What do you want?"

"Goods to the value of £2,498.78," he smiled knowingly.

Dad gulped again. "I'll call the police!"

"I shouldn't bother, mate. I've already told them I'm coming. I'm the bailiff. Danny Thumper – Bailiffs Direct. Pleasure to meet you."

"But this is outrageous! I was in court only this morning. The judge said we were OK for at least two months—"

"Ah..." smiled Thumper. "Different debts. I'm here to collect for unpaid gas and water bills."

I could tell Thumper meant business. He and his crew got to work pretty quickly, stripping our home of all our electrical goods – the fridge, the freezer ... then I saw the TV going past, followed by the DVD player, games console ... and the final insult – my star-gazing telescope that had taken me six long months to save up for.

This was all so wrong. My fear of Thumper and his crew turned instantly to anger. "Oi, that's mine!" I shouted, grabbing it. "I paid for that!"

"It ain't yours any more," laughed one of Thumper's men, wrestling it clear from me with a twist and a shove. I followed him outside and watched my pride and joy disappear into the back of a metallic silver van guarded by a pair of vicious-looking pitbulls.

"Hate. Love. Settle down!" yelled their master.

I watched Thumper keeping a running total of all our things by punching numbers into a calculator. "Yep, call it fifty quid for that lot," he muttered before yelling, "Sofa suite and beds next, lads! Keep it coming."

"What are you expecting us to sleep on?" I asked.

"It's not my problem, mate." Thumper pointed a chewed biro at Dad. "Ask your old man. He got you into this mess."

Finally Thumper lifted his eyebrows and totted up the total. "That should do for the time being. Sign here, please."

As Dad reluctantly scrawled on the paperwork, Thumper flicked through a pile of final-demand bills stacked up on the sideboard. "Here, are all these unpaid?"

"I'm not telling you," said Dad, handing back the pen.

"I collect for these two companies as well. I'll get in touch with them and let them know your situation."

"Oh yeah. Great. If it's not, like, too much trouble?" Shufty said, fuming.

"No trouble at all," said Thumper, as he and his crew sauntered back to the van.

The Quads and I followed them out to escape the explosive atmosphere building between Shufty and Dad.

Thumper grinned, ducking his head as he climbed into the front of the van. "We'll be back

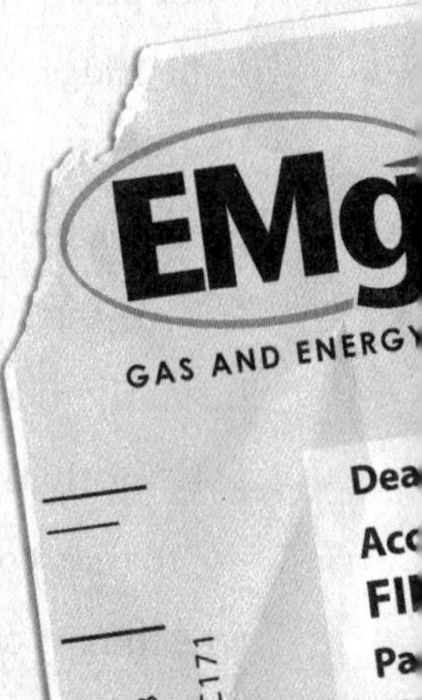

ONE OF DAD'S MOST IMPRESSIVE BILLS →

to clear the sheds, outhouses and musical instruments and all that rubbish. That jet engine's got to be worth something."

The rest of his crew boarded the van. They slammed the doors and coolly drove off. They weren't in any sort of hurry. In fact, they were obviously eyeing up the outbuildings and planning their next raid.

"Is that man ever going to bring our stuff back, Ace?" asked Thursday quietly.

"Not unless we find some money from somewhere." I dug a newspaper clipping out of my back pocket, and nodded to myself.

It was time to move to Phase One of the Secret Plan. I took my mobile out and wrote a text message. Hesitating slightly, I pressed send and walked towards the barn.

Shufty stormed out of the kitchen. "Where are you off to, Ace?" she asked grumpily.

"Jake's. If Thumper hasn't stolen my bike, that is. I've got work to do."

count Number 446647-122

15 65 5

You can contact our Customer Services department Monday to Friday, 8am to 8pm. Automated service is available at all other times.
See reverse for details

NSTALMENT FINAL DEMAND
Overdue amount £1,967.75

YYYHS6868689W0

ur CRANKSHAW,
nber 446647-122
MAND
your third instalment of £1,967.75 for your gas bill has not been
payment is not received within 5 working days your payment contract
celled and the full balance of £3,200.56 will become due.
y will then be pursued by a debt collection agency appointed by EMg
y or by court action.
course of action for which you will be liable.

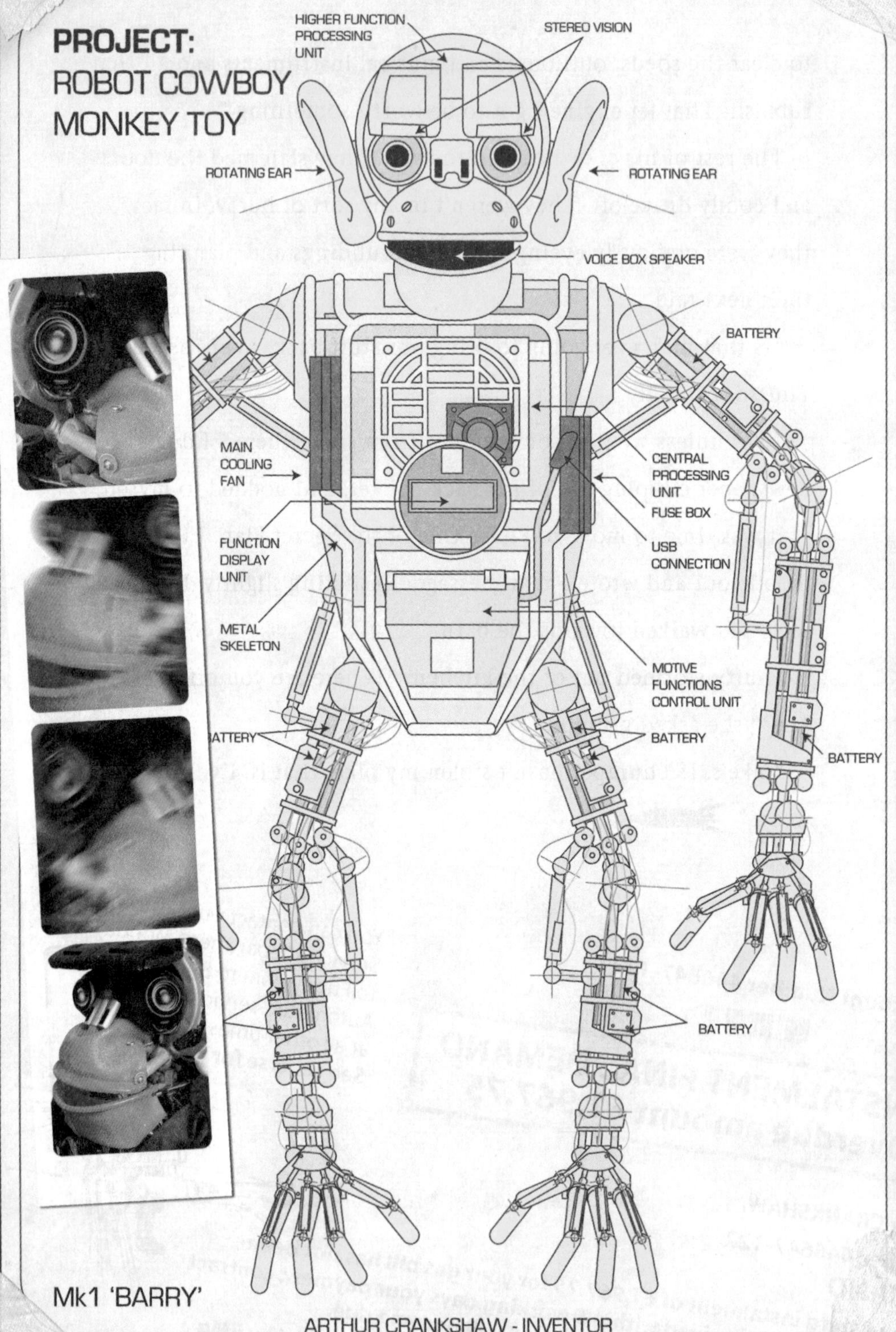
PROJECT:
ROBOT COWBOY
MONKEY TOY
HIGHER FUNCTION
PROCESSING
UNIT
STEREO VISION
ROTATING EAR
ROTATING EAR
VOICE BOX SPEAKER
BATTERY
MAIN
COOLING
FAN
CENTRAL
PROCESSING
UNIT
FUSE BOX
USB
CONNECTION
FUNCTION
DISPLAY
UNIT
METAL
SKELETON
MOTIVE
FUNCTIONS
CONTROL UNIT
BATTERY
BATTERY
BATTERY
BATTERY
Mk1 'BARRY'
ARTHUR CRANKSHAW - INVENTOR

BARRY
BARRY
BARRY IS DAD'S BEST INVENTION-
A FULLY FUNCTIONING, WALKING
SQUAWKING, INTELLIGENT TOY
WHOSE SOFTWARE WAS CREATED
USING DAD'S OTHER GOOD
INVENTION, THE 'BRAIN-O-MATIC
3000'. BARRY IS LIKE AN EXTRA
MEMBER OF THE FAMILY, AND
THE QUADS LOVE HIM TO BITS.
DAD SOLD THE DESIGN TO ZIRCON
FOR £500, WHICH WAS A BIT RUBBISH
BECAUSE ZIRCON THEN CHANGED
THE NAME TO THE 'ZIRCOBOT' AND
MADE MILLIONS OF DOLLARS OUT OF
THE IDEA. WE'RE NOT SURE WHY BARRY
IS DRESSED UP LIKE A COWBOY,
BUT IT COULD BE TO DO WITH DAD'S
OLD BAND 'THE MANIC COWBOYS'—
AN EARLY VERSION OF BARRY APPEARED
IN THEIR MUSIC VIDEO.
BARRY IS COOL! BARRY ROCKS!

JAKE & ACE'S NEW BAND

LEAD GUITAR/HARMONICA

'ACE' CRANKSHAW

DRUMS/RECORDING ENGINEER/ CLEVER COMPUTER STUFF/ SAMPLES

JAKE 'DRUMS' DRUMMOND

POSSIBLE OTHERS

LEADSINGER – ALF GUPPY?
- PROS – GIRLS FANCY HIM
- CONS – CAN'T SING

KEYBOARDS
VIC CASH

BASS GUITAR – TREV NICHOLS
- PROS – CAN PLAY 12 BAR BLUES (JUST)
  – HIS DAD DRIVES A BIG VAN, SO GOOD FORSHIFTING OUR EQUIPMENT TO GIGS
- CONS – SMELLS BAD.

POSSIBLE BAND NAMES:

✓ THE CROUCHING MONKS
COSSACK BRASS RUBBERS
ITCHY FREAKS
THE GLUM FARMERS
YESTERDAY'S TOMORROW
? WEST OF VENUS
CAPTAIN ACE AND THE STARGAZERS ✓✓
? CAFÉ WHA?
BOLONEY BROTHERS
THE FOOLISH SCHOLARS
✓ THE DIRK AXEMAN PROJECT
MILLIPEDE SHOE SHOP

DEBUT ALBUM TITLE IDEAS

THE LAB RAT BREAKOUT
✓✓ ROBOT • MONKEY • COWBOY • HERO
THE THAMES DELTA SESSIONS
THE ABOMINABLE UKULELE INCIDENT
THE GRAVESEND HARMONIC PROPHECIES

P.A. AMP
BASS AMP
P.A SPEAKER
GUITAR AMP
DRUM KIT
BASS
VOCALS
P.A SPEAKER

← ONE OF JAKE'S MANY (fake) U.F.O. PICTURES

JAKE'S HIGHLY FLAMMABLE FART EXPERIMENTS
↓ (HE GETS THE FLASHY LABELS FROM HIS MUM'S OFFICE)

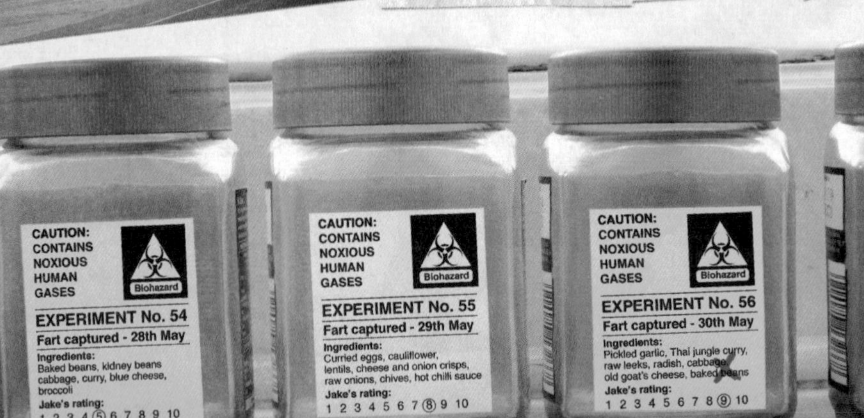

COFFIN-DODGERS

"I've searched the internet for you, man," said Jake, easing back in his office-style chair and nodding towards his computer screen.

He was chewing on a raw leek, and his room reeked of ... well ... it was a smell unknown on the planet, but best described as rotten eggs with an extra spicy topping. He was attempting to generate the most poisonous fart ever produced by the human digestive system. Jam jars containing the bottled results of his noxious experiments lined the windowsill.

The walls were plastered with images of space rockets (real and fictional), UFO pictures from around the world, and famous drummers. We wanted to be in a band together one day, and we'd been trying to come up with a name for ourselves for ages.

Under the window four shelves were wedged tight with books on his (and my) one true love – rockets and space.

"What are you planning to do with it?" he asked.

"What did you think I was planning to do with it?" I replied, not wanting to give too much away. It was a Secret Plan, after all.

"Look, Ace, when you texted me, man, you didn't make it clear. You said you wanted a rocket. Different rockets do different jobs. They aren't one size fits all. Let's start with the basics. Do you want short-range or long-range?"

"Hey?"

"Are you planning a tactical battlefield strike, man ... or, err ... planning to nuke someone with an intercontinental ballistic missile? It's a simple choice."

"Neither. I don't want to start a war, Jake, mate. I ... I..." I had to tell him. I had no choice. "I want to fire a rocket at the Moon." I unfolded the newspaper article.

Jake's eyes skimmed over it, his eyebrows twitching up

2 ▸▸

● WORLD NEWS

OUR ARCH ENEMY

ZIRCON ANNOUNCES LAUNCH OF MOON SHOT COMPETITION WITH $10m PRIZE

HE STILL OWES DAD

MOON

By **FELIX McQUARRIE**
in New York

AT ZIRCON Headquarters in New York yesterday, amid fanfare and flashy graphics, ailing billionaire Zack Zircon announced he was putting up a $10m prize for any non-governmental body able to land a probe on the Moon.

It would appear that these non-governmental bodies will have to be multibillionaires with vast amounts of cash to burn if they are to enter the most spectacular race ever conceived. Make no mistake, the sheer size and ambition of this competition is without precedent in human history.

With a cough and a wheeze Zircon dubbed this extraordinary contest 'The Great Space Race', and the natural next step in amateur space exploration.

The reclusive Zircon's connection to space is long-standing, so his race, although incredible in scale, must be taken very seriously. His conglomerate of companies banded under the heading 'Zircon Science Industries' have supplied satellites and related technology to many countries worldwide for both civil and military use. He has also diversified into the growing artificial intelligence field, manufacturing the hugely popular ZircoBot, a product worth an estimated $50m in the worldwide toy market last year alone.

Closer examination of the race reveals it has little to do with furthering mankind's scientific knowledge or have any broader ambitions such as kick-starting a new wave of space exploration, rather it has much more to do with promoting another of Zircon's business interests – namely the launch of the ZircoSpaceParc in Illinois, a colossal roller coastered theme park now in the final stages of construction.

Challenged on the issue that building space rockets for fun must rank as one of the most expensive pastimes known to mankind, Zircon assured the assembled press and media that he had already signed up several billionaires, and was certain the competition would take place.

When questioned that $10m seemed a drop in the ocean to the winner when weighed again the production and launch costs of the rocket, he replied: "It isn't really about ~~the~~ CRANKSHAW'S money. It is about the prestige of being the first person on Earth capable of landing a probe on the Moon by means of their own phenomenal wealth. Have no doubt - this is a very rich man's game. The winner shall be remembered for all human history. And who can put a price on that?"

Who indeed? Blastoff of The Great Space Race will mark the opening of the ZircoSpaceParc next summer. Whether or not the probes land on the Moon, this amazing publicity stunt will surely be the most elaborate, impressive and expensive ever staged.

with surprise. "Ace, you're not seriously thinking ... wait. It's Judgement Day today, isn't it?"

"Yep."

"It didn't go well, then?"

"Nope."

He looked at the newspaper article again. "And now you want to enter Zircon's competition?"

"How did you guess? If we can enter Zircon's Space Race, we're in with a chance of winning $10 million. It's just getting back what we are owed from four years ago."

"And ... err – let me get my crystal ball out. To enter Zircon's Space Race you need me to find you a rocket?"

"Yeah, Jake. Something like that."

"Wouldn't it be easier to relaunch your dad's pop career than try your own moon shot, man?" asked Jake. "He was actually famous in the 1990s."

This was true. Dad used to front a techno/bluegrass/house band called the Manic Cowboys. Their 1993 dance hit "Lasso That Steer, Cowboy" had hung about in the European dance charts all through the summer of '93, making him a temporary fortune – enough to buy The Mill, at least.

"I'm telling you," I said. "We need serious cash, or the judge will kick us out of The Mill, and Zircon's Space Race is the best and fastest answer."

Jake didn't say anything. Instead he Googled the Great Space Race website. "Ace, mate, look, there are seven other competitors in the race, plus Zircon himself – and they are all multibillionaires. Look at 'em."

← THE NEWSPAPER CLIPPING WHERE I GOT THE IDEA FOR MY SECRET PLAN!

The GREAT SPACE RACE

HOME NEWS CONTACT US APPLY TO ENTER WIN TICKETS

COMPETITO

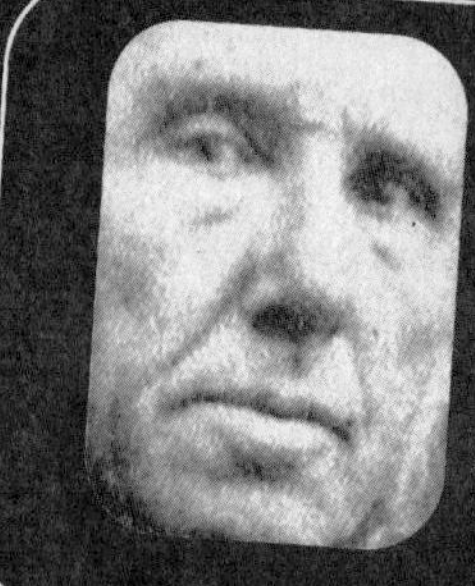

COMPETITOR 1

ANTON PETROV

TEAM PETROV

- AGE 82
- NATIONALITY RUSSIAN
- BUSINESS INTERESTS Oil extraction
- ESTIMATED WEALTH $30bn (US)
- INTERESTS Making money

PAGE 1 of 3

273892300 2030304 400404043_3_3

www.thegreatspacerace.

All were about as old as the pensioners we played to at the ice rink. They were old. Really old. He clicked through them, just to show me the competition. There was Anton Petrov (Russian oil billionaire), Andrea Crompton (Canadian banker), Gaston Chevalier (French nobleman), Jakob Northrup (German car-parts entrepreneur), Jimmy Pak (North Korean owner of an electronics empire), Robert Shredder (American owner of a whole bunch of African diamond mines), and finally a British eccentric, Sir Conrad Neemis (casino and gambling supremo).

"Just a bunch of coffin-dodgers," I said.

"Loaded coffin-dodgers. Like, completely cash-rich."

"Yeah, but we can give it a go," I encouraged.

Jake rocked back, laughing. "OK. In one corner, a group of international multibillionaires – just look at these guys ... from

France ... Russia ... America – all with more cash than it's actually possible to imagine. In the other corner, step forward Eric 'Ace' Crankshaw, a fourteen-year-old lad from Gravesend with all the spending power of someone with a weekend job washing cars at Murphy's Magnificent Motors. Oh, let's think for a moment ... I wonder who'll win?"

"Yeah, but it's worth a go."

"But these guys have a two-year head start on you," said Jake. "Their rockets are in the final stages of construction. You, on the other hand, don't even have a rocket, and it's four weeks until blast-off, man. In America. Not sunny Britain. Forgive me for putting a downer on the idea."

"Please," I pleaded. "Just see what you can find."

Jake looked long and hard at me, and he could see I wasn't joking. "OK, I'll look into it," he said, without a single tiny glimmer of hope in his eyes. He didn't believe in the Secret Plan. I could tell. He was just feeling sorry for me on Judgement Day. "How much cash have you got, Ace?"

"£170.89. That's the lot."

Jake pulled a face like he'd just been asked to shin up to the Moon using the nearest lamppost.

I had to handle the situation carefully. My plan would be dead in the water without him and his particular expertise. "Do you reckon you can find one?"

Jake lifted his leg and leaked out a brutal fart that smelt almost metallic. "The market for second-hand rockets is weak at the moment, so you're looking to invest at the right time. Leave it with me."

Eight days after the bailiff's visit, Shufty called a meeting in the attic of the old grain store.

This was where Crank Up The Volume practised. We had it pretty well set up in there. In the middle of the room was an ancient wood-burning stove we used for brewing up tea and keeping us warm in the winter. On one side we had Shufty's piano and Monday's drum kit. On the other side there was a battered pine table and chairs and an old sofa. Dad had made us some music stands which cluttered up the place, but all in all it was a pretty neat little den.

But today I could tell making music was not on Shufty's mind.

"Right, you lot, shut up!" she started off, banging the table with an ancient mallet that had been hanging on one of the rusty nails along the back wall. "Meeting is now in session."

"Where's Dad?" asked Wednesday.

"I've banned him," said Shufty. "In fact, the reason I've called you all here is to announce that I've taken over running this family – effective immediately."

I knew she was angry with him, but this was unheard-of – a New Regime.

"Since Thumper's visit, I've decided to mount a coup. All decisions about the family will now have to go through me. We're

SHUFTY'S PIC OF HER MASTERPLAN →

cutting Dad out of it. There's no other way."

"Have you told him?" I asked.

"I've informed him by letter."

"But he stopped opening his post months ago," said Thursday. "Said he got sent nothing but bills."

"Ignorance is no defence in law," Shufty said with a smile.

"He's not going to like it," I said.

"He'll never know, Ace, as long as you don't tell him."

Shufty pulled down a canvas screen to reveal a blackboard (normally used to write up song lists). Then she laid out a crumpled piece of paper she'd got from her back pocket and began to chalk up a new list on the board.

"This is it. This is what has got to happen."

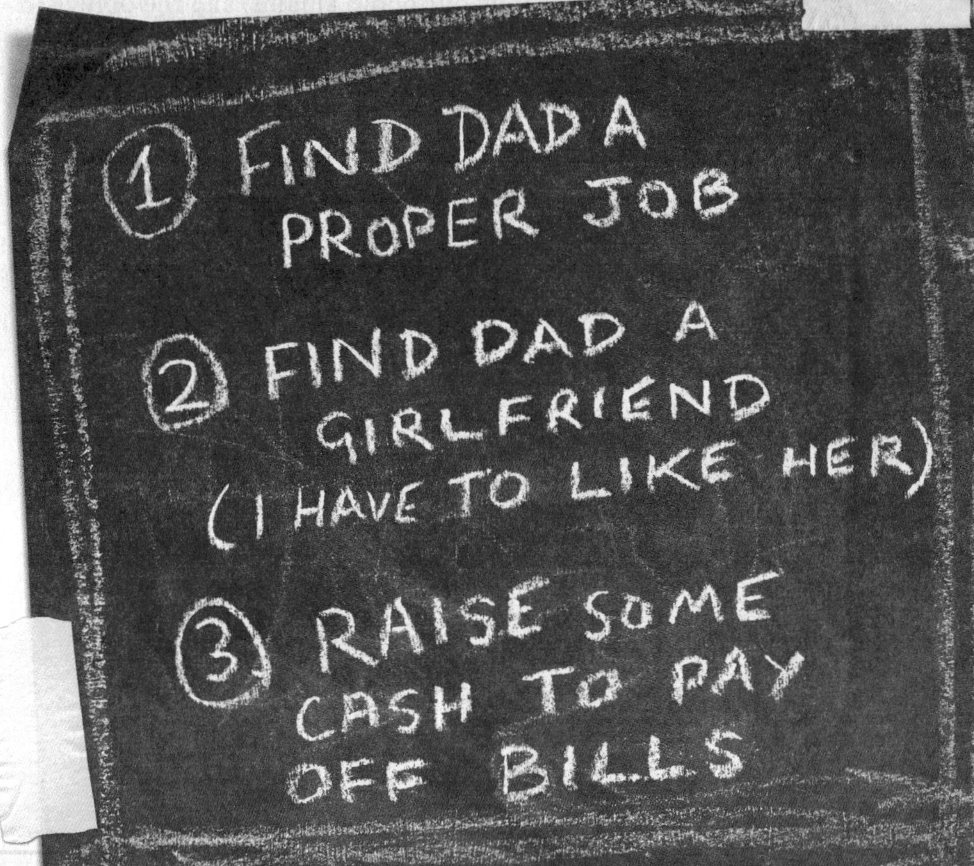

I WAS NEVER SURE THIS PART OF SHUFTY'S PLAN WAS GOING TO WORK. I WAS RIGHT. ONLY 5 HITS IN THREE WEEKS! (AND NO TAKERS)

"The job search is your problem, Ace."

"Oh, so I get the easy one, then," I said. It would've been simpler to ride a unicycle backwards up Mount Everest without oxygen.

"Tomorrow you will pretend to be Dad on the phone, and call an employment agency using the pay phone in the village."

"How do we get him to an interview?" I laughed. "He'll smell a rat. This is a rubbish idea."

"We'll worry about how we get him there once we have an appointment. Second point. His love life. Do you have your drawing of Dad for the website, Thursday?"

"What?" I asked. Things had been going on behind my back.

"I'm putting Dad on datemysingledad.com. They need a picture of him. Thumper took our photo albums, and the only other pictures I've found won't do."

She produced some photos of Dad dressed as the village idiot for last year's medieval fête, and another of him taken just after he'd set his trousers alight in a welding accident.

"I see what you mean," I said. These totally embarrassing pix weren't going to lure potential girlfriends into the barbecue-jet-set world of the Crankshaws.

Thursday unfolded his artwork. It was a portrait of Dad, all right, but it made him look even more crazy than Shufty's snaps. Part montage, part drawing, it featured hair made of pieces of painted straw and Dad clutching a real quarter-inch Whitworth spanner actually stuck down on to the paper with glue.

"We can't use that," I scoffed. "Nobody would take him seriously."

www.datemysingledad.com/578849
Most Visited
DAD — AS DRAWN BY THE QUADS
MUSICIAN • INVENTOR • SCARECROW !
Profile photo
See Arthur's profile
Main menu
Arthur
Add to your favourites
FLAMMABLE HAIR
HUMAN – OR ALIEN ?
SPANNER
Done

PHOTOCOPY OF THE QUADS' DESCRIPTION OF DAD!

"We can use it," insisted the Quads.

"It's the best we've got," said Shufty. "It'll melt someone's heart. I'll scan it in at the library, then upload it with the description."

"Description? Description of Dad?" This was going to be good.

"Yeah, the Quads have been working on it all afternoon."

Monday cleared his throat. "We've made it just like the ones in the newspaper, Ace. Listen." And he read out:

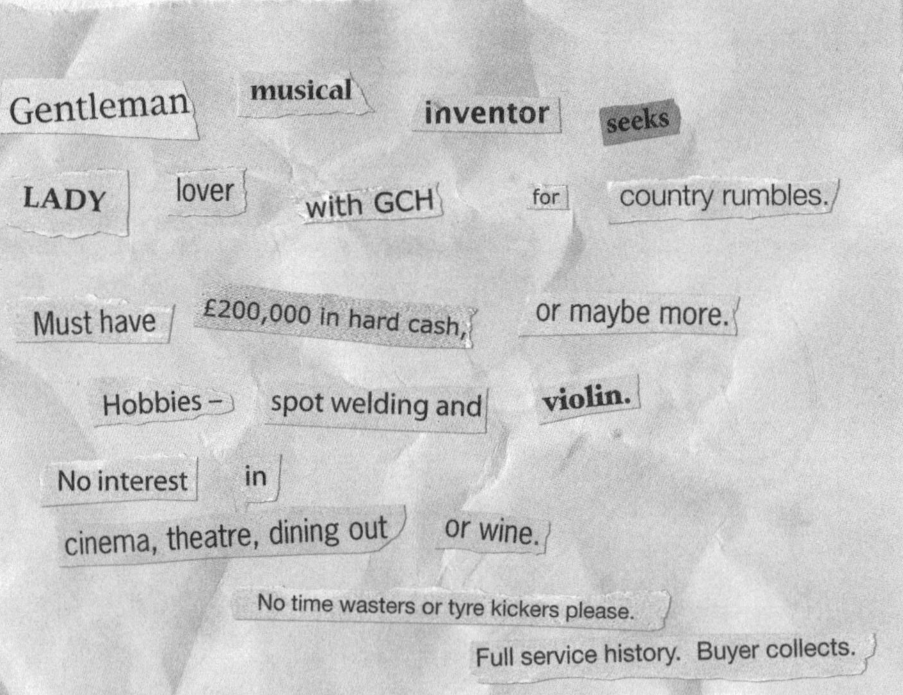

"Is that the best you can do? It's not GCH. It's GSOH. Good *sense of humour*. GCH means she's got gas central heating."

The General wagged her finger at me. "Don't you start, Ace, OK? They've been working very hard on this."

"Yeah, Ace," said Tuesday. "We've made Dad look *hot to trot*.

He's ready to *burn up the dance floor.*"

"What? Dad?" I realized the Quads had been reading the magazines they'd been cutting up, and had discovered phrases they had no real understanding of.

Thursday whispered, "Ace ... Ace ... women won't be able to resist Dad's *magnetic manly allure...*"

"...or the *salon fresh shine of his heat-damaged hair,*" added Monday, slapping down another piece of straw loaded with way too much glue.

"But in the advert, you've made him sound like a cross between a second-hand car and a house for rent," I said.

"Leave it out, all right?" snapped Shufty. "You need to stop worrying about the dating advert and start worrying about how to find Dad a job. And we need to organize some gigs. Get some cash flow. Come up with some creative solutions."

My phone bleeped. It was a text message from Jake.

"Got to go," I said, jumping up and legging it to the stairs.

I'd almost given up on Jake. Over a week had gone by without my getting much of a word from him other than "I'm working on it".

"Where are you off to?" yelled Shufty.

"I've got some plans of my own to get us out of this mess."

"What sort of plans?"

"Secret plans."

"Creative solutions, remember, Ace!" Shufty shouted after me as I bolted down the stairs.

"Don't worry. It's creative, all right."

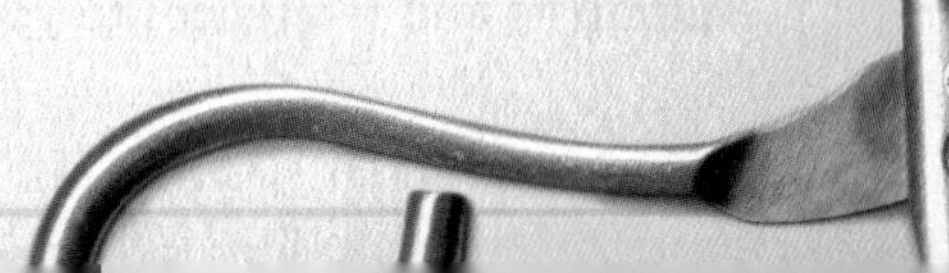

SP SERIAL 687

Jake didn't even look up from the computer screen when I arrived at mission control. The stench in his room had taken on a new and riper edge. He was snacking from a jar of pickled garlic perched on his mouse mat. "You're in with a shout here," he said. "Quick – we're running out of time."

"Hey?"

"Here," he said, handing me an A4 print-out with a simple message reading:

SP SERIAL 687 – Quantity 1 – Date of manufacture – 1974 – Royal Air Force surplus – Unused – Boxed – Free UK delivery.

I moved a book on South American UFO sightings from his chair, and made myself comfortable.

"What's SP serial 687, Jake?"

Jake reached down for a well-thumbed book lying on the floor by his desk. Its cover said *Classified – Top Secret*. What was this? It looked like the genuine article. He flicked through it to a page marked with a strip of torn paper. There were no pictures anywhere on its hundreds of densely printed pages, just loads of codes, serial numbers and references to government

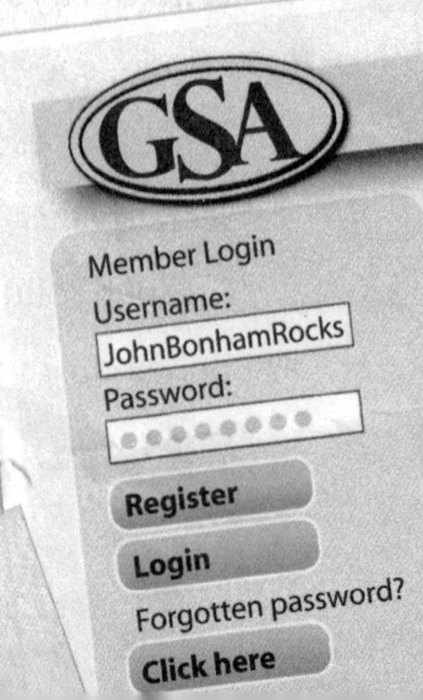

aerospace projects. Only Jake would own a book like this.

"There," he said, stabbing at a paragraph. "See – SP serial 687. Production name GS1 – Ginger Streak 1."

None of this was getting any clearer. "OK," I asked. "What's Ginger Streak?"

"A rocket, man. Like you asked for. I found it on this government internet auction site."

"Will this Ginger Streak thing get to the Moon?"

His answer was not encouraging. "Might do. Might not. Cancelled British project from the 1970s. Untested."

I peered at the computer screen, then at the top-secret book. We were bidding for a bunch of serial codes. There was no mention of a rocket. Only someone with Jake's expertise and a similar top-secret book would know what the government was actually selling off.

"In two minutes she'll be all yours."

"Joker," I laughed.

Jake pointed with his garlicky finger at the

ONLY JAKE WOULD KNOW ABOUT A WEBSITE AS DULL / GEEKY / OBSCURE AS THIS

ERNMENT SURPLUS AUCTIONS ONLINE

Search

YOU ARE BIDDING ON 1 ITEM - TIME REMAINING 32mins

SEARCH SP SERIAL 687

me to GSA DIRECT

ER LISTINGS

Item	Quantity	Description	Guide Price	Your Bid	Time Remaining
YUU - 177811 11	32	Toothbrushes - Used - Free UK delivery	For disposal	No bid	22 minutes
* SP SERIAL 687	1	Date of manufacture 1974 - Royal Air Force surplus Unused - Boxed - Free UK delivery	For disposal	£5.00	32 minutes *
DKK-R3142638	120	Unused - Boxed - Free UK delivery	For disposal	No bid	42 minutes
	1,100	Used - Free UK delivery	For disposal	No bid	52 minutes
		UK delivery		No bid	1 hour 2 mins
					1 hour 2 mins

SP SERIAL 68

wall, where there was a blurred picture of a rocket blasting off. "No joke, Ace. Ginger Streak should look a bit like that."

"Someone'll snipe it at the finishing line," I said, kicking back and discounting the actual possibility of real-life rocket ownership. I was a Crankshaw. Nothing ever went to plan. It would never happen.

Jake grabbed his drumsticks and began beating the hell out of the labelled jam jars on his windowsill which contained the bottled results of his unhealthy experiments. "Ace," he said, suddenly stopping and settling back in the seat, "here we go. Last ten seconds..."

I was still the sole bidder.

Jake put on a fake American accent. "Captain Ace Crankshaw. Blast-off in 10, 9, 8, 7 ,6, 5, 4, 3, 2 ... 1!"

The screen flashed: *Bidding closed on this item.*

"You've won, Ace!" Even Jake – one of Gravesend's most talented geeks – seemed disbelieving for a second or two. He clicked on the item and rechecked what he'd just done. Twice.

I sat down on the bed. "No way?"

His email pinged almost immediately. *You have one new message.*

JAKE'S BEDROOM IS LITTERED WITH STUFF LIKE THIS
... ONIONS, GARLIC AND TOP-SECRET BOOKS!

TEST LAUNCH IN AUSTRALIA. JAKE RECKONED THIS ROCKET HAD SLIGHTLY DIFFERENT PAINTWORK TO 687

Jake opened it fast and read out, "*You have won a bid on: SP SERIAL 687. Winning price £5.*"

"Give me that book again." I checked the code twice. If Jake was right, I'd just won a rocket.

"Errrhh..." struggled Jake. "Congratulations, man. She's all yours."

My instant reaction was to feel a little bit sick. My hands began to tingle and shake. The Secret Plan was working, all right. I was now the proud owner of a space rocket. "OK..." I said, although I was far from OK. I looked at the rocket picture on the wall.

"When do you want your ship delivered, man?" asked Jake, scrolling through the email.

I didn't answer. I was still working through the scenarios in my mind. What would Dad say? What would *Shufty* say? The General would not be pleased, that was for sure.

"Ace, when do you want the rocket delivered? Ace?"

I felt light-headed, now. Strange. I thought as fast as my shocked brain could manage, struggling out an answer. "Saturday. When we're playing at the Mermaid. Nobody will be home."

"Sorted," said Jake, pinging off a reply.

I grabbed my coat and made for the door, my legs slightly wobbly.

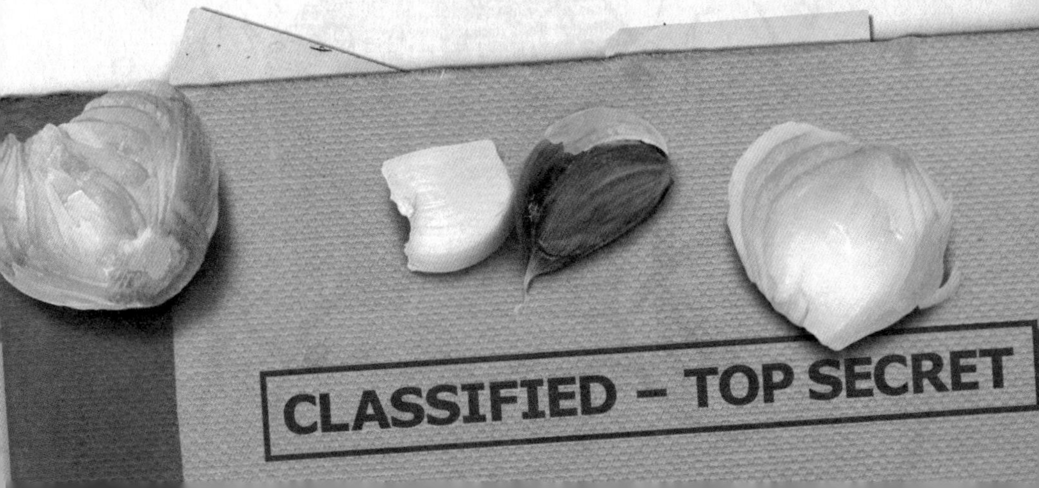

"Hey – *Ace Crankshaw, rocketeer guitarist*. It's got a good ring to it."

This had suddenly got serious.

Then a warm glow of excitement grew in my stomach, just like the feeling you get after eating a hot curry or a spicy pizza with extra chillies. The chance of winning the Space Race was suddenly real. I, Ace Crankshaw, could save the family from financial ruin.

Everyone would be in a good mood after our gig at the shopping centre, and it would be the ideal time to reveal my Secret Plan: to enter Zircon's competition with Ginger Streak and win back the $10 million Zircon owed us.

The more I thought about it, the more perfect the inevitable result seemed.

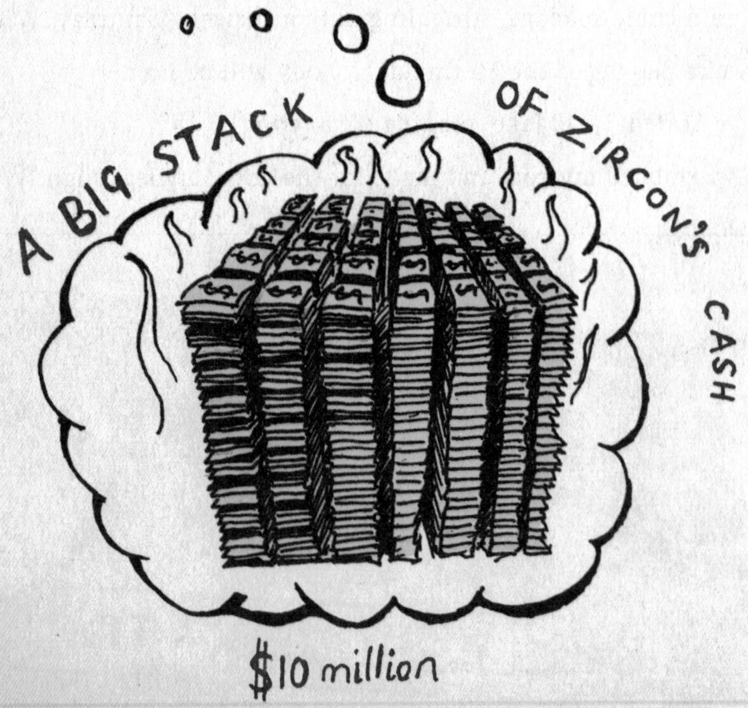

Herds of Saturday shoppers were already stooging around the Mermaid Shopping Centre by the time we arrived to play our gig – a great place, I guess, if you've got cash to burn, not so great if you're stony broke.

We'd done a fair few gigs over the years, so the idea of playing to shoppers wasn't that scary.

We began to set up our instruments on the small stage next to the escalators. They had a PA system with speakers, a white grand piano, and even a drum kit, so it was a huge improvement on the ice rink. The manager, a bloke called Grimwinter, fussed about. The instant he'd met us all, I could tell he thought it was a bad idea.

"Your family seem, er, quite young," he grumbled to Dad. "Are you sure they can all play, Mr Crankshaw? Have they learnt their scales, and so forth?"

"Quads, why don't you show Mr Grimwinter what you can do?" said Dad with a grin.

Monday jumped on to the drum kit and let rip with a phenomenal thirty-second solo which echoed around the place like machine-gun fire. It stopped the shoppers dead in their tracks. Thursday broke into a phat bass line, then Tuesday and Wednesday finished off with saxophone and trumpet solos. Barry, who always plays in the band with us, began smashing his cymbals together.

"All right for you, Mr Grimwinter?" asked Dad.

The audience began to clap and whistle, wanting more. Then Grimwinter saw Dad's weird-looking two-horned violin. His face twisted in horror. "What in the name of goodness is that thing?"

"My Stroh."

"Is it loud?"

"Very. It can take the skin off a rice pudding at fifty paces."

It was clear Grimwinter was having second thoughts. Massive second thoughts. "I know you're called Crank Up The Volume, but could you keep the volume down just a bit? The idea is to entertain the shoppers, not frighten them away." He retreated to his office to worry.

Dad had once described his Stroh as the band's "unique selling point". Shufty preferred to call it "uniquely ridiculous". She was right. My dad's a born entertainer, though, and our gigs were as much about him with his stupid violin as they ever were about playing music.

As the shoppers gathered round, Dad moved to the front of the stage and got things going with his usual comedy routine. "I'd like to introduce the band...!"

DAD'S CRAZY STROH VIOLIN
BASS HORN
GRAMOPHONE STYLE RESONATOR
TREBLE HORN
CHIN REST
THE STROH CONCEPT WAS INVENTED OVER A HUNDRED YEARS AGO TO MAKE VIOLINS MUCH LOUDER FOR THEATRE ORCHESTRAS AND FOR USE IN EARLY SOUND RECORDINGS. IN 1899 (WHEN THE FIRST OF THESE BEASTS WAS PATENTED) YOU COULD'NT BUY ELECTRIC AMPLIFIERS OR EVEN MICROPHONES, SO THIS WAS YOUR BEST AND ONLY CHOICE IF YOU WANTED TO "ROCK DA HOUSE"

He turned away from the crowd and towards us.

"Shufty, meet Ace, Ace, meet Shufty...!"

The shoppers seemed to love it. We'd heard his gags so many times we just pulled faces at him, which made them laugh even more.

THE FANS ↑

Then Dad whispered back to us through gritted teeth, "Just keep it snappy in the choruses, and try to look a bit more cheerful, kids. If we don't play, we don't eat."

Sadly, this was true.

We were there to provide background "muzak" – music to shop to. As far as I could make out, Dad had chosen the same dire set list we'd played for the OAP tea dance at the ice rink – nothing much from after 1945!

Nevertheless, we all got into position, Barry marching on, crashing his cymbals, ears spinning, and we launched into our first number.

I have said a lot about the general rubbishness of us, the Crankshaw family, but there's one thing we're good at – playing music. Line up the Quads, give them their musical instruments, and they'll entertain. Suddenly, they are no longer annoying little brothers, but stumpy little stars with talents way beyond their age. People are always totally impressed by how good they are. Dad, Shufty and I aren't half bad either. The band name is utterly rubbish, but we rock.

When Crank Up The Volume plays it is one of the rare occasions when we all actually get on with each other. On stage our stresses are somehow forgotten. Even Shufty and I get on with

each other (most of the time) in a way we don't anywhere else. I don't know why.

That morning we were playing better than ever. Tuesday's trumpet solos were spot on and the crowd was getting bigger and bigger. We were a hit at the Mermaid!

As the first set of songs was coming to an end, the thought of Ginger Streak being dumped on our lawn just wouldn't go away. Although we were given a cup of tea and a sandwich during the interval by Grimwinter (now a little less worried than he had been), I was so nervous I couldn't eat or drink.

Phase One of the Secret Plan was almost in the bag, but Phase Two had really started to plague my mind.

It was all very well *having* a rocket, but not much use if I didn't actually enter the race. I had to do something about it quickly.

Luckily, under the New Regime, Shufty had taken it upon herself to send grovelling emails to all the people Dad owed money to. So she'd brought her laptop with her to the shopping centre because there was free Wi-Fi there, the grand piano serving as her temporary office during the interval.

I had to get on to Zircon's website and enter the race. The entry deadline was getting close. I could have done it at Jake's, but he'd done enough for me already, and I wanted to do this bit for myself.

I grabbed Shufty's laptop when she was playing her favourite solo and got to work quickly, finding the webpage and entering all my details. She glared at me and mouthed "Leave it alone" as she played. Needless to say, I ignored her. This was it. The Secret Plan was working, and that $10 million was getting closer and closer to my bank account.

My finger hesitated over the return key for a couple of seconds. This was a life-changing moment. I caught my breath, then sent the application. I'd done it. Next stop, the Moon!

Shufty finished her tune and, as the shoppers were giving her a round of applause, she grabbed the laptop back. Then she saw the Space Race webpage. "Why are you looking at that?"

"Oh. No reason, really."

"Well, stop running my battery down, and leave my stuff alone, OK?"

Dad started on a short history of the Stroh violin. He was just firing off a small explosive charge from the instrument's horn (to demonstrate its uses as a military weapon) when I noticed Danny Thumper, the bailiff, and his dogs, Love and Hate. The gruesome trio were grinning at us menacingly from the crowd.

He was back.

"What's yours is mine, Crankshaw!" he yelled, while the two dogs strained at their leads. "Give me the instruments, the laptop and the car keys!"

Dad launched into the next number while jumping off stage, scampering towards the escalators and shouting back, "Keep playing, kids – if we stop, we don't get paid!"

Climbing the escalators two at a time, he didn't miss a note, and Barry followed him, crashing his little cymbals, ears spinning as fast as a washing machine.

I watched as Thumper unleashed the slavering dogs in Dad's direction.

"Faster, Dad!" shouted Shufty.

Dad hadn't seen the pit bulls hot on his heels and

THE GUITAR PLECTRUM I USED AT THE MERMAID GIG

thought Shufty was making some sort of musical comment.

"This tune is marked *Allegro*, Shufty," he called out. "Don't rush! Keep in time..."

"Does he honestly think I'm talking about the music?" replied Shufty as Hate sank his teeth into my father's backside and hung on.

"Ahaaaaaaaaahaaaaaaaa!" Dad, yelling with pain, made it to the top of the escalator, but Love had soon overtaken him, cutting off his escape route. Then Thumper bounded up the escalator after them all, leaving Dad no choice but to come back down.

Despite having two pit bulls hanging off him, and Barry the robot monkey on his back, Dad continued to play his violin, never missing a note of the tune.

This was turning into quite a spectacle.

Dad, spotting the ornamental pond and waterfall beside the stage, quickly swerved off towards it, vaulting into the waist-deep water.

Barry, who up until now had been clinging on to Dad for dear life, was programmed to avoid getting wet at all costs, so jumped clear. He landed with a "hoo-ho-ho" and straightened his waistcoat. It seemed the dogs weren't sure of the water either, and let go of Dad's rump.

Dad, still playing the Stroh, waded as fast as he could to the cascading waterfall feature beside the statue of a mermaid, who was the patron saint of the shopping centre. He was trying to hide behind the tumbling water, but from the stage we could see him as clear as anything.

"Come out from behind there!" bellowed Thumper, reaching the pool himself and diving in.

Grimwinter had heard the shouting and barking. He shot out of his office at top speed, screeching at Shufty, "What in heaven's name is going on here?"

Shufty stood up and grabbed the microphone. "This is a number called 'Sing, Sing, Sing' ... Monday – drums!"

With growing panic, I dug out my music for the next tune, but I could tell Dad was on the brink of disaster. How were we meant to help him?

By now Thumper was in hot pursuit and had almost reached Dad. The old man was clutching his Stroh in one hand and grasping a section of what appeared to be solid rock in the other. But as he tried to haul himself up, a huge section of plastic strata came away in his hand and fell into the water. He jumped and tried to grab the next piece of the outcrop, but it wouldn't support his weight either.

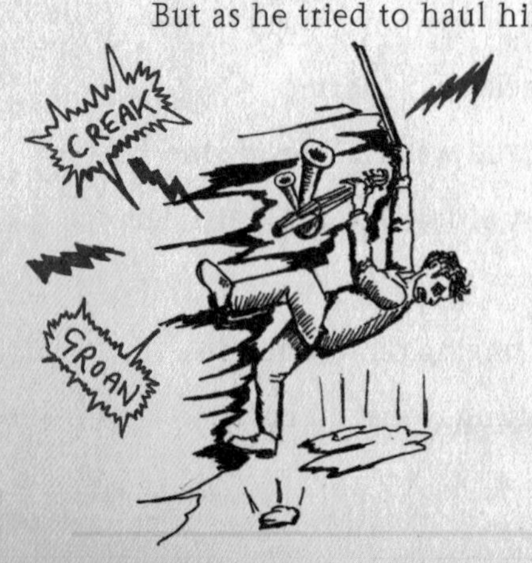

Tuesday's drumming had distracted Grimwinter for a colossal six seconds, but he soon cottoned on to the damage being inflicted on the mermaid's decor by Dad's escape. A crowd of bored shoppers, fascinated by what was going on, began to form around the waterfall.

It was as if Dad was competing in some sort of game show. Some people were on Dad's side and were shouting, "Don't forget yer crampons, mate, it's a long way to the summit!" and the others, gunning for Thumper, were screaming, "Set the dogs on him!"

Thumper didn't need any encouragement. He'd swum across the water feature by now, and was grabbing at Dad's leg.

Dad jumped up for the next outcrop, and managed to get a grip, until the rock gave way with a sudden jolt. He fell, bringing the mermaid statue crashing down with him. The statue cracked the pond's retaining wall with a bang. Immediately a surging tide of water rushed across the marble floor towards the shoppers.

They ran away, screaming in terror, as the lights fused and there was an enormous blue electrical flash from a room beside the stage. The entire lighting system blew, plunging the building into darkness.

Dad surfed back to the stage on the wave of water, Stroh violin held high, yelling, "The gig's over. Permanently! Leg it!"

We grabbed our stuff and elbowed our way through the crowd, sprinting for the Land Rover. I cast a last glance at our enemy. I could just make out the silhouette of Thumper wading his way out of what remained of the pond. The dogs had lost interest and were busily chomping their way through a koi carp apiece, while Grimwinter was yelling, "You'll never work in retail entertainment again, Crankshaw!"

WE UNPLUGGED FROM THE MERMAID — PERMANENTLY.

CAPTAIN CALAMITY CRANKSHAW AND

THE MERMAID

KEY

1 CRANK UP THE VOLUME (US) ARE BUSY PLAYING MUSIC FOR THE SHOPPERS AT THE MERMAID CENTRE

2 THUMPER AND HIS DOGS (CALLED 'LOVE' AND 'HATE') TURN UP DEMANDING WE HAND OVER OUR MUSICAL INSTRUMENTS, SHUFTY'S LAPTOP AND THE LAND ROVER KEYS

3 DAD DECIDES THE BEST THING TO DO IS RUN AWAY. BARRY FOLLOWS AFTER HIM

4 DAD MAKES FOR THE UPPER LEVEL OF SHOPS, TAKING THE 'UP' ESCALATOR TWO STEPS AT A TIME. HATE BITES DAD ON THE BUM AND HANGS ON.

5 MEANWHILE LOVE OVERTAKES AND CUTS OFF HIS ESCAPE ROUTE.

6 WITH THUMPER HOT ON DAD'S HEELS, THE OLD MAN DECIDES TO DO A U-TURN AND HEADS FOR THE DOWN ESCALATOR. BARRY JUMPS ON DAD'S BACK WHILE LOVE BITES INTO THE OLD MAN'S LEFT BUTTOCK

7 DAD COMES UP WITH A NEW PLAN - TO SWIM FOR FREEDOM. HE SWERVES OFF TOWARDS THE POND AND JUMPS IN.

8 BARRY AND THE DOGS DON'T LIKE THE LOOK OF THE WATER AND LET GO. DAD WADES IN, DEEPER AND DEEPER

THE MERMAID CENTRE
Mr C. Grimwinter, O.B.E
General Manager

PAGE 2

MERMAID REPAIR BI
'COLOSSAL' AS MALL
IS FORCED TO CLOSE
FOR TWO MONTHS

49
DISASTER
9 HE NOW COMES UP WITH A NEW TOTALLY RUBBISH STRATEGY— HE ATTEMPTS TO HIDE BEHIND THE WATERFALL. THIS DOESN'T WORK
10 WITH THUMPER APPROACHING FAST, DAD MAKES ANOTHER BID FOR THE UPPER FLOOR BY CLIMBING THE FAKE ROCKS. THESE BREAK OFF AND ENDS UP BACK IN THE WATER
11 HE TRIES AGAIN. MORE FAKE ROCKS BREAK OFF AND HE FALLS – CRASHING INTO THE MERMAID STATUE.
12 THE MERMAID TOPPLES OVER AND SMACKS INTO THE POND'S RETAINING WALL. THE WALL CRACKS AND THE WATER STARTS FLOOD OUT. THIS SWAMPS THE SHOPS AND BLOWS UP THE ELECTRICS.
13 DAD SURFS OUT ON THE TIDE AND ORDERS A GENERAL RETREAT
14 WE PACK UP AT TOP SPEED AND RUN FOR THE EXIT
SHOPS
WATERFALL
10
11
12
9
SHOPS
MERMAID STATUE
FLOOD WATER
13
SHOPS
14
GRIMWINTER'S OFFICE
EXIT
CAPTAIN CALAMITY CRANKSHAW
BARRY
STROH
CALAMITY SHIFTS INTO TOP GEAR DURING THE CHASE
CHOMP
CHOMP
LOVE
HATE
'HE'S RUINED THE PLACE' BLUBBERS MERMAID MANAGER
IN AN EXTRAORDINA

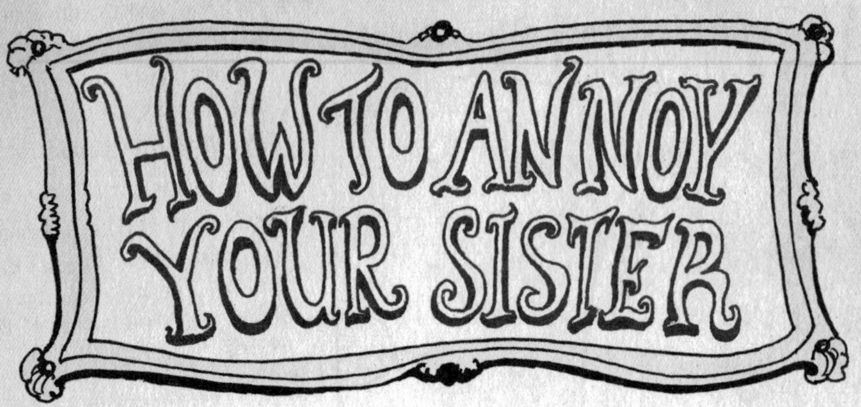

We slumped into a miserable, doom-laden silence as we drove home. This was not the ideal setting I'd had in mind to reveal the Secret Plan, and the dirty great rocket which was probably now parked on our front lawn.

Shufty sat with her arms crossed in the front passenger seat, her face a mixture of anger, disappointment and bitter frustration. The gig was meant to be a new dawn, but instead it had just made everything much, much worse.

Monday got to the root of the problem. "Ace ... Ace ... you know when you break something in a shop and have to pay for it, well ... will Dad have to pay for the entire Mermaid Centre coz he *really* broke that ... and he flooded all the shops ... and he broke the electricity as well?"

"Have a bag of crisps," I said, chucking the Quads some grub. If they were eating, there'd be less chance of them blurting out painful truths.

In this volatile atmosphere, several times I dared myself to say, "Hey, guess what? I've bought a space rocket," but I just had to look at Shufty smouldering like a volcano about to erupt, and I'd lose my nerve. Dad had one eyebrow arched and a slightly pained expression as if he expected the inevitable outburst at any time. Either that or he was still a bit sore from the dogs. He cast the

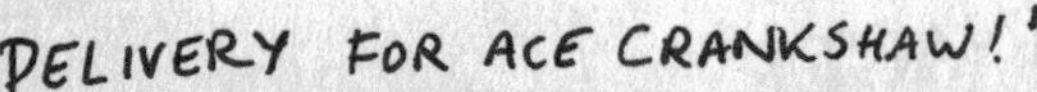

occasional glance at Shufty, and she just dead-eyed him back with a "well-what-do-you-want-me-to-do-about-it?" look.

We had reached a new level in the Dad-versus-Shufty war.

As we arrived home, I saw Jake at the bottom of the drive on his bike, waving.

Oh no. I knew this could only mean one thing.

"What's he doing here?" asked Shufty. "Get rid of him. And Dad, don't you dare stop to talk to him. OK?"

Then I saw them.

Then everyone saw them.

Six HGV trailers parked slap-bang on the lawn.

The first was loaded with the unmistakable body of a rocket – the largest chunk of Ginger Streak lying horizontally under a tarpaulin with its two main engines pointing directly at the house.

"Cor ... what's all that stuff?" said Monday. "It looks really expensive. Is that yours, Dad? Is it for another barbecue

JAKE'S PIC OF THE ROCKET BEING DELIVERED!
THIS TRAILER HAS THE UPPER STAGES ON IT

PHASES OF THE MOON

NEW MOON | WAXING CRESCENT | FIRST QUARTER | WAXING GIBBOUS | FULL | WANING GIBBOUS | THIRD QUARTER | WANING CRESCENT

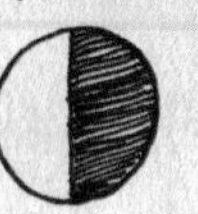

invention? Shufty won't like it, will you, Shufty?"

"What the...?" breathed Shufty.

"It's mine," I blurted out. "I was going to tell you ... but..."

"What's yours?"

"All of it."

Silence. The Quads hadn't quite worked out what it was, but were peering at it, their cupped hands pressed to the glass. I had seconds left before they realized.

"Ace, old son. What is it?" asked Dad, the row with Shufty temporarily shelved.

"Errr ... yep." I did a fake cough, and tacked on "Ginger Streak" to the end of it in a sort of mutter.

"What is Ginger Streak?" asked Shufty very slowly.

"Ummh..." I mumbled, still unable to bring myself to say the word.

Dad turned round, a slow, knowing smirk dancing on his lips. "Tell me, Ace, is it *the* Ginger Streak I'm thinking of from the seventies, or is that just a coincidence?"

My heart was pounding. I was speechless. What had I done?

"Go on. Tell me. What is it and why did you buy it?" said Shufty finally, turning round and fixing me with a stare.

The Quads finally worked out what it was. Thursday yelled at the top of his voice, "It's a space rocket!" and they began bouncing up and down screaming, "Ace has bought a space rocket! Ace has bought a space rocket!!"

"Yep. It's a rocket, so I can enter the Great Space Race."

"Zack Zircon's Space Race? Our arch enemy Zack Zircon's Space Race?" Shufty's eyes twitched left to right, searching me for an answer.

"It's a cash-raising idea. We can win $10 million. It's the best idea anyone has come up with—"

"I can't actually believe this ... get rid of it," said Shufty. "Call whoever delivered it and tell them to come back and take it away." She grappled with the Land Rover's door, kicking it open and marching off towards the kitchen, not giving the trailers a second glance. Dad was about to speak, but she stopped and turned. "And, Buzz Lightyear, make sure you get your money back, because we're going to need it. Every penny. *Comprendez?*"

Dad, meanwhile, flashed a smile, which grew to a grin, then a laugh. "I think you're on to a winner with this, old son. Yes ... a real winner." He jumped out of the Land Rover and wandered off in the direction of his workshop.

"Wicked, man. Your own ship," said Jake, wheelie-ing to a stop on his bike. "Bigger than you thought?"

"That's an understatement," I said, getting out of the car, followed by the Quads.

"I should charge you a finder's fee," Jake grinned.

Dad came back clutching a menacing-looking jemmy for opening the crates on the trailers. "Let's take a look," he said. "Where do we start?"

I pointed at the first crate and he swung into action.

"This rocket idea could work, Ace," he added, clenching his teeth and straining to open the crate.

As the lid finally came away, the Quads, Jake, Barry and I all gathered round to see what was inside. It looked like some sort of Iron Age computer underneath a pile of straw.

"What do you think it does?" asked Thursday.

"Oh, that's easy," replied Jake. "It's the mission-control computer. Very advanced for its time."

"How do you know this stuff?" I asked.

"I just do, man."

"Well, fella," said Dad, rubbing his hands together. "I can't wait to unpack the rest of her." There wasn't a hint of doubt about the rocket plan to be found in Dad's knuckleheaded grin as he began to prise open lid after lid.

What had we got ourselves into? More to the point, what had *I* got us into? Was this really the only way to save our family? There must be an easier way. All those thoughts were churning around inside my head, but I suddenly didn't care. Why? Because I now owned a rocket, and it was totally and utterly the most exciting day of my life.

The General gazed down at us from her bedroom window with a fuming, unblinking stare. I was ecstatic with my very bargainatious five-quid purchase; she on the other hand was totally and utterly ... how would I put it? Seething? So seething she couldn't speak? It was worse than that. I think in her mind I'd just moved into Dad's league, and I was being rated as a new and dangerous enemy to the Crankshaw family's future. Hmm ... I marked down her attitude to the rocket as furious. Furious to the max. Yep, a full ten out of ten to me on the sister-baiting scale.

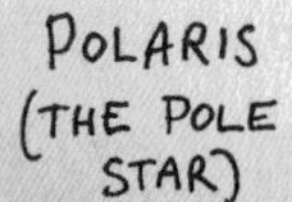

When school finally broke up a few days later and the summer holidays began, things were still far from relaxed at The Mill.

For a start, Dad was unable to sit down after his encounter with Thumper's pets at the shopping centre. So now, to keep busy, the old man had decided to mount a defence campaign against Thumper, sealing off the drive with a padlock and chains and adopting "siege precautions", as he described them. Military preparations were under way for the bailiff's inevitable return.

But, of course, there was also the rather large problem of Ginger Streak sitting in the garden. There were six massive trailers with six massive loads of stuff on the back. This rocket was huge. I had no idea what to do with it all. I mean, where do you start? I hadn't a clue.

On top of that, I hadn't heard anything from the Space Race people to confirm my application since I'd fired it off at the shopping centre.

So with all the operations taking place to keep Thumper at bay, and Ginger Streak being a major preoccupation, we'd all failed to realize that Dad's fame was being incubated by the world-wide web like some gruesome alien egg.

Shufty had found several camera-phone movies of Dad playing the

OH YEAH – I COULD DEFINITELY ENTER THE OLD MAN INTO THE 'WORLD'S MOST EMBARRASSING DAD' COMPETITION.

16.2 MILLION VIEW ONLINE CLIP OF DOG CHASE VIOLINIST

BY BILL HENRY

VIOLINIST and inventor ARTHUR 'CALAMITY' CRANKSHAW – destroyer of the recently opened Mermaid Shopping Centre – has become an internet sensation.

Inventor Crankshaw set about destroying the multimillion pound centre in a bizarre chase involving a pair of angry dogs and a robot monkey toy.

Phone movies shot and posted online by several terrified shoppers have been viewed by 16.2 million people, making Crankshaw a worldwide hit. These clips show the demolition derby in close-up.

Stroh violin with a pair of pit bulls attached to his nether regions, shot by shoppers at the Mermaid. She pulled up a YouTube page, and there he was for all the world to see ... and the world *was* seeing him, to judge by the ridiculous amount of hits.

Only one day after it had happened, a staggering 899,736 people had seen it. It had a maximum five-star rating. Twenty-four hours later the number rose to nearly five million. By day three my dad had been laughed at by 16.2 million people worldwide. By day four, the old-fashioned TV news channels and newspapers were reporting this hit rate as an important national news story.

Should I have been surprised then to find Ki-Ki Sapphire, the presenter of TV's woeful *Ki-Ki's Afternoon Cuppa*, being helped by her cameraman and sound recordist to climb over the locked gate?

She flashed her trademark smile. "Hi, I'm Ki-Ki."

"I know," I answered, slightly embarrassed. "Errr ... hi. Ummhhh ... I'm Ace."

"I was wondering if I could speak to your dad."

"Is it about Ginger Streak?" I asked.

"Ginger who?"

"Ginger Streak."

Ki-Ki looked confused. "I want to interview your father about the shopping-centre incident."

"Why?" I said. "Are they after him for damages?"

"Damages? No, I want his side of the story. I want to know how he actually felt as the dogs bit into him. He's famous around the world, you know. A celebrity..."

"What, for having some dogs bite him on the backside?"

"That's all it takes these days, Ace. Have you seen the film? It's very, very, very good," she laughed. "He needs to get an agent."

"I don't need to see the film," I said grumpily. "I was there. Unfortunately."

"Is your dad about?"

A bang and a "Deee-yerrr ... yoowwwhhhh!" indicated that he was still making delicate adjustments to his latest anti-Thumper device. Then, as if Ki-Ki's arrival wasn't tricky enough, over her shoulder I saw the alarming sight of Love and Hate charging towards the padlocked gate like greyhounds after a rabbit, followed seconds later by a massive yellow JCB excavator.

"Thumper!" I yelled.

"Who?" asked Ki-Ki.

"The bailiff. He's here for our stuff."

"Do you think he'll wait until I've spoken to your father?"

"I doubt it – look!"

Thumper was accelerating towards the front gate. Dad's dainty padlock wouldn't stand a chance. Thumper changed down a gear for more power and, in a huge cloud of climate-changing exhaust fumes, he lowered the scoop and crashed through the gate at speed.

Surprisingly, Dad had planned for this, and as the gate was pushed over it tripped the first booby trap – a set of spikes which hinged up out of a small trench and tore into the digger's tyres. On hearing the tyres explode and the JCB judder to a halt, the

DROPPED D GUITAR TUNING D A D G B E INSTEAD OF → E A D G B E

dogs double-backed to check on their master, their paws rasping on the gravel as they changed direction.

Ki-Ki, high heels in hand, and her crew sprinted up the drive to the safety of the old pigsty.

"Dad! He's here!" I yelled over the grinding of gears and barking behind me.

The workshop doors swung open and the old man ran out almost slap-bang into Ki-Ki. "If you're here for money, I haven't got any," he said.

"No," said Ki-Ki. "I want to interview you, if that's all right?"

"Oh yes." He laughed falsely. "Is it about the barbecue design?" He might have been talking to Ki-Ki, but his focus was firmly fixed on Thumper, the dogs and the stranded digger.

"What barbecue design?" asked Ki-Ki.

"The jet-powered barbecue," replied Dad, craning his neck to get a better view of Thumper. "It's a revelation in alfresco dining. Burgers cooked in three seconds flat."

Ki-Ki followed Dad's gaze to the scene ahead and suddenly changed the subject.

"Are those the dogs from the shopping centre?"

The next chapter of the horrific Mermaid saga was unfolding before her very eyes. The crew knew it too. The sound man was hurriedly turning on his equipment, while the cameraman shouldered his camera, the pair edging around to get the best angle of Dad and the stranded digger.

TELEVISION REVIEW

Ki-Ki's Afternoon Cuppa

★☆☆☆☆

Is it just me or does the return of **Ki-Ki's Afternoon Cuppa** *(Mon-Fri 3pm)* mark a new cultural low? This *surely* is the zero on the ruler by which all daytime TV shows are measured?

But last year's winner of *The Worst Show on TV* is back, after Ki-Ki danced her way to the ballroom finals with her ratings grabbing tango earlier this year. Yes, Ki-Ki is TV hot property again.

The titles fade to reveal Ki-Ki enthroned on the famous red velvet chair, the queen of her own fantasy land. Beside her the props department pump steam through the spout of a fake teapot with such force that it looks as if our hostess has worked up enough boiler pressure to pull a 10-carriage train.

Then she opens her mouth to reveal those teeth. They're even whiter and brighter than you remember, with a glare as blinding as the epicentre of a nuclear blast. Bedazzled, we begin our nightmare return journey aboard Ki-Ki's saccharin express.

An innovation on last season's run is Ki-Ki's attempt to be more 'hands on', she tells us. A new feature, snappily entitled *Ki-Ki Reports*, sees our beaming presenter loose in the real world and attempting what looks like a form of journalism.

Camera crew in tow, Ki-Ki sets out to find what she calls 'real stories about real people'. All well and good until we meet th[illegible]

← KI-KI'S SHOW – 30 MINUTES OF UTTER DRIVE

Dad knew he couldn't delay any longer. "Would you be so kind as to help my son to operate one of the water cannons?" he asked, pointing in the direction of the tripod-mounted hose hidden in the bushes. "If we can get rid of the man with the dogs, I'll be happy to give you an interview on any subject of your choosing."

"Me?" asked Ki-Ki. "I'm not getting involved. We're impartial journalists."

The Quads and Barry ran out of the house and saw what was going on. Barry went berserk, rushing towards Dad, his ears twirling so fast one of them flew out of its socket.

"Man the defences, kids!" commanded Dad. The Quads saluted and moved off to their positions. "Defence plan four!" he called after them. "Direct assault in daylight. Shufty? Shufty, where are you?"

"Here," she said, wandering out to see what the commotion was. "Oh, great – Thumper. That's all we need! He's here for the rest of our stuff."

"Shufty – start the engine for the water cannons."

"This plan is stupid," said Shufty, none the less jogging off to her allotted position at the pump house by the stream.

"Ace, help me with the TDV."

"The what?"

"The tactical defence vehicle."

The tactical defence vehicle was just the old Land Rover rebranded with a flashy new name. For the last two days, this had been the centre of Dad's attention. He'd welded a huge water tank to the back of it and connected up a high-powered pump and hose to it.

"Bump start, Dad?" I asked, from long experience.

"No need. I've charged the battery specially."

The starter motor wheezed once, then died from lack of power. Dad jumped out and cranked the engine into life with an old-fashioned starter handle. The spearhead of Dad's battle plan gasped and shuddered into life in a belch of smoke.

"Jump aboard, Ace and keep your eyes peeled for those pit bulls. Pass me my flying-helmet and goggles, fella."

Barry gave a shriek and climbed in beside me, handing me his loose ear, while Ki-Ki and her crew jumped up on the tailgate.

"Mind if we join you?" she asked.

"Be my guest. The barbecue is this way," said Dad.

We went about a hundred feet before the huge weight of the water tank and extra passengers broke the Land Rover's rusty back. There was a loud bang as the chassis split, and the gearbox exploded with a dull thump. One of the front wheels splayed out, and the vehicle slewed off the track and slid towards the ditch by the veg patch. The Land Rover ground to a halt. Water dripped, then began to pour from the poorly welded water tank.

"I saw a car like this at a circus once," chortled Ki-Ki. "It was driven by a clown."

"Please keep quiet, whoever you are," flustered Dad.

The camera crew dismounted, took up a new position in the ditch alongside and focused on the attack. Dad grabbed the CB radio handset. "Big Dog, this is Big Dog. Charlie 1, can you read me, over?"

I could see movement down near the gate. Thumper was taking no chances and was deploying a platoon of hired hard nuts. This didn't look good.

The CB crackled into life. "Big Dog, Big Dog, this is Charlie 1."

Charlie 1 was Monday, our recon expert, whose battle station was in what Dad called the "crow's nest" at the top of the house – sometimes known as my bedroom. His job was to relay information back to Dad on the state of the battle. Dad could then coordinate his forces (or so the idea went).

The plan was to use a series of high-pressure water cannons linked up to the pump house by the millpond "to deter any advancing forces", as Dad described it. My bedroom was an ideal vantage point because it had four windows pointing in every direction, with good views of all approaches to the house. Dad had also installed a contraption in my bedroom he called the Anti-Thumper Alarm, which was meant to help with the blind spots.

"Big Dog here," Dad said, slowly. "Reading you loud and clear. Ahhh, we're hung up in the ditch by the back gate. The TDV is temporarily out of action. Report the enemy's position, over."

Monday answered slowly and clearly, "Big Dog. Big Dog. They're sneaking up from the direction of the cesspit and the pond. They've occupied the potting shed, the garage and the greenhouse. Over."

Dad pushed his goggles up on to his forehead. "They're trying a pincer movement. Watch the flanks, Charlie 1. I'll try to get the pump working on the Land Rover ... TDV, I mean."

Dad was now trying to power up the high-pressure pump by yanking at one of the Land Rover's three gear-sticks. In theory this would connect the pump to the engine, but with a blown gearbox, he wasn't having much luck.

"Charlie 2 has fallen back to the herb-garden strong point and

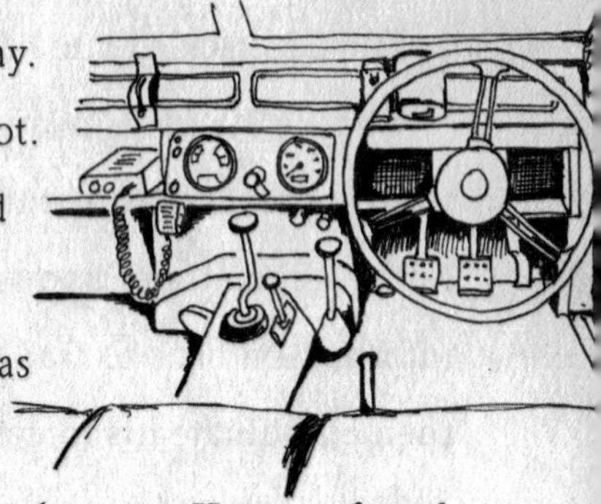

is holding the south side," said Monday.

Charlie 2 was Thursday, our best shot. In the background there was the sound of a high-powered watery battle with shouts and yells from Thumper's men as he hosed them down.

I tried to work out what Thumper's plan was. He was after the jet engine. He'd said as much. And the instruments, for sure. But what about Ginger Streak? It was possible he didn't know about the six trailers of 1970s space kit yet.

"Do you think he'll take the rocket as well?" I asked Dad. "It's mine, after all, not yours. I paid for it."

"Rocket?" said Ki-Ki with surprise. "What rocket? Is that the stuff on those low loaders?"

"Yes. Ginger Streak. I thought that's what you were here to interview me about, not Dad and the dogs. I've tried to enter us into the Great Space Race so we can earn some money."

Ki-Ki's mouth dropped open. "The Great Space Race? Zircon's Space Race?"

"Yes. Have you heard of it?"

"Of course I've heard of it," said Ki-Ki. "Everyone has heard of it. Do you think you can get to the Moon with that thing?"

"It's the only chance we have of clearing our debts," I replied. "We're going after Zircon's $10-million prize."

"Are you serious?"

"Serious? Check it out." I pointed towards Thumper's advancing troops. "They're here for the rest of our stuff, so we don't really have any choice now, do we?"

Dad forced the gear-stick into place with his boot, then tried to start the engine. It coughed twice, then died.

Ki-Ki sparked into action. "There's a story in this. Yes – bankrupt family enters the richest race in history. We'll put you on my show tomorrow. We'll sneak through the hedge, get you all aboard my people carrier, then head straight for London." She ran off towards the hedge, followed by her crew.

There was a loud bang from the pump house, and a geyser of water blasted through the tiled roof. After a full three minutes of battle, the defence of The Mill seemed to be in its final stages.

The radio crackled to life again. It was Shufty, and she sounded highly irritated. "Dad. Are you there ... Dad?"

"This is Big Dog, over."

"Shut up and listen," Shufty snapped. "They're swarming up the drive and we've just lost water pressure. We can't hold them back again if they have another try. No water. No water jet. Over and out ... OF WATER."

"There must be a blockage in the intake," said Dad, grabbing for the CB handset. "All units. This is Big Dog. Set off the smoke bombs and regroup to the TDV. We're pulling out. Grab the musical instruments, if you can. Over."

"They're at the back door. I put them out ready," shouted Shufty, her voice distorting. "I knew this water-jet nonsense was a waste of time."

It didn't take long for clouds of sulphurous smoke to start billowing across the garden. One by one the Crankshaw army retreated to the ditch beside the crippled Land Rover. The Quads arrived first.

"Cor ... those men we've hosed down with the stinky old pond water don't look very happy that we've ruined their clothes," said Tuesday.

"Ace ... Ace ... does this mean we're in even more trouble now Dad's plan has gone really, completely and totally wrong?" asked Thursday, slightly out of breath. "Does this mean we'll have to pay for cleaning the mud off those really angry men's clothes coz we don't have two pennies to rub together to pay for it, you know?"

"Why are you asking me?" I said. "Ask Captain Calamity Crankshaw over there. This was his big idea."

POWER CHORD

B5

Shufty was last in, clutching her accordion case, her laptop and the last few family valuables. Her face was like thunder. "Oh, you've really done it now, haven't you, Dad? They'll take everything. What do we do next?"

Dad was about to defend himself against Shufty's verbal attack, but Barry, who'd seen the fanged mouths of Love and Hate approaching, started pointing and screeching. The dogs were sniffing out Dad's scent, keen to renew their acquaintance. They stopped, sniffed again, then plotted a course directly towards us at top speed.

"Crikey!" Dad cried, clutching his recovering rear end. "Over the top! Leg it! Leave the monkey! Leave the monkey!"

Shufty was already off before he gave the final order to escape. Big Dog was being chased by two real dogs, both with a dangerous glint in their eyes. They raced across the vegetable patch towards us, fangs glinting in the sun. Despite Dad's last order, I couldn't leave Barry, who was jumping up and down in terror, so I grabbed him and swung him up on my back. He clung on around my neck and I raced off at top speed. The camera crew followed behind us, filming everything.

I could tell by all the "hoo-ho-ho" noises Barry was making in my ear that our pursuers were close behind. The image of one of Thumper's mutts attached to my backside gave me the sort of adrenalin-fuelled speed normally seen only at the closing stages of track and field events at the Olympic Games. Dad overtook us all, clutching his rear end with one hand and the Stroh violin with the other.

Ki-Ki's head appeared in a gap in the hedge, from where she called and beckoned us to her waiting people carrier.

In a rare moment of intelligence, Dad lifted his Stroh violin to his chin and, using all its colossal stopping power, played a really high, screeching note. Love and Hate pulled up short. Their heads tilted and their eyebrows twitched up, and they began to whimper and slink away with their tails between their legs. This gave us vital seconds to clamber into the waiting car. The crew's sound recordist was last to arrive, using his boom mike like a medieval jouster to ram through the hedge.

We'd escaped.

Just.

Ki-Ki floored the accelerator and we pulled away up the lane with a squeal of tyres, passing Thumper, who emerged from the side gate, waving his fist at us. We couldn't hear the exact swear words he used, but he'd gone a bright red and the veins were bulging on his neck and forehead like oil pipelines.

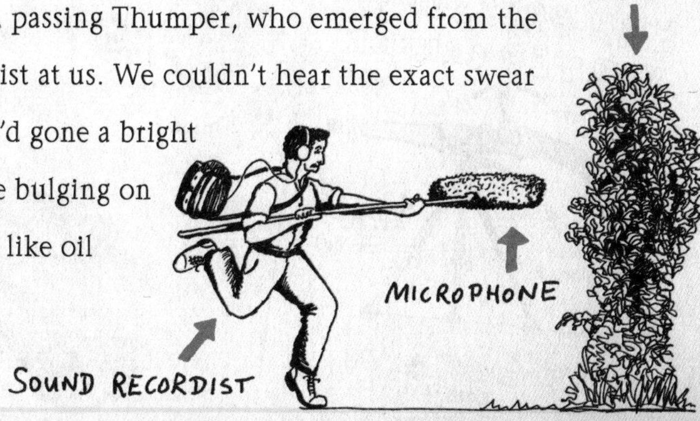

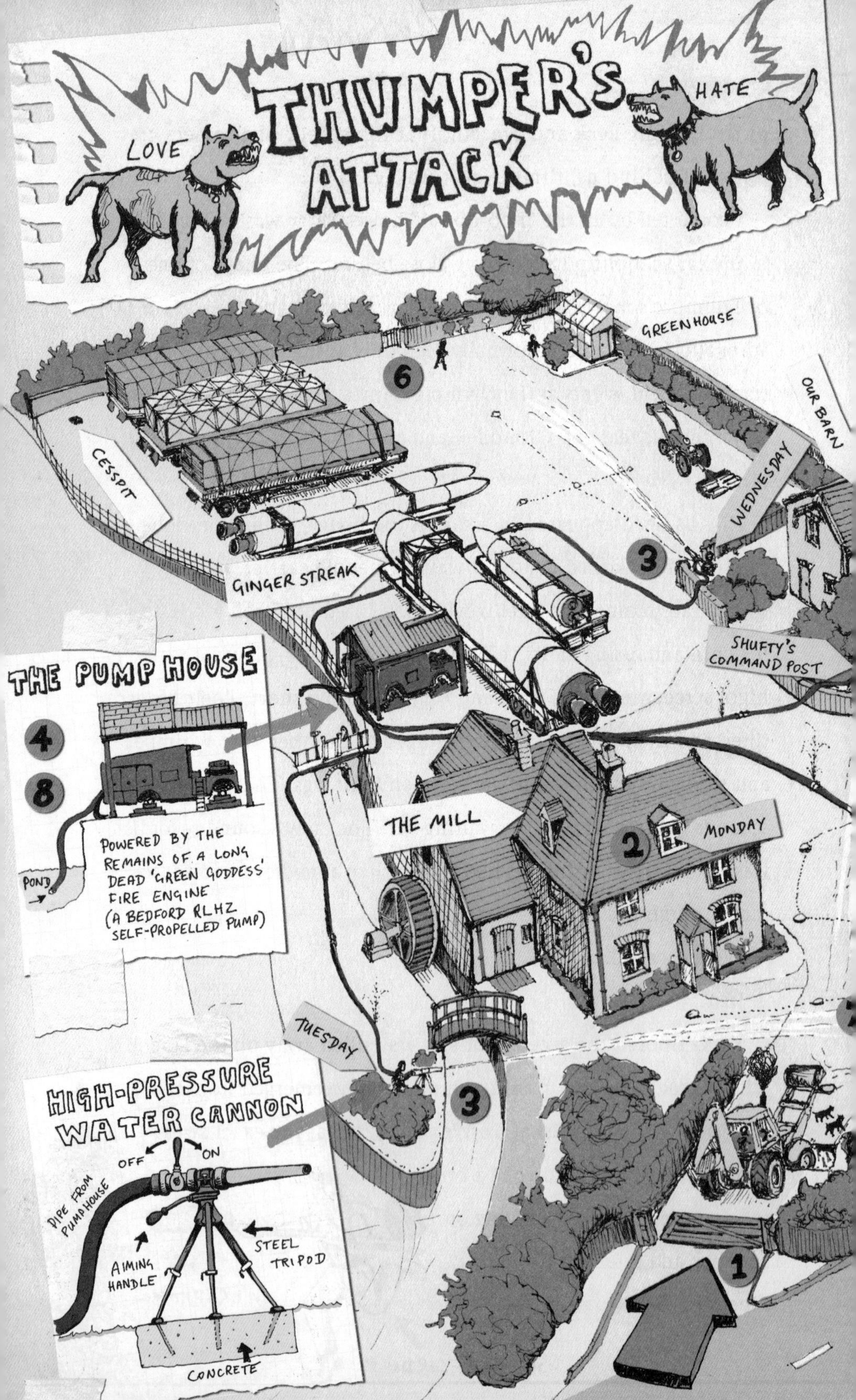
THUMPER'S ATTACK
LOVE
HATE
GREENHOUSE
6
OUR BARN
CESSPIT
WEDNESDAY
3
GINGER STREAK
SHUFTY'S COMMAND POST
THE PUMP HOUSE
4
8
POWERED BY THE REMAINS OF A LONG DEAD 'GREEN GODDESS' FIRE ENGINE (A BEDFORD RLHZ SELF-PROPELLED PUMP)
POND
THE MILL
2
MONDAY
TUESDAY
3
HIGH-PRESSURE WATER CANNON
OFF
ON
PIPE FROM PUMPHOUSE
AIMING HANDLE
STEEL TRIPOD
CONCRETE
1

T.D.V.
TACTICAL DEFENCE VEHICLE
SERIES IIA
LONG WHEEL-BASE LAND ROVER
DATE OF MANUFACTURE: 1968
2¼ LITRE ENGINE
BADLY WELDED WATER TANK
WATER GAUGE
AERIAL FOR CB RADIO
WATER PUMP
HIGH-PRESSURE WATER CANNON
STARTER HANDLE
ROTTEN CHASSIS
WORKSHOP
KI-KI'S CAR
JET BBQ
POTTING SHED
OLD PIG STY
GARAGE
SMOKE BOMB
DITCH
THURSDAY
THUMPER'S VAN
5
9
11
10
6
3
KEY
1 THUMPER RAMS THE GATE BUT IS STOPPED BY DAD'S BOOBY TRAP
2 MONDAY TAKES UP POSITION IN THE "CROW'S NEST" AS LOOKOUT.
3 TUESDAY, WEDNESDAY AND THURSDAY MAN THE HIGH-POWERED WATER CANNON.
4 SHUFTY STARTS THE WATER PUMP THEN RUNS BACK TO HER COMMAND POST
5 DAD AND I SET OFF IN THE T.D.V. — BUT THE CHASSIS COLLAPSES UNDER THE EXTRA WEIGHT OF THE WATER TANK AND TV CREW
6 THUMPER'S HARD NUTS ADVANCE ON ALL FRONTS
7 CRANKSHAW ARMY OPENS UP WITH WATER CANNON
8 THE ANCIENT PUMP BLOWS UP
9 DAD ORDERS GENERAL RETREAT TO THE T.D.V.
10 SMOKE BOMBS SET OFF BY SHUFTY TO CAUSE CONFUSION TO THUMPER
11 WE ESCAPE THROUGH HEDGE

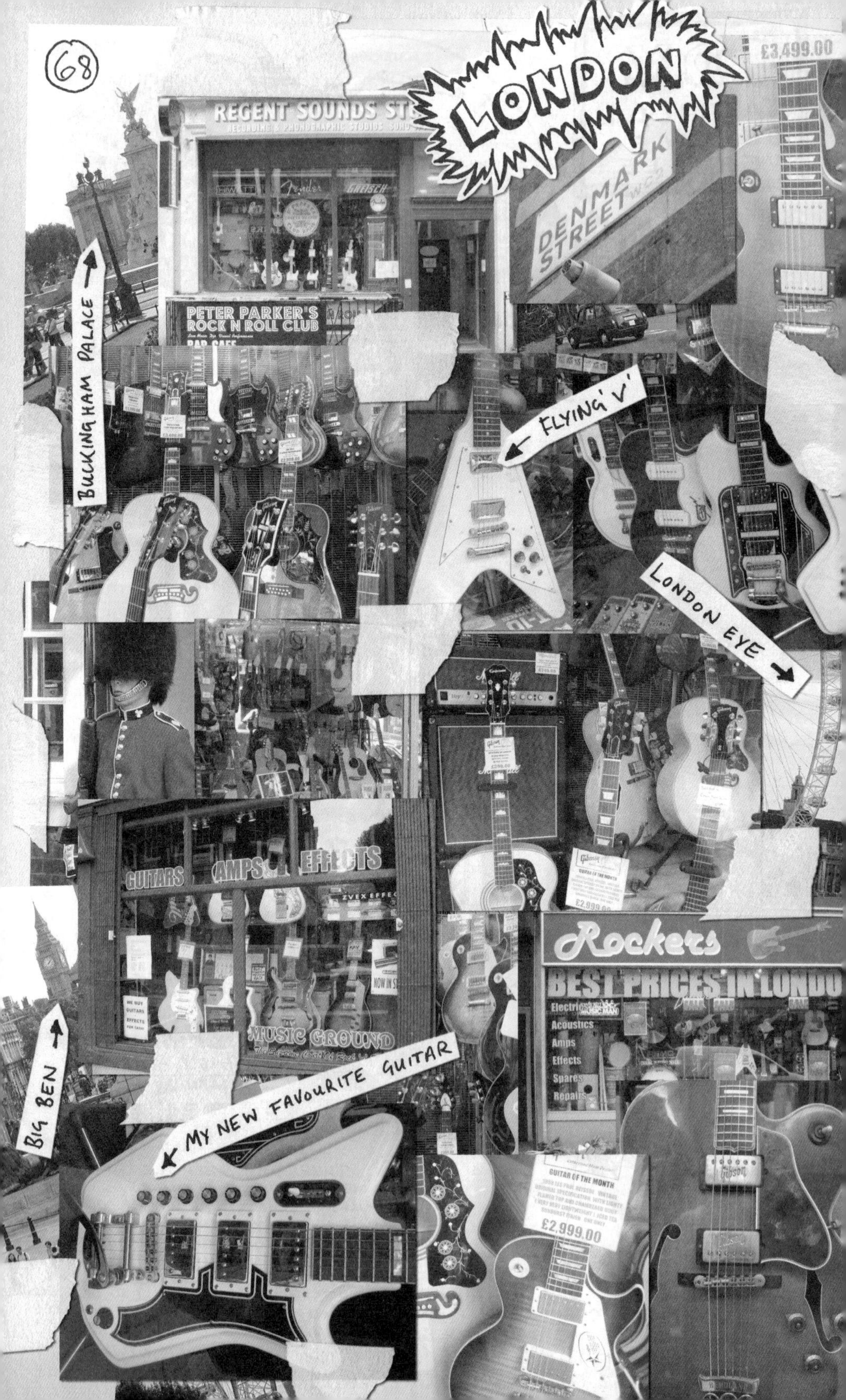

LONDON
REGENT SOUNDS ST
PETER PARKER'S
ROCK N ROLL CLUB
DENMARK STREET WC2
£3,499.00
BUCKINGHAM PALACE
FLYING 'V'
LONDON EYE
GUITARS
AMPS
EFFECTS
MUSIC GROUND
Rockers
BEST PRICES IN LONDO
Electrics
Acoustics
Amps
Effects
Spares
Repairs
BIG BEN
MY NEW FAVOURITE GUITAR
GUITAR OF THE MONTH
£2,999.00

TALKING TO THE ENEMY

Once we'd arrived at the posh hotel near the London Eye where Ki-Ki was going to put us up, she revealed her master plan. She wanted us to do a ten-minute interview slot on her show the next day, live to the nation. She wanted to rerun the now famous YouTube clip and its terrible sequel "Revenge of the Bailiff". In return we got a night in the hotel, a morning of sightseeing and all the grub we could stuff our faces with – paid for by the TV company.

Our interview went out at five o'clock the next day, right on schedule. Introducing Dad as "the most famous person on the internet", Ki-Ki then showed the new footage from The Mill. And, as the Quads tucked into the artfully arranged fruit on the coffee table, Dad switched into "entertainer mode". It was as if the whole show was going to be some sort of huge advert for his jet-propelled barbecue invention.

The whole ordeal seemed to go on and on, and just as I thought we were finished, Ki-Ki turned to me, flashing her trademark smile. "Ace, I was fascinated to hear you're entering Zack Zircon's Great Space Race with a real British space rocket." Ki-Ki smiled her fake smile again.

She seemed to have taken it as a given that Zircon had accepted my application. But I still hadn't heard a thing.

DENMARK STREET – THE BEST PLACE IN LONDON A.K.A. GUITAR HEAVEN

A.K.A. 'TIN PAN ALLEY'

Camera Three edged closer, focusing on my face. The red light on top of it indicated that I, Ace Crankshaw, was now speaking to the nation.

This was the first mention of the Space Race. I wasn't prepared. I thought we were there to talk about the Mermaid incident.

"Errrrr," I managed impressively. "Yep, well, ummmhhh ... I've, errrrr .... bought a rocket."

They showed a picture of Ginger Streak stranded on our lawn like a beached whale, obviously filmed during the heat of the Thumper battle.

"What inspired you to do such a thing?" asked Ki-Ki.

"Errrrrrr..." I bumbled on. "I want to pay off our debts. But Dad's flat broke, so ... umhhh ... we might not, you know, be able to get to America to join the race after all."

Then Ki-Ki said, "I'd like to introduce you to someone very special."

The camera pulled back. An old man with two walking-sticks hobbled in and eased himself into a chair beside our sofa. But hang on, I thought. I recognized this guy! This was Billy Nansen, the multibillionaire businessman who owned the international airline Nansen Air! He looked really unwell. His face was a purplish colour from the effort of walking, and he wheezed like Dad's Land Rover. He waved his

hand as a hello, but the effort was almost too much for him.

"I admire your plan." He paused a moment and coughed some more. "Ki-Ki here sent me a picture of your rocket last night. I understand you are in some financial difficulties. Well, I have some good news for you. I have ... telephoned the debt agency and have stopped them ... from bothering you..." He coughed, making a sound like someone unblocking a drain with a sink plunger. "...until after the race. Next stop..." he waved his hand skyward, "...the Moon."

"Ace ... Ace ... that old coffin-dodger sounds like he's got bits of snot and green cough-bogies rattling round in his throat, doesn't he?" said Monday, for all the nation to hear.

Forget the cough-bogies. Had our luck changed?

Shufty, head in hands with boredom, turned towards Nansen, as if seeing him for the first time. Her left eyebrow arched upwards, her eyes focusing on our apparent saviour with disbelief. She spoke for the first time in the entire interview. "You're going to help us?" she asked excitedly.

"Yes ... yes. Yes, I am."

"Oh, thank you very much," said Dad. "And I wonder ... would you be interested in investing in a very promising barbecue idea as well?"

Shufty booted him in the shins. "Thank you very much, Mr Nansen," she said. "We'd be delighted to accept your help."

Nansen leant forward to shake my hand, but the effort was too much. He gave up, and began to splutter and gurgle again.

"I have another surprise for you," said Ki-Ki.

What next? I thought. How much better could this get? My

rocket plan was beginning to work out! We had an investor. A Crankshaw project actually had a financial backer!

The screen behind her flickered into life. A caption at the bottom of the screen read: *Live from Zircon Corporation, Chicago.*

"That's him!" hissed the Quads, their fruit suddenly forgotten.

Zircon.

The enemy.

I went cold. I tried to take in his cruel face, withered and deflated with age. The skin hung from his cheeks and mouth like a slobbering dog's. But it was his eyes that unsettled me most. They were like a hypnotist's, drawing in my attention, twinkling, glassy and green. The TV lights gave his skin a weird lime tinge to match. Man, he was scary.

"Welcome, Crankshaws," breathed Zircon.

"Mr Zircon, thank you so much for your time," said Ki-Ki. "I have the Crankshaw family here, and they're as keen as mustard to enter your astonishing race to the Moon."

None of us was expecting this. I mean, Zack Zircon!

I could see Shufty out of the corner of my eye. She was immediately seething, her eyes narrowing. There he was. The bloke who'd ripped Dad off to the tune of millions and millions of pounds.

"Mr Zircon." Dad bit his lip, momentarily lost for words. "Errr ... long time ... errr ... no see."

A thousand thoughts rushed through my mind. I jumped in, "Why haven't you replied to my application to enter your race, Zircon?" I was surprised at the strength of my voice. "I've got a rocket. I sent you all our details."

Zircon pulled out some papers. I caught a glimpse of Jake's pictures of the Ginger Streak. Those were my actual emails! The ones I had sent – actually there in Zircon's shrivelled, claw-like hands.

"I have your application here," said Zircon, his voice deep and eerily loud over the studio speakers.

"And what the nation wants to know, Mr Zircon, is will you be accepting the Crankshaws into your race?" Ki-Ki asked boldly.

Zircon scratched his cheek slowly, considering his response. He turned the edges of his mouth down, then relaxed and breathed in slowly, examining the Ginger Streak pictures with something close to reluctance. "Do you think Ginger Streak will fly?" he said finally.

"It'll fly," spat Shufty. "You can bet it will. I'll make it!"

Shufty's sudden change of heart was almost as shocking as our actually speaking to Zircon. I turned to Dad, who looked equally confused. In a surprising turnaround, the General was now supporting my scheme. Shufty was on our side.

"Can you have your rocket ready in two weeks' time?" wheezed Zircon. "That is the date set for blast-off. We won't wait for you."

"I will pay for Ginger Streak to be transported to America," said Nansen. "They'll be there, Mr Zircon, don't you worry."

Thursday yelled, "We'll be first to the Moon, you'll see!"

"So you will accept the Crankshaws into the race?" asked Ki-Ki.

Zircon took a sip of water from a glass beside him. "Next week I shall be presenting the other competitors to the world at the Zircon Plaza, my headquarters in New York. If you can make it there, I'll accept your application."

At that, the screen went dead.

I didn't trust him. I know he'd already ripped us off, but there was something else.

Shufty nailed it as we were led off the TV set behind Nansen. "That was too easy," she said, more to herself than to anybody else in particular.

"What do you mean?" I asked, catching up with her.

"Zircon," she said. "He's up to something."

"But you *are* going to help us now, Shufty? We need you."

"If there is an outside chance, no matter how small, of getting that slimy Zircon's $10-million prize, it's worth going for. With Nansen backing us, who knows what might happen?"

The Quads began to cheer. The General was on the team, and I suddenly felt 100% more certain of success.

"Tell me about this rocket, Ace," said Shufty with a reluctant smile. "How do we get it to the Moon?"

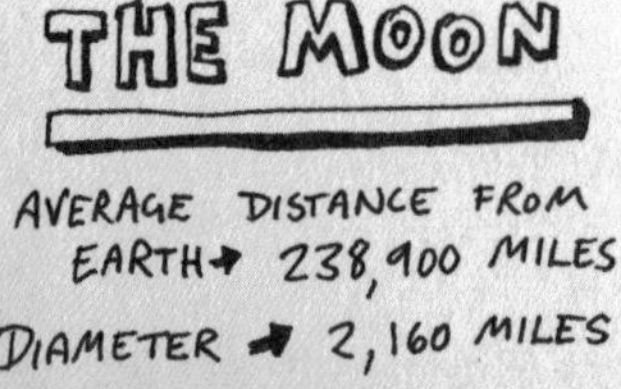

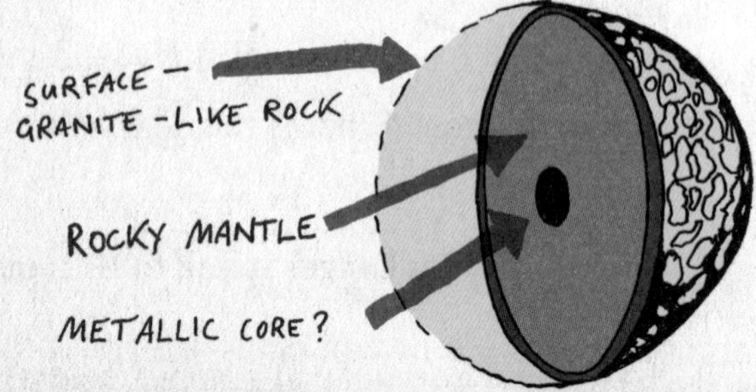

MILITARY SATELLITE
MANUFACTURED BY ZIRCON SCIENCE INDUSTRIES - SPECIAL PROJECTS DIVISION
CLIENT - CLASSIFIED

• MISSION STATEMENT •

Zircon Science Industries is the lead player in global communication and software technologies with a growing presence in intelligent application research.

From military satellite design to ZircoBot development and manufacture, Zircon Science Industries have proved time and again the ability to deliver complex projects on ... udget.

CREATING THE IMPOSSIBLE

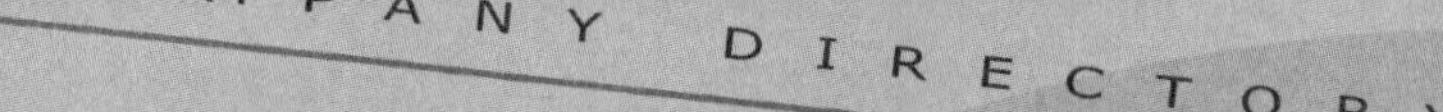

COMPANY DIRECTORY

- SATELLITE TECHNOLOGIES
- STRATEGIC SOLUTIONS
- HARDWARE DESIGN
- SOFTWARE ARCHITECTURE
- INTELLIGENT APPLICATIONS
- RESEARC...

NEW YORK
JIMI HENDRIX PLAYED HERE *
CAFE WHA?
CAFE WHA?
RADIO CITY
THE ONLY INVITATION THE CRANKSHAW FAMILY HAS EVER HAD!
ZIRCON
SCIENCE INDUSTRIES
The Crankshaw Family
Please join us at the Zircon Plaza
to celebrate the official launch of
The Great Space Race
3pm onwards
Champagne buffet
Strictly by invitation only

N THE WAY TO THE OPENING CEREMONY

MONKEY WARS

Four days after our appearance on nationwide TV, we were lined up on a stage in New York for the opening ceremony of Zircon's Great Space Race. Nansen had paid for us to be flown out there on his private jet.

The world's press stood between us and a cheering crowd of space fanatics.

The other competitors were already on stage – six men and one woman. These guys looked loaded. I mean, *mega*-rich. They sat in a line away to the right of us, along a table with their names written on cards in front of them, looking like part of a geriatric seven-a-side football team at a press conference. Petrov, Crompton, Chevalier, Northrup, Pak, Shredder and Neemis. I recognized them from the website. They looked even more decrepit in the flesh. It didn't make much sense to me. Surely they couldn't have been in it for the money, so why were they here?

Then there was us. The Crankshaws. Quite a contrast to the competition. We were scruffy-looking and broke. Only Shufty was wearing jeans without holes in the knees, and we all badly needed a haircut.

But, as I looked in total awe at all the cameras and space fans, the excitement of launching a rocket welled up inside me again.

* Jimi Hendrix (1942 – 1970) Number 1 rock god and guitar legend

We had everything riding on this. It had to work.

An orchestra started to play a dirge like a national anthem.

"Ladies and gentlemen," said the MC over the PA system. "May I present ... Zack Zircon."

There was a massive round of applause as Zircon appeared on stage in an electric wheelchair. A bottle of medicine, being pumped into his veins to keep him alive, swung dangerously from the end of a pole connected to the back of his chair. He swerved to a stop in front of the microphone.

"He's on his last legs," said Wednesday a little bit too loudly perhaps.

"Ladies and gentlemen," he gasped, short of breath, "it is with great pleasure that I welcome you to the Zircon Plaza, to the launch of the Great Space Race competition. I have been blessed to have a career spanning several fields – software development, satellite design and, lately" – he waved his decrepit hand – "... monkey toys.

"I have dreamed all my life of a day when people could fly to the Moon, in the same way they might take a trip to a shopping mall..."

I noticed Dad wince when he heard these words.

"Using my vast fortune, I have built a theme park for the people, so they can enjoy the thrill of space even when they're ... stuck here on the ground."

Some flashy graphics, bursting on to a screen behind, revealed the new theme park. The place had everything – rollercoasters, overpriced burger bars and people walking about in stupid space costumes. All the stuff we'd never, ever been allowed anywhere near on our family holidays. I couldn't wait to have the life frightened out of me on the death-defying rides once I got there.

"I give you – the ZircoSpaceParc."

There was a round of applause and whooping from the crowd.

ZIRCON ON STAGE

Monday, sitting near a live microphone, piped up right on cue. "Ace, is this the sort of theme park you told us Dad would never take us to coz he's a cheapskate, work-shy dreamer?"

The crowd heard every word as clear as a bell and began to laugh.

"Thanks, Ace," said Dad.

"No problem."

Zircon wiped some spit away from the corner of his mouth. "So, then, I say welcome, welcome. Welcome pioneers, adventurers, latter-day Columbuses and Magellans ... welcome to the most spectacular race yet in the history of the world."

More wild cheers from the crowds echoed around the plaza.

"The challenge is anointed: each of the competitors will be supplied with a small Zircon lunar lander designed by me, to be carried to the heavens in their rockets. The prize will go to the first competitor who lands their probe on the surface of the Moon. All rockets will launch simultaneously from the ZircoSpaceParc, Illinois, in the most spectacular blast-off the world has ever seen. The winner of the $10-million prize money will be declared when the first success signal is received. I, of course, cannot resist racing myself. Nine rockets, then, one Moon

PAGE FROM ONE OF ZIRCON'S FLASH BROCHURES SHOWING THE COMPETITORS' ROCKETS. GINGER STREAK NOT LISTED COZ WE JOINED THE RACE SO LATE.

and one huge prize. I declare the Great Space Race open for business. Next stop – the Moon!"

Behind us pictures of each competition rocket were flashed up on a stadium-sized screen. All of them looked spectacular. Ginger Streak was last. They showed the picture Jake had shot with his camera phone. To say we looked cheap beside our rivals was an understatement – so cheap-looking the audience began to laugh again.

"Are they laughing because our rocket looks like a load of old rubbish?" asked Monday into the microphone.

There was another round of laughing. A cycle courier on the edge of the crowd shouted up to Monday, "You're seriously going to the Moon with that old tin can, buddy?"

"Yeah," said Tuesday to the heckler. "At least we own a space rocket, and I'll tell you this for free, it's a lot cooler and much faster than your ropy old push bike with stickers all over it and no lights. You'll get knocked over on a dark night, you will—"

Enough was enough. Shufty leant forward and yanked the lead out of the microphone and told Tuesday to behave.

My mind was fixed on Zircon, the enemy. He finished up, his voice as cold as an ice box, "Pioneers, you have ten days to prepare your rockets. Good luck." He swivelled round and drove himself off stage to the cheers and applause of the crowds.

Almost immediately we were ushered off stage and up to the penthouse level of the Zircon Plaza, where a lavish reception was being held for all the competitors, VIPs and selected members of the press.

Dad, Shufty and I were surrounded by journalists asking about

TEAM PETROV

COMPETITOR: Anton Petrov

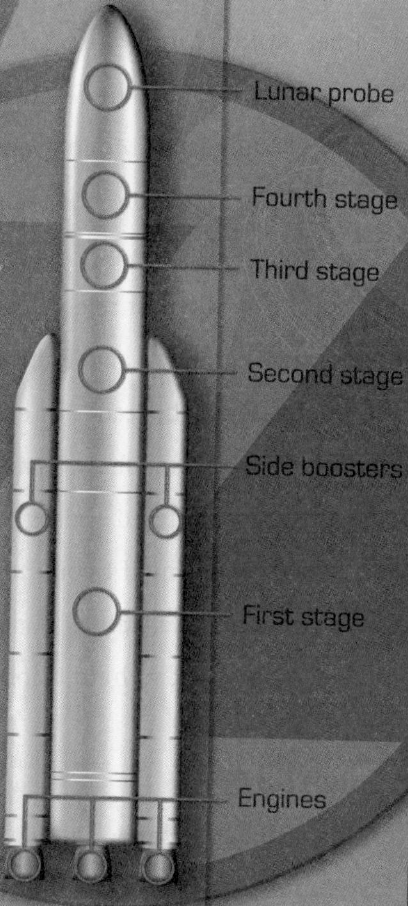

Lunar probe

Fourth stage

Third stage

Second stage

Side boosters

First stage

Engines

COUNTRY
Russian Federation

ROCKET NAME
Tatyana

‘My rocket will win the Great Space Race because it is the best design, powered by the latest Tunguska Class II engines’

THE COMPETITORS

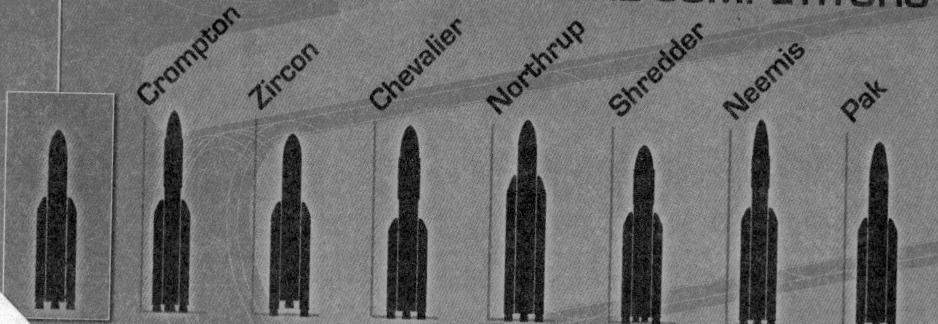

Crompton

Zircon

Chevalier

Northrup

Shredder

Neemis

Pak

THE QUADS GET STUCK INTO THE FREE GRUB

our rocket. The Quads, on the other hand, went straight over to the buffet to load up with food. They moved like a highly trained military unit. Some of the grub was stacked beyond the reach of their clawing little hands, so Monday and Tuesday used a chair to clamber up on to the long table, then walked along it – this way they had full access to the menu. Every type of food was taste-tested, then either accepted or rejected. The stuff they liked was chucked down to Wednesday and Thursday, who were waiting below with two plates each, ready to receive.

"Mr Crankshaw, Mr Crankshaw," said a woman, crabbing in beside Dad as he was offered a glass of champagne. "Mr Crankshaw, I was wondering if I could have a word with you."

The woman was almost as tall as Dad, and the same sort of age, with her hair scraped back so hard it looked as if it was stretching the creases out of her face.

"Of course," said Dad.

"I'm writing a research paper on 1970s rocketry," she went on, "and I'd love to take a look at Ginger Streak. I've been trying to track your rocket down for a number of years. I thought it was lost to history. This is such a rare opportunity. I ... I plan to be over in Britain for the next few weeks, so I could come and visit you easily."

"I'm sorry," said Dad. "We're going to be very busy preparing for the race. There is so little time until the launch, and there's so much to do."

"Oh, I don't mean to get in your way," the woman said with a false laugh. She nervously scanned the room over Dad's shoulder. "Nothing like that. Perhaps I could actually help you?"

"Help? We don't need any help. We've got Mr Nansen backing us now," Dad boasted.

The woman smiled again, and tilted her head. She wasn't going to be put off that easily. She said more softly, "I could assist you in programming the complex guidance computer, to guide your rocket into space and land the probe on the Moon. I expect you already have someone, but I do have some experience in that field, if you don't."

"I know a bit about computers myself," said Dad, scratching his chin. "Know much about trajectory and guidance?"

"Well, in a way I do, yes."

Dad still didn't believe her. "Really? What, exactly?"

"Well now, after receiving a doctorate in astrophysics from Oxford in 1989, I joined the mission directorate of NASA, where I worked on the Shuttle's navigation and flight systems. To cut a long story short, since then I have become an expert in aerodynamics, thermodynamics and fluid mechanics..." She started rummaging in her bag and found a business card. "I've been around spacecraft all my working life. I like to think of myself as something of an expert on them. I could give your team quite an edge over your competitors."

Her credentials were mind-blowing. She was a rocket scientist! A real, live rocket scientist. We needed her, and Dad knew it. So did Shufty. Our luck really had changed. First Nansen with his cash, now a rocket scientist offering to help us. The $10 million was virtually ours.

Dad looked at me.

I looked at Dad.

Shufty looked at us both.

"Do you really want to join the team?" asked Dad.

The woman nodded. "You see, the Ginger Streak was a rare British rocket, and for my work I'd love to study her guidance systems. Programming a flight path would be an ideal way to see how the rocket works. It's of huge historical interest." She looked nervously about and said in a whisper, "Maxine Lavisham, by the way. Professor Maxine Lavisham."

Her name badge said *Jane Sweet, Journalist*. She tried to cover it with her hand, but we'd all seen it. "Don't take any notice of that," she laughed nervously. "It was rather difficult to get in here, and I really did want to speak to you before you flew back to Britain."

"When can you start?" I asked.

"Well, let me see," she beamed. "I fly over to Britain tomorrow."

"Do you want a cut of the prize money?" asked Shufty.

"Oh, no, nothing like that," smiled the Prof. "Would it be OK if I brought my assistant with me?"

"If you want to stay, you need to bring your own beds," said

THE PROF'S PRESS PASS – OBVIOUSLY STOLEN
NEITHER THE NAME NOR THE PHOTO MATCHED

Monday. "The bailiffs took ours."

"Do you know the address?" I asked. "The Mill, Gravesend. Second left after the Green Man pub."

Two security guards paced purposefully towards us, pointing at the Prof. She clocked them and began to edge away. "See you in England," she said, making for the lobby, where a lift had just arrived.

"Ma'am? Ma'am? Stop there, please," said the security guards, breaking into a jog. She stepped aboard, giving us a wave, just as the doors slid shut and seconds before the guards could get to her.

"What an extraordinary woman," said Dad.

Extraordinary or not, she was essential to pump some much-needed expertise into the Crankshaw space programme.

At that moment, Barry – who up until this point had been quietly sitting with the Quads while they were polishing off their food – suddenly jumped up on to the buffet table. He seemed intent on reaching the other side of the crowded room, recklessly knocking over plates of gourmet grub and making a metallic screeching sound. I soon saw why. Six Mark 5 ZircoBots – the newest model of monkey toys with sleek chrome styling and shifty-looking eyes – were chasing another smaller ZircoBot. Barry was making a beeline for what appeared to be a monkey-toy stampede.

Dad and I sprinted after him. Barry could cause thousands of pounds' worth of damage! Neither of us wanted to be kicked out of the Space Race because of old Bazza wrecking Zircon's posh reception. Not now! Not after we were suddenly so near $10 million. It would be just our luck.

But before we could catch up with Barry, he fearlessly launched himself into the monkey ruck with an epic jump. The Mark 5s went berserk. Arms and legs were punching and kicking, all to a soundtrack of ear-shattering mechanical screeches. Sparks of electricity arced out of their thumbs and forefingers, just like the high-voltage shock released by police stun guns. I'd never seen anything like it on a ZircoBot. The Mark 5s were armed and dangerous.

They surrounded Barry and pinned him to the floor, electrocuting him with massive amounts of voltage. I wanted to rescue Bazza, but a Mark 5 hissed at me, threatening me with his sparking left arm. I backed off. Dad, who was never really scared of anything very much, grabbed a fire extinguisher and blasted powder at the scrum. The Mark 5s began to back away. Dad fired twice more. Through the clouds of extinguisher powder, I saw Barry again, sprawled face down and missing an arm. I risked it and grabbed for him. His body felt limp and lifeless, but at least I had him back.

The Mark 5s began to retreat, dragging their prey with them. Through the extinguisher powder I could just about make out their captive. It appeared to be a very early monkey-toy model – like Barry.

As the guests gave Dad a round of applause, and he turned to bow (always the showman), the Mark 5s had scampered away and were slipping out of sight. The bewildering battle seemed to be over.

"Dad, I think that was—"

"What, Ace?" said Dad, handing the extinguisher to the security guard.

"I think they had Eve with them. I'm sure it was her."

Dad looked as if he didn't know what I was talking about.

I tried again. "You know, *Eve*."

"Eve? What? Our old Eve? *Really?*"

Eve was the prototype monkey robot Dad had sold to Zircon all those years ago. And here she was. I was almost certain of it.

"Yes," I said, piecing together what I'd seen. "I think that was who they were after. Barry jumped in and tried to help his sister."

"Well, they got Barry, good and proper. He looks cooked."

I gently lifted Barry up to check the damage. When I tried to reboot him, there was no response. Only a wisp of smoke drifted out of the hole where his twirling ear should have been. Whatever the Mark 5s had done to him had been pretty severe.

The Quads swarmed round, but when they saw Bazza's limp body they burst into tears. He was their toy, mostly. I felt pretty sad myself. Barry's eyes gazed blankly out. He was as dead as a dead robot monkey can be. Game over.

• ZIRCOBOTS •

Zircon Science Industries is the lead player in global communication and software technologies with a growing presence in intelligent application research.

From military satellite design to ZircoBot development and manufacture, Zircon Science Industries have proved time and again the ability to deliver complex projects on time and on budget.

Our core target aspiration is communicating and executing the interconnectivity of digital resource assets.

Our aspiration is to provide global business synergy between products and customers.

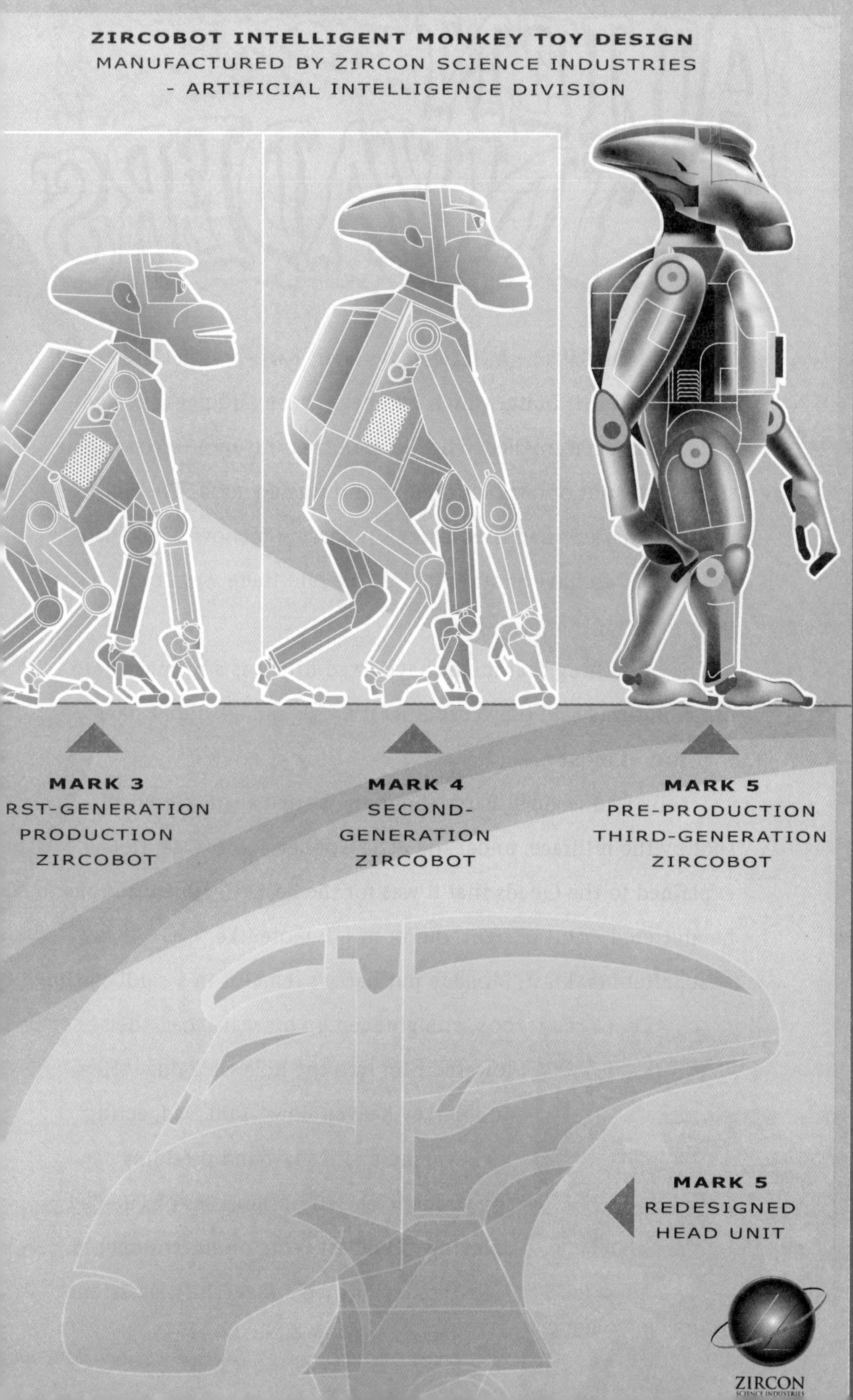

ZIRCOBOT INTELLIGENT MONKEY TOY DESIGN
MANUFACTURED BY ZIRCON SCIENCE INDUSTRIES
- ARTIFICIAL INTELLIGENCE DIVISION

MARK 3
RST-GENERATION
PRODUCTION
ZIRCOBOT

MARK 4
SECOND-
GENERATION
ZIRCOBOT

MARK 5
PRE-PRODUCTION
THIRD-GENERATION
ZIRCOBOT

MARK 5
REDESIGNED
HEAD UNIT

Alien Invaders

Back home at The Mill two days later, Barry was declared dead by Dad. His brain, which had never been 100 per cent right, had clearly been totalled. The old man tried his best to coax some signs of life out of our old friend, but it was no good. The fight with the Mark 5s had fried Barry's innards somehow. The Quads begged Dad to have another try, but he said there wasn't much point.

The only thing that might have fixed him was a primary hard drive. But Dad said they cost at least £450, and we didn't have that sort of money.

Finally Dad decided Barry should be buried at his favourite spot by the millrace, under the little wooden footbridge. He explained to the Quads that it was for the best. To Shufty and me he muttered, "Out of sight, out of mind, more like."

So, after breakfast, Monday put Barry's remains in a cardboard box, straightened up his waistcoat, then lowered him into the hole we'd dug. "He's in monkey heaven now," said Dad, acting as Reverend Crankshaw and presiding graveside to the straining notes of Tuesday playing "The Last Post" on his trumpet. Wednesday pushed a makeshift headstone

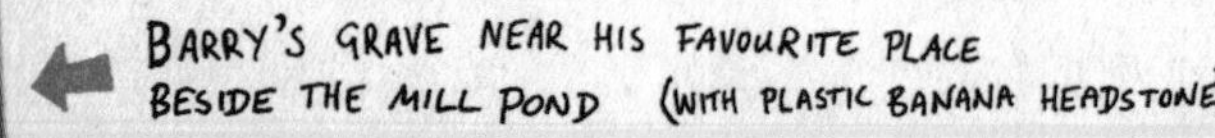

BARRY'S GRAVE NEAR HIS FAVOURITE PLACE BESIDE THE MILL POND (WITH PLASTIC BANANA HEADSTONE)

– a plastic banana – into the mound of fresh earth to mark the spot.

As we ambled back to the house, a vast chrome motor home (more like a spaceship than Ginger Streak) wallowed up the drive and eased to a stop.

"It looks like a UFO mothership," I said. "Wow!"

A tinted electric window lowered and the Professor poked her head out.

"You found us, then?" said Dad.

"Easily," replied the Prof, pushing her iridium sunglasses up to hold the hair off her face. She was wearing a T-shirt with "All science is either physics or stamp-collecting" written across the front of it. I was aware of a shadow behind her. Her assistant, no doubt – a brainbox with even more qualifications than her. "I've brought my own accommodation, Mr Crankshaw."

"So I see," said Dad. "She's a beauty."

"Is that the rocket?" the Prof asked, nodding towards the trailers.

"Yep, all waiting to go. Or we could just strap the engines on the back of your motor home and blast that into orbit instead, ha, ha, ha!"

I could see the Prof didn't really think Dad's joke was all that funny. She looked with suspicion firstly at us, then at Dad, then at the half-finished inventions littering the garden, and finally at the rocket. She winced slightly at what she saw. "Where shall I park? We'll need power."

"Just there on the drive is fine. We can run a power cable out to you."

MY MUM'S OLD FENDER STRAT.

I INHERITED IT ON MY 12 BIRTHDAY (+ HARMONICA

The Prof edged the mothership towards the allotted place and switched off. An argument kicked off inside, muffled by the silvered walls of the craft.

After about a minute the door finally hissed open. "I'm not meeting them," came an American voice from the inside. "This is a dumb idea. Turn us around and let's get back to civilization. You promised me a tour of Britain. Not this dumb place."

"Please come and meet them," pleaded the Prof.

"I told you I don't want to, all right? You said we were coming here to this lousy country to go on vacation, and now we've got to sit around while you do more research. This is NOT a vacation. I mean, what is this place? It's falling apart. It's some kinda hick's paradise. There are rusting piles of junk everyplace. I didn't sign up for a Scooby-Doo adventure."

The Prof appeared at the doorway a couple of seconds later, trying to cover over the argument by flashing a massive fixed smile.

"Your assistant sounds a little reluctant," said Dad.

"We can make you a cup of nettle tea," said Thursday. "It's all right, it doesn't sting when you drink it."

"Thank you. My son doesn't drink tea, unfortunately. Especially not nettle," the Prof said quickly.

"Son?" I asked. We hadn't bargained on this. "He's your assistant?"

"That's right. My son." The mothership's door hissed shut, leaving the Professor standing outside, defeated. There was a whirring sound from the roof and a TV satellite dish elevated and unfurled.

"Oh, I don't like this," grumbled the General. She turned to me with sisterly concern. "I mean, we don't want her kid hanging around here and slagging us off as hicks. This is our place. We'll set up a lookout. Keep an eye on him." I didn't think this was necessary, but with Shufty's martial law in place, orders were orders. "Monday, you take first watch. Any movement, raise the alarm."

"Right," Monday nodded.

"Well, Mr Crankshaw," said the Prof. "I need time to settle in. I suggest we make a start on your rocket first thing tomorrow."

At that moment, Love and Hate broke cover and crashed through the hedge. Without a second thought, Dad launched himself off in the opposite direction and ran slap into the arms of Danny Thumper, who'd crept up on us SAS-style from the direction of the barn.

"Got you, Crankshaw. Love. Hate. Sit!"

"You can have everything. Just keep the dogs off me," Dad said bravely.

Thumper laughed like a drain. "I've just checked inside one of those crates what's just been delivered. I'll tell you this, and I'll tell you now, so unblock your ear 'oles. You're not going to reach the Moon with that heap of junk!"

"Don't you think so?"

Thumper grabbed Dad by the collar and lifted his feet clear of the ground, slamming him into the wall. "Nansen has warned me to steer clear of you. Temporary-like. You've got yourself a reprieve, mate. I don't like it, Crankshaw, but there it is. Seems they think you're some sort of hero in the making. Going to do Britain proud." He laughed through gritted teeth.

"It's true."

"Where's that monkey toy? The prototype ZircoBot. You didn't tell me about that, did you? It might be worth something."

"He's dead. His brain was fried in New York. He was virtually ripped apart."

"I see," murmured Thumper, seeing tears in the Quads' eyes. "The ZircoBot prototype will be top of my list for repossession once Nansen's out of the picture, I'm warning you."

"We've buried him," yelled Thursday. "He's worthless to you now. Let him rest in peace."

"Love and Hate will be watching you," Thumper snarled. "And I'll be watching you ... like a hawk."

Thumper still had Dad pinned to the wall. The old man tried to look cheerful. "We'll be making a start on the rocket first thing, Professor. We'll win that prize money, you'll see."

Thumper finally let Dad go. The old man slid down the wall as the bailiff stomped off, followed by his pit bulls.

The Professor looked a bit alarmed by what had just happened. "Shall we say 5 a.m.," she said, surveying the six low-loader trailers. "We certainly have lots to do."

"Five in the morning?" gulped Dad. "Right. Why not? Nothing I like more than an early start."

UNEARTHING THE SPACE DINOSAUR

In the cold light of dawn next day, I wondered whether somehow the Prof's arrival was too good to be true. Perhaps she was up to something, just like Zircon was. Why had she used a different identity in New York? What was her game? I had an uneasy feeling. The same uneasy feeling I'd had after Ki-Ki's TV show when Zircon had let us join his race.

Despite my growing worries (shared almost certainly by the General, I reckoned), some things had definitely changed for the better on Planet Crankshaw: Dad was actually doing something useful. Yep, there he was, at twenty past five in the morning, astride our Second World War vintage tractor, unloading the trailers, and giving me a jaunty "look-at-me-actually-doing-something-useful" wave.

The tractor bounced towards the barn, a wooden packing case from the fourth trailer swinging dangerously on the end of straining ropes behind it.

My half-asleep brain finally clicked what was going on here. I jumped up on the back of the tractor, which was still covered in morning dew. "Have you told Shufty about this, Dad? She won't like it."

"The Professor says she needs a laboratory. She won't cause you any problems. Quiet as mice, these scientists, you'll see. She

THE BLUE STREAK 1955 — 1972
BRITISH ROCKET FUEL — OXYGEN AND KEROSENE

doesn't mind you practising music upstairs, either."

"That's big of her."

The Quads appeared, woken, like me, by the clatter of the clapped-out diesel engine. They loved the tractor and ran towards us, already overexcited by what was going on.

"Ace," said Dad. "Keep the Quads out of the way. This is dangerous work."

I jumped down and rounded them up as best I could.

"Keep it coming," yelled the Prof, as she beckoned Dad into the barn. "This one should be the first of the main ground-control computer consoles."

The decrepit tractor inched forward in wild jerks until – with a squeal of brakes – the case was inside the barn. The hydraulics gave a gasp and dumped the cargo on the floor with a bump.

The Prof untied the lifting straps from the crate, then Dad backed out in a cloud of diesel smoke.

"All yours!" Dad grimaced as he waved the fumes away. He parked up, switched off and jumped down.

The Prof examined the first crate as we all crowded round. A mouse scarpered out and ran for cover.

"Perhaps he heard the Moon was made of cheese and fancied a free ride?" said Thursday.

The Prof was in no mood for jokes. She set about pulling out clumps of straw with the speed and frenzy of someone bailing out a sinking boat. Little by little the shape of a large metallic desk was revealed. It was an old-style console, with a bank of switches and dials surrounding a grey-screened TV monitor with rounded corners. Man, it looked old-skool. The side panel fell off with a clatter, revealing the interior. It was an electrician's paradise – miles and miles of fiddly wiring. This was the thing we were relying on to guide our rocket to the Moon.

"It's the main engine starter panel," said the Prof seriously. "And that's the main engine's ignition button, I think."

"But it's made from an old car cigarette-lighter," I said.

"Not just any cigarette-lighter, Ace," said Dad, proudly pulling it out and examining it. "It's an Austin Allegro's cigarette-lighter."

"Yep," confirmed the Prof, pressing it in to test. "A simple solution. Simple and foolproof. Push it in, and when it makes contact the main engines will fire."

"Austin Allegro?" asked Thursday. "Who's Austin Allegro?"

"It's not a *who*, it's a *what*," explained Dad. "The Austin Allegro was a car. They were quite the thing in 1974. British Leyland engineering at its very best. Cutting-edge, Thursday, cutting-edge. If this rocket is as well built as the Allegro we'll be in space in no time, you'll see. This is far better than I dared hope."

"I never thought I'd see the day," the Prof marvelled. "It's colossal. It's fantastic..."

AUSTIN ALLEGRO BUILT BY BRITISH LEYLAND BETWEEN 1973 AND 1983. EARLY VERSIONS LIKE THIS HAD A SQUARE STEERING WHEEL

"Is it Roman?" asked Thursday.

It wasn't that old, but it was nothing like a modern computer. As you well know, modern computers are neat and small. They fit in your pocket and contain 40,000 MP3 files. This load of junk must have weighed ten tons and needed a tractor to move it.

Shufty strolled in, inspecting what was going on with a great deal of suspicion (I should point out here that she considered the barn very much her territory). "Morning," she said cautiously, peering at the packing case. "Busy, I see?"

I ignored her. "How much memory does it have, Professor?"

"A hundred kilobytes," answered the Prof. "Maybe a little more."

Shufty laughed. "A hundred kilobytes. Are you serious? That's nothing. My keyring stick has masses more memory than that."

"This was an extraordinary achievement back in '74," said the Prof. "We are privileged to see it."

"Privileged to see it outside a museum," said Shufty. "It's as old as Dad."

The Quads began to press buttons and fiddle about with the controls.

"Enemy ships on the scanner, Captain!" yelled Thursday.

Monday grabbed a pair of old-skool headphones hanging off a hook on the main panel and put them on. "Arm the lasers and give me full shields."

"Ginger Streak is very old and rusty," said Thursday. "Do you think she'll hold together?"

"He's right," snapped Wednesday. "Our ship is a cheap load of old scrap-yard junk. Perhaps we should try to reason with them first, Captain, by hailing their leader using this worn-out old TV screen."

BOLT-TOGETHER TECHNOLOGY FRO

"No. Thumper the Merciless can't be trusted. We can't wait any longer for breakfast, either. Blast his ships and be done with it, then power up the toaster for some grub."

While this space battle was going on, the Prof pulled out a load of paperwork and bound manuscripts with technical drawings from a shelf in the central console. These were crinkled with damp, and didn't look too promising to me.

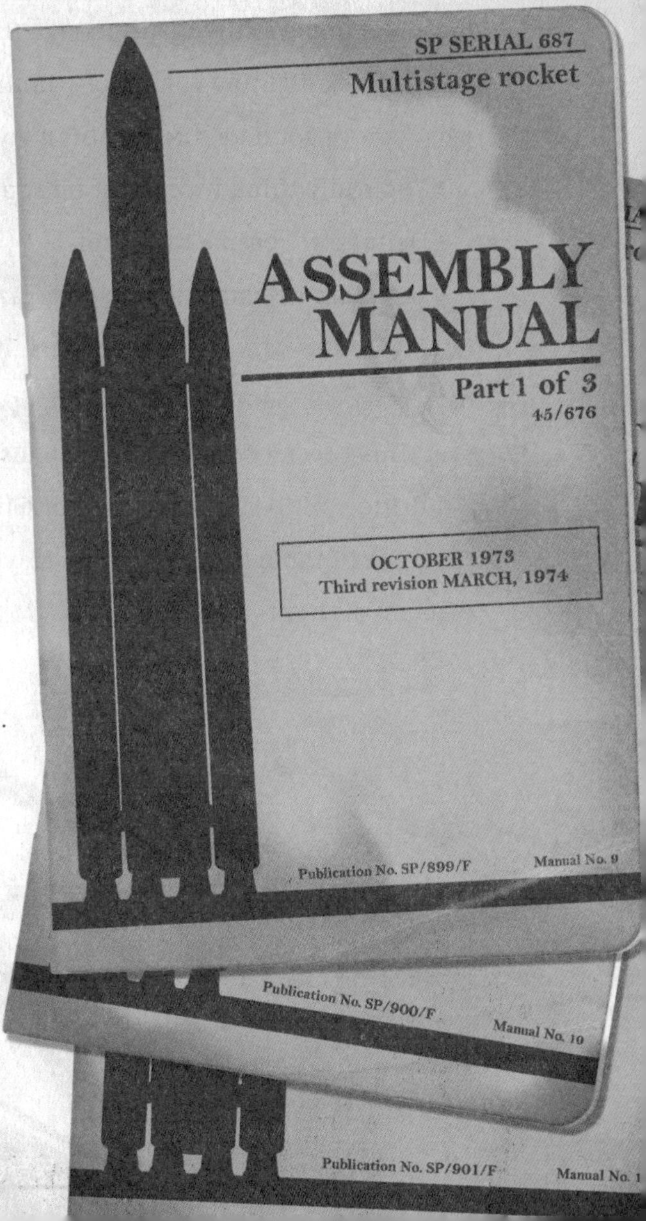

They did to the Prof, though. "This is fascinating!"

"Manuals?" asked Dad.

"Yes, Mr Crankshaw," enthused the Prof, flicking through them. She chucked one over to him. "You'll need these to help you bolt the rocket back together."

"Please call me Arthur. No one calls me Mr Crankshaw, unless they want money from me."

"Then call me Maxine. Max for short," she said with a warm smile.

Dad didn't answer for a second or two. He was pulling a face I'd never seen before. "Well … I'd be delighted, Max."

Did he like the Prof? What's more, did she like him? Shufty's eyebrows shot up. I could see her examining the Prof with fresh eyes.

The Prof put her hands on her hips and surveyed the ground-control set-up. "It looks like it's all here," she declared. "If we can programme a flight path to take the probe to the Moon, then you'll have a fighting chance of winning this race. Now I've seen what you've got here, I really think you can do it."

"You really think we can get into space?" I asked.

"Definitely!" beamed the Prof.

That night I clambered into bed, gazing at the ceiling covered in glow-in-the-dark moons and stars. It had been a whirlwind few days. So much had happened. And, apart from poor old Barry, everything seemed to be running unusually smoothly.

I drifted off to sleep dreaming of Ginger Streak blasting off into space, and I thought maybe – just maybe – things were going to turn out all right.

MY 3 BLUES HARPS (HARMONICAS)

JAKE AND I PLAN TO REINVENT THE BLUES WITH THEM

"Ttzzzzzzzz! Ttzzzzzzz!"

Dad's Anti-Thumper Alarm, buzzing like a wasp trapped in a jam jar, made me sit bolt upright, heart pounding. I looked at the clock. It was 4.32 a.m.

"POTTING SHED" was flashing away in red on the panel.

It could be a fox, I thought.

"Ttzzzzzz! Ttzzzzzz!"

"CESSPIT" flashed.

"Ttzzzzzz! Ttzzzzzzz!"

"ROSE GARDEN" was now flashing.

Whatever was moving around out there was getting closer. I rolled over in bed and drew back the curtain to check what was going on below. A shadowy figure was crouching down beside one of Dad's abandoned projects.

Then the buzzer went again.

Again? Were there two people outside? It was too dark down there to see that far out.

This was strange.

"POTTING SHED".

"Ttzzzzzz!"

"CESSPIT".

I gazed into the gloom. Yes! A second figure was following the first.

ANTI-THUMPER ALARM
(PATENTS PENDING)
FRONT GATE
CESSPIT
GREENHOUSE
POTTING SHED
ROSE GARDEN
VEG PATCH
TOP GATE
GARAGE
WORKSHOP
BARN
PUMPHOUSE

DAD'S RIDICULOUS 'ANTI-THUMPER ALARM'
THE TELEPHONE CONNECTED TO THE HIGH-PRESSURE WATER CANNON POSITIONS IN THE GARDEN

"Ttzzzzzzz!"

"ROSE GARDEN".

They disappeared. I felt hot and cold – the blood was rushing in my ears. Could they be burglars after Ginger Streak?

Then an icy thought struck me.

What if it *was* Thumper? What if, by some fluke, Dad's crazy alarm system was warning me of the very thing it was designed to? What if Thumper and one of his hard nuts were here to take more of our stuff in a sneak attack?

Like my guitar.

Like my guitar that was sitting in the practice room.

Like my guitar that was sitting in the practice room in the barn which the figures, reappearing out of the gloom, were now approaching.

I had to get there before them. Quickly changing into my jeans and hoodie, I slipped downstairs and out of the kitchen door. It was chilly outside as I pulled the hood up and slunk across the yard towards the barn. There were no lights on in the mothership – they must have been tucked up in unimaginable luxury in there. I opened the barn door just enough to squeeze in and climbed the familiar stairs to the practice room.

It was almost pitch-black inside, but I knew my guitar would be propped in the corner, just where I always left it. My hands were shaking as I reached out for the neck and found ... nothing. I flapped my hand around in the shadows, but with a sinking feeling I knew it was gone. But where could it have gone if whoever was outside hadn't taken it? Thumper? Had he already been in and nicked it?

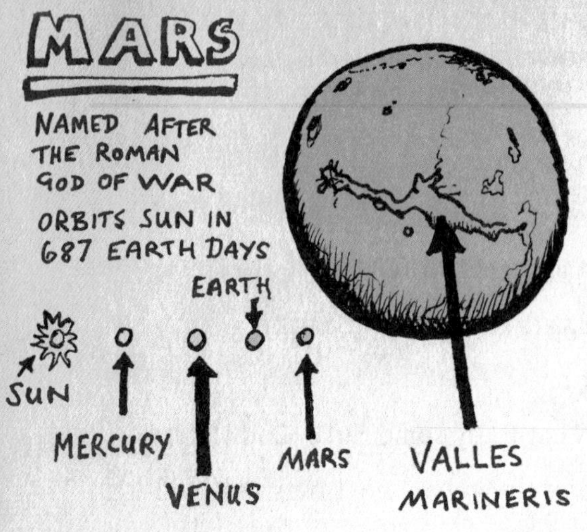

I heard the door downstairs creak open. I had to hide. There was only one real option. I jumped up and grabbed the roof beam above me and hooked myself up. There was so much adrenalin pumping through my veins, it was easy. There were a few planks up there which formed a platform of sorts – Barry used to sit up here when we practised. I hoped it would hold my weight. I rolled on to the planks and made myself as small as possible. This wasn't ideal, but in the circumstances it would have to do.

One of the figures reached the top of the stairs. It paused, feeling for the wall, then walked into the attic, arms outstretched like a zombie. The figure was just below me, now. Two feet away. I held my breath. Whoever it was was so close I could hear them breathing. They were a ghostly outline between the crack in the two planks.

"What is she up to?" I heard a whisper. Only ... it was an American voice. I relaxed enough to breathe. It wasn't Thumper after all – it was the American. The Yank. Of course. But what was he doing here on our territory?

The Yank moved towards the window and wiped off some of the grime, cupping his hands to peer out towards the veg patch. Outside there was the other figure. I caught her profile in the moonlight. It was the Professor. What were they both doing out here?

"It's started," the Yank muttered to himself. "Lavisham madness is definitely setting in. Wandering around out in the dark in the middle of the night, Ma. Next thing you'll be wanting to build a rocket and fly to the Moon ... oh, but that's right. You *are* building a rocket. With this crazy inventor and his hillbilly backyard space programme run by a bunch of hick kids."

Hillbilly? I didn't know what that meant, but it sounded like an insult. Should I jump down and tackle him? Take him to task over his invasion of our territory? In the dark he appeared to be taller than me. An unknown enemy. Jake had always said "Know your enemy". I didn't know my enemy. Was he wearing a judo jacket? He was wearing something like it. Had he come looking for a fight? I decided to lie still.

The Yank suddenly dipped down as his mum altered course towards the barn. If he didn't make his move back to the mothership, he would be trapped. I watched the shadow of his judo suit dissolve into the darkness. He moved quietly downstairs and left without a sound. A few moments later I heard the slight hiss of the motor home's door as it opened. He must've made it. I let out a long breath – but almost immediately heard someone pushing through the undergrowth at the back of the barn.

Then the door slowly creaked open downstairs. I guessed it was the Prof this time. Was she going to start work on the computer? At this hour? At 4.42 a.m.? I'd be stuck up here until dawn if she was. Then I heard clearly in the stillness of the night the harsh pips as she dialled a number on her mobile phone.

"Hello?" said the Prof. She sounded nervous.

There was silence for a couple of seconds. The tone of her voice changed, and she began to sound more friendly than I'd ever heard her before.

"No, I can't find it ... I've been searching everywhere ... yes, I got your email ... I think Crankshaw must be part of Zircon's operation ... he invented the ZircoBot after all ... you're going to need to dig out as much information as you can – on the other competitors as well. We'll need everything we can find ... and I don't suppose you've heard any news about Jed yet...?"

She wandered off to the other end of the room, and her voice became muffled and indistinct. I lay perfectly still. A minute or so later, she paced back.

"...the FBI and the CIA don't believe me. It's useless. They think I've lost my mind. No ... we're on our own here. But I've absolutely no doubt now. This race has nothing to do with landing a probe on the Moon for $10 million. It's a scam. We just need firm evidence to back that up ... OK, I'll keep you posted."

She hung up, and seconds later I heard the door being locked. She was off. I craned my neck to see out of the other window, and just managed to glimpse her feet as she climbed the step to board the mothership.

I swung down and landed on ... someone. There was another person in the room. I nearly died of fright. "Thumper!" I yelped in terror.

"No. It's Shufty, you idiot. Keep your voice down. What are you doing here?"

"What are *you* doing, more like?"

"I came over to save your guitar," replied Shufty. "I heard someone creeping about in the garden and thought it was

Thumper ... or the Yank."

"It was the Yank. He was here."

"I know, you dummy. I've been hiding behind the drum kit."

"Did you hear the Prof's phone call?"

"Yes – every word."

"What is going on here?" I asked.

"No idea. She said the Space Race was a scam."

"Trust us to enter a race that isn't a race at all," I said.

"I knew there was something wrong with Zircon's Space Race all along," said Shufty. "Here – take this."

"What is it?"

"Your guitar, Ace. Keep it hidden. I could easily have been Thumper. Let's get back to the house."

We climbed downstairs as quietly as burglars. I opened the door fractionally, and checked it was all clear. No sign of Thumper. No sign of anyone. Shufty tapped me on the shoulder and we edged back through the inky shadows towards the kitchen door. We were almost there when the headlights of the mothership came on full beam. I froze, which was stupid. I mean, we couldn't pretend we weren't there. I held my hand up against the dazzling light. I could make out the Prof behind the steering wheel with an angry expression on her face.

Eventually, I just grinned and half waved. "Just getting my guitar."

She didn't answer. She sat there for a couple more seconds, and then killed the lights.

VOYAGER 1 AND 2 SPACECRAFT

LAUNCHED 1977

(STILL WORKING)

SPEED 38,000 MPH

Once we were in the kitchen, Shufty pulled me towards the window, peering out at the mothership. The Prof was still sitting there, gazing towards us.

"What was she searching for out there?" asked Shufty.

"How should I know?" I said. "There's nothing in the garden. It's just full of Dad's old junk. The Yank didn't know what she was doing out there either, and he's her son. How do you expect *me* to know? If she's after the secrets to the barbecue design, then she's welcome to them."

"Things don't stack up with the Prof," considered Shufty. "Like they don't stack up with the Space Race. I don't trust her. We need to get to the bottom of this, and fast."

"I know, all right," I said.

"You started all this, Ace, with that stupid rocket of yours. Find some answers."

"I did it to get us some money. Ten million dollars."

Shufty didn't look impressed. "The future of this family rests firmly on this ridiculous plan of yours now, so I hope you know what you're doing. Launching a rocket at the Moon? You're turning into Dad. It's your fault if it goes wrong, OK? I'll be blaming you."

LUNA 1 RUSSIAN 1959

A.K.A. 'FIRST COSMIC SHIP' 'MECHTA'

- FIRST SPACECRAFT TO CHECK OUT THE MOON.
- STILL ORBITING THE SUN BETWEEN EARTH AND MARS

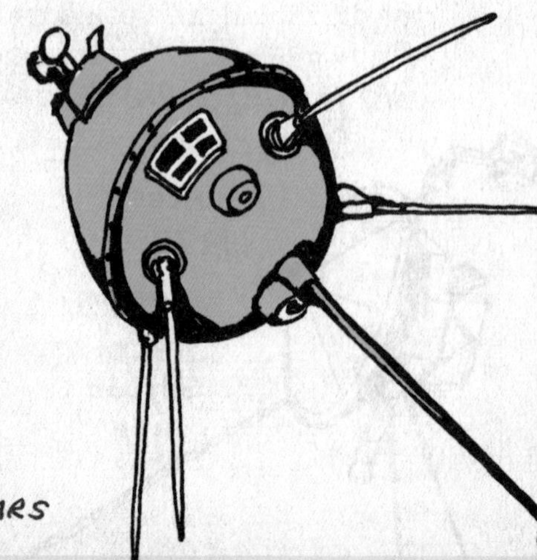

Monkey Business

Thanks to Ki-Ki Sapphire, the interest around our rocket attempt was gathering so much momentum that by the following day a full press pack had set up camp in the fields all around The Mill. There were so many cameras, journalists, broadcast trucks, satellite vans and motor homes it was as if a circus had arrived in town.

At this, Thumper had taken security measures to whole new levels. He had already spent a couple of days with a nail gun, building a wooden hut at the end of the drive and establishing a cordon around The Mill. He'd installed one of those lifting barriers like you get at car-parks and had a clipboard with a list of people he deemed suitable to enter. "Nobody gets in or out of my rocket facility without my say-so."

Love and Hate had their own little kennels, too. They lay there most of the day, gnawing on bones. Occasionally they would chase off a photographer foolish enough to think he might be able to snap a picture exclusive for a newspaper.

Strolling past Barry's grave after lunch to fetch some wood for the stove, I saw something I couldn't immediately account for: the plastic-banana headstone had been moved and planted in a completely different place. Not only that, the ground looked freshly disturbed.

I jumped off the little footbridge and skulked down to examine it more closely. I burrowed my hand into the soil. We hadn't buried him very deep, and after thirty seconds I discovered the terrible truth – there was no cardboard-box coffin and definitely no Barry. He'd gone.

There was something sticking out of the bottom of the plastic banana. It was a piece of rolled-up paper with a message scrawled on it:

I'm holding your ZincoBot hostage.
The Professor doesn't know.
Suggest we talk.
Come to breakfast tomorrow at 9.am
after I have rested and jacuzzied
No cops or the deal is off.
FRANK. (The guy in the Winnebago)

The uncomfortable truth was that instead of fighting with the strange ninja-vampire-zombie-Yank, we really did need to talk to him. The answers lay in the mothership.

Shufty was up for just storming in and taking Barry back off the Yank straight away. I talked her out of it, but only just.

Next morning, at the appointed hour, the General and I marched towards the motor home. She was seething so much she could hardly speak. "Just don't make friends with him," she ordered.

"Right," I said.

She pounded on the window of the mothership five times. After a good minute, the door swooshed open.

Frank greeted us with a casual, "Oh, hi," and ushered us in. We passed through the famous doorway, so long wondered at, into the forbidden land. The Yank was wearing sunglasses, jeans and a T-shirt, with a dressing-gown over the top. That was it! That's what he'd been wearing in the barn. Not the judo suit of my crazed imaginings.

He was drinking a glass of freshly squeezed orange juice which tinkled with ice cubes. "Kick back and take a seat."

"Wow!" I said as we walked into the saloon. "This is great."

It was styled like a luxury hotel. Soft flute music came from speakers set into leather-lined walls. A rack of champagne glasses above the espresso machine glinted in the spotlighting.

"You seem impressed."

"You bet I am," I let slip. Shufty gave me daggers.

"The truck is German," said Frank. "The interior was handcrafted by Italian artisans in Turin, I'm told. No expense has been spared."

"And the jacuzzi?" I asked.

Frank pushed a button on a remote control. The wall opened to reveal the sunken bath with a bank of freshly laundered soft towels stacked beside it. "This is in party mode. I thought it was perhaps a little over the top for a breakfast meeting. We have business to conduct, after all."

8 GALAXY MOTHERSHIP - GENERAL LAYOUT

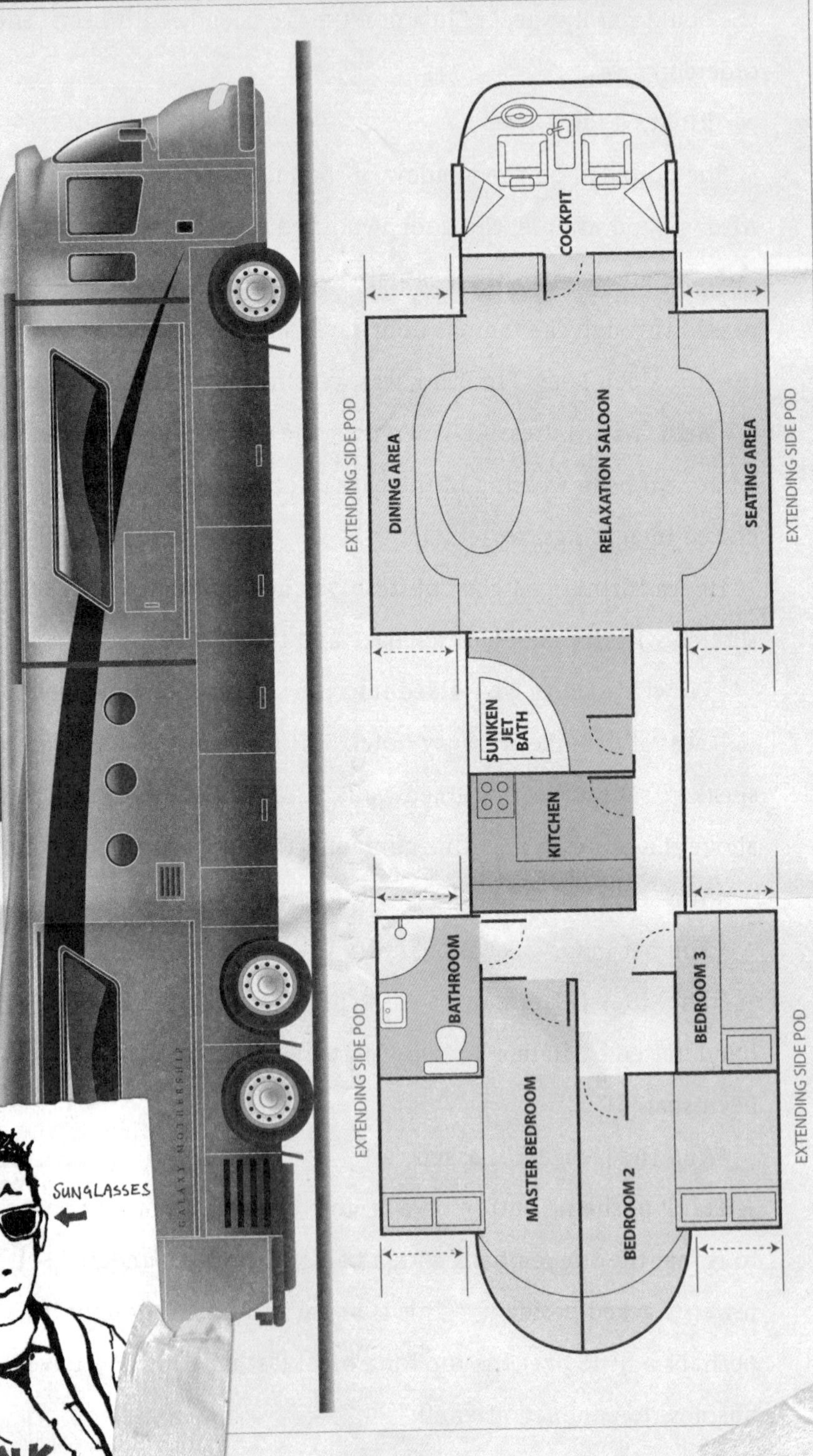

GALAXY MOTHERSHIP

COCKPIT

EXTENDING SIDE POD

DINING AREA

RELAXATION SALOON

SEATING AREA

EXTENDING SIDE POD

SUNKEN JET BATH

KITCHEN

BATHROOM

BEDROOM 3

EXTENDING SIDE POD

MASTER BEDROOM

BEDROOM 2

EXTENDING SIDE POD

SUNGLASSES

DRESSING-GOWN

FRANK

"Show-off," coughed Shufty, unimpressed.

Frank hit the button again and the wall slid back. No wonder he never left the place. He showed us to the dining table where fresh fruit, coffee, waffles and croissants lay waiting for us. "Be my guests. Have some food, please."

"We want our Barry back," said Shufty sharply.

"He's quite safe."

"Yes, but you had no right to take him. He was dead and buried."

"I read the reports on the internet," said Frank. "Barry's death at Zircon's launch party was well covered by the journalists present. Those Mark 5s did quite a job on your ZircoBot. One reporter described him as being cooked."

"Cooked or not, we want him back," I said. "Now."

"Hey, slow down. I'm proposing an alliance. He's my bargaining chip."

"What? What alliance?" I asked, confused.

"I've tried to keep you out of my affairs, but, reluctantly, I have come to the conclusion I need your ... how shall I say ... assistance." Frank took a slug of orange juice and opened a file on the table in front of him. "I've been reading my mother's notes on the ZircoBot. I had no idea they are run on your father's own unique operating system and software. Mom knew about Eve, but the second prototype Barry was a complete surprise. Seeing him on the Mermaid clip was clearly a revelation to her. So much so that she printed this out."

He lifted out a freeze-frame action shot of Barry taken at the shopping centre, mid- "hoo-ho-ho".

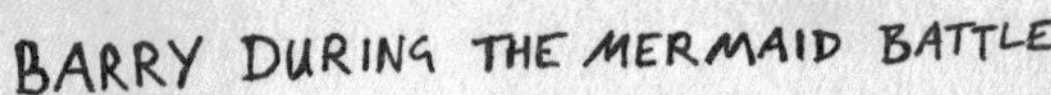

"Barry was the first prototype," said Shufty. "He didn't work as well as Eve. Eve was the one Zircon bought."

"Did Zircon know about Barry?" asked Frank.

Barry had never been part of Dad's bad deal, and Dad had always told us not to tell anyone Barry existed "because of contractual and legal obligations with Zircon", whatever that meant. But of course Barry had been shown to a gazillion people on the web, so that plan hadn't worked. His cover was well and truly blown. It seemed pointless to pretend any more, so that's why we had taken Barry to New York with us in the first place – that, and to keep the Quads happy.

"Zircon didn't know about Barry, not until the shopping-centre fiasco that catapulted my dad back to fame," I mumbled. "It was pretty difficult to keep Barry a secret after that."

"No kidding?" Frank paused, his expression turning to a sly half-smile. "Look, there's something you can help me with ... a favour, if you will."

He'd already got Barry, so what could he possibly want now? Shufty looked totally confused, too.

"I need your dad," said the Yank. Shufty and I looked utterly confused. I was tempted to say he could take the old man away for free. "OK ... I believe my mum's helping to put Ginger Streak back together is nothing more than a cover story. I think what she really wants is to find Barry. It's possible Barry has some vital information."

"He's not going to tell us anything now, though. He's dead," I said.

"Say, do you think you could reboot Barry from your dad's old computer system?"

"No," I said. "He's been totalled. Look, if you knew your mum wanted Barry, why didn't you just give him to her when you found him?"

"Barry's in great demand around here," said Frank. "Barry is therefore a commodity of high value. You see, I'm a businessman at heart ... or I will be. And in business you never give away an advantage without getting something in return. The ZircoBot is clearly yours, not my mother's, and certainly not mine, so view me as strictly neutral here. I do not intend long-term ownership of the monkey. Think of him as being on loan to me, if it makes you more comfortable."

"Oh, I feel, like, a thousand per cent better knowing that," said Shufty, insulted. She crossed her arms and glared – never a good sign with ol' Shufts.

"There's $10 million floating about. I don't sleep nights when I hear that kinda cash is up for grabs," said the Yank. "To my mind, Barry is most definitely mixed up in this Space Race caper."

I couldn't see how old Bazza could be mixed up in all this. I mean, how could he be? He was just a monkey toy. I decided to keep my thoughts to myself, and not give too much away to the American.

Frank continued, "It's a very tangled situation here. If Mom won't tell me what's going on, then it's my duty – my absolute duty, do you understand – to get to the bottom of it myself. Besides, I've got little else to do."

"So why do you need our dad?" I asked.

"To send him on a date. With my mom, of course. With those two out of the picture for a couple hours, we'll have time to restore Barry's computer brain. See what he knows. Find out why the Mark 5s fried him in New York. Obviously, I need you guys to help me."

Blimey.

"You mean bring Barry back from ... the dead?" asked Shufty, in horror.

"Exactly," replied the Yank, taking another sip of juice. And there was I thinking Barry would never play the cymbals again.

"It's possible ... look, it's possible there's some data left in Barry's secondary drive," said Shufty, thinking hard. "That drive wasn't too badly damaged. If we can get a replacement for the destroyed primary drive, we might be able to recover some data. We'll have to tell the Quads, though."

"Is that necessary?" said Frank. "I don't like to have too many people on the team, if you know what I mean."

"It's their toy, mostly," said Shufty. "They're already on our team, whether you like it or not, anyhow."

I thought for a moment, and I detected a possible problem with the Yank's plan. "Frank, won't your dad have something to say about your mum going out on a date with, errr ... our dad?"

The Yank lifted his sunglasses slowly with his index finger so we could see his eyes. "Oh, my dad ran off with Miss Venezuela. We don't like to talk about him much. Is this plan OK with you guys?"

I shrugged. Shufty reluctantly shrugged. "We can send them down to the Half Moon for scampi and chips. Can you guarantee your mum will take the bait?"

"Oh, sure. She wants to know everything she can about Barry. This will be a superb opportunity. What about your dad?"

"He'll be there. I'll make certain," said Shufty.

Frank knocked back the last of his orange juice and flipped down his sunglasses. He reached into a drawer and pulled out the muddy cardboard box. I hesitated before carefully opening Barry's coffin lid. Inside, the one-armed robot chimp gazed out with his blank-eyed stare.

"OK," said the Yank. "We have a deal. We've just bought ourselves two hours to resurrect your old friend Barry here and find out what he knows."

"One last thing," said Shufty. "We'll need that replacement primary drive. They're expensive."

"OK. Where do we get one?"

"Jake," I said. "He'll find us one. Can you afford it? Coz we sure can't."

"No problem. I may be only sixteen, but I already run several successful business ventures back at my high school in the States. I'm an independently wealthy man."

A SIGHT I NEVER THOUGHT I'D SEE AGAIN!

"Sure?" checked Shufty, who, as usual, was keen to keep an eye on costs.

"Sure I'm sure. Send me the bill. I'll put it against tax. I'll arrange some working capital for you this afternoon."

It sounded as if he was showing off, but I'm not sure he was. I liked him. He had a sort of laid-back swagger which was quite funny to be around. He was the type of guy who would make a million dollars before he was twenty-five. There was no doubt about it.

We left Frank and wandered back to The Mill. The General was already forming a battle plan. "Right. I'll sort out Dad and the date with the Prof. He's going out with her whether he likes it or not. I'll set it up for tomorrow night. Meanwhile, Ace, you get on to Jake at the human-fart factory and put in an order for a new hard drive for Barry. OK? I think the Yank is on to something here."

Shufty would never admit it, but now that she'd talked to Frank, a lot of her curious, instinctive hatred of him had suddenly disappeared. Maybe it was because he was seeking answers to the same questions we were. We didn't know it yet, but he was an ally ... and blimey, we were going to need some good allies to get through the Great Space Race alive.

AGONY UNCLE ACE

Time was short to sort out a new hard drive for Barry's brain. Jake reckoned his dad was the best hope of rustling one up, because he worked up in London near a shop that sold exactly what we needed. Jake emailed his old man with the master plan.

Three fart-saturated hours later we got a reply. Jake read the email and explained, "He's not happy about it, but he'll pick it up in his lunch hour tomorrow."

"When does he get home tomorrow night?"

"Depends on traffic. Seven ... seven-thirty."

The date was being lined up by Frank for 7.15 p.m. That wouldn't give me long to get from Jake's back to the barn, but what else could I do?

Shufty spent most of the evening trying to persuade Dad to go on the date with the Prof. He wasn't having it. Excuse after excuse was invented. Countless reasons surfaced as to why it was a bad idea, the most weird being "because her neck is too long". What was she – a giraffe? Her neck wasn't any longer than anyone else's as far as I could see.

I pushed off to bed at that point. There wasn't much else to do – no TV, no computer games, nothing. I crashed out on a mattress made up of cushions and rugs, and lay there thinking about the Barry plan. I still had my doubts. Frank was at a bit of a disadvantage because he'd never actually met Barry when he was alive and functioning. If he had, then perhaps he wouldn't have been half so enthusiastic about resurrecting him from the dead like Frankenstein's monster. Or should that be Crankenstein's monster?

A painful-sounding yell woke me up a few hours later. I looked at my watch. It was 1.05 a.m. It sounded like a Dad yell. I wasn't sure what he'd done to himself, but I yawned and stumbled down to the kitchen to see if he was OK.

MY GLOW-IN-THE-DARK GUITAR PLECTRUM – GREAT FOR NIGHT TIME GIGS

He was standing by the empty space where the cooker had been, nursing an injured thumb. He was gazing at a picture stuck to the wall of Mum on a freezing-cold Welsh beach. Her hair was blowing all over the place in the wind, and she was eating an ice cream, most of which was all round her mouth. We'd only ever had two family holidays, and that one had been Mum's last before she went into hospital for the last time.

Dad was talking to the picture softly. "I'm trying my best. I really am. If this doesn't work, then—"

"Dad?" I said, quietly.

"Ace!" he said, turning around quickly. "You gave me a shock, old fella."

"Are you OK?" I asked. "I heard you upstairs."

"Yeah," he replied unconvincingly. "I was talking to your mum."

"Oh?" I said. We all talked to this picture a bit. It was as if she was always there, watching over us. Dad always said we

should never get sad about her. She didn't like sad things, and it went against her "naturally upbeat" attitude to life. This seemed different, though. This was in the middle of the night.

"Who am I trying to kid, Ace? I'm a bit like this fuse panel," he said, pointing to the vital part from the computer's central console. "All the parts are here, but somehow nothing I try ever works. Your mum made sure things happened. And things were going pretty well for us, you know, before she died. I loved your mother, Ace, more than anything in the world. I still do."

"We all do," I said.

He fiddled with the fuse panel. "Shufty wants me to go on a date with the Professor."

"Yeah ... I sort of ... heard." I went bright red. This wasn't the sort of stuff we chatted about. Ever. No. We talked about Land Rover gearboxes and the benefits of the imperial measuring system over the metric. Not love. Girlfriends and stuff. Even worse, a girlfriend for Dad.

He nodded at the fuse panel. "We need to get this thing to work." He'd obviously been trying to fix the fuse box with the hammer when he'd hit his thumb. He waved the handle at the Iron Age electronics. "The rocket is coming together. We can make the deadline, all right. It's really in very good shape. Dry-stored in a deep mine is my guess. I think we're really in with a good chance, especially with the Prof on the team. Ginger Streak is really in A1 condition. Well, ummmhh ... apart from this fuse panel."

"Dad? Is ... is that really the right tool for repairing a fuse panel?"

"Probably not," he replied, suddenly defeated. "Er ... about this date with the Prof ... I don't think I should go on it. I don't feel right about it."

Where was Shufty? This was her department. I couldn't tell him we just wanted him out of the way for the night so we could bring back Barry from the dead. We'd shaken on the deal with Frank and promised not to say a thing.

The old man checked over his shoulder to see if anyone was listening, then said secretively, "You know ... Ace, old fella ... how ... er ... how do you ... ummhhh ... feel about the Prof, anyway?"

"I don't know, do I?"

"Whenever I think about going out on this date, I think about your mum" – he waved the hammer vaguely at the photograph – "and it's no good."

"Mum wouldn't have liked all this," I said, pointing at the blank spaces where the fridge and cooker had once stood before Thumper had nicked them. "If you found someone, it might make stuff easier."

Enough. This was as far as Agony Uncle Ace was prepared to go. Anyway, did I really want the Prof as a stepmum? I hadn't really considered the fallout from this dating plan, should it actually be successful. We'd just strolled into a minefield. I mean, it seemed they were both about to take this date seriously.

"Sure, Ace?"

"Sure, Dad. Absolutely positive." Those were my final words. End of subject.

He thought about it for several moments. "Thanks. Ummmhh, OK, I ... I will go on the date. Just to make you all happy. I'll never hear the end of it otherwise."

Superb. We were back on track. "Hey, do it for yourself, Dad, not me."

"OK, OK. And listen to me..." He was serious again. I was still bright red with embarrassment and wanted to leg it. "Ace, old son, we will make it into space. I absolutely promise."

I stared into his eyes and I could see tears forming. Somehow, and despite myself, I almost believed him. Almost – but not completely. I totted up the likelihood of us, the Crankshaws, really launching a rocket into space, even if it had been dry-stored (whatever that meant). "Don't make promises you can't keep, Dad."

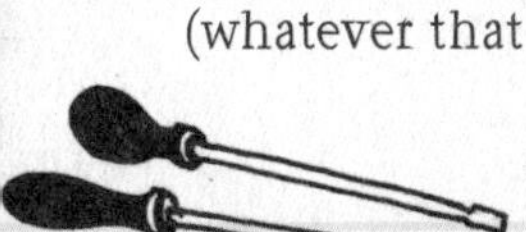

THE DODGY FUSE PANEL

← DAD'S FAVOURITE SCREWDRIVERS

He idly tossed the hammer down on the table, knocking the fuse panel. "I've always been a bit of a disaster. Now you don't trust me—"

"Dad!"

"What?"

"The fuse panel! Look!" Lights were beginning to glimmer weakly.

Despite his dodgy promises, I suddenly felt glad to be there, in the kitchen, in the middle of the night, with my nightmare dad. Just me and him and a Neanderthal lump of electronics on which our entire future now firmly rested. I nodded a couple of times and smirked at him.

MY GUITAR-STRING WINDER

Dad was beaming. "The problem was just a loose connection – so small, I missed it. At this rate, Ace, we really *can* have Ginger Streak ready on time."

Well, we could launch Ginger Streak, but if the race was a scam we weren't likely to win much, I thought. But I didn't want to spoil the moment. "Shufty will be happy," I said.

"Yes ... and the Prof says the guidance software is almost written. Son, we can really do this. We can really enter the race with a working rocket!"

"No, Dad. Shufty'll be happy about you and ... and the date."

"Oh! Oh, good. Umhh ... I almost forgot," said Dad.

Well, there's a surprise. Thanks to yours truly – Agony Uncle Ace Crankshaw – the date *and* the fuse box were fixed. Not a bad night's work.

Jake's dad, suited and booted after a hard day at the office, turned up at 7.32 p.m. with the replacement hard drive wrapped in an old carrier bag. He didn't look too stoked to be running errands for me. I paid him with Frank's money, chucked the goods in my rucksack, jumped on my bike and pedalled off as fast as I could for home, shouting a chirpy "thank you" over my shoulder for good measure. The entire exchange took less than fifteen seconds. The General was running a tight timetable and I was now late. Very late.

I wheelied into our drive and banged on the back brake, just avoiding a smart-looking man and woman standing right in the way. They both wore dark suits and carried matching black leather briefcases. Thumper seemed to be directing them (by waving his clipboard) down the road towards the village, and with a very serious look on his face. It wasn't his normal way of dealing with the press.

Anyhow, I didn't have time to stop. I swerved past them, piled on the power to get up the slight climb to the barn, skidded in an arc to a stop, jumped off and leant my bike against the door, all in one easy movement. Sweet.

The doors of the barn were open. Everything was ready. Barry's brain op was to take place at the far end of the room downstairs

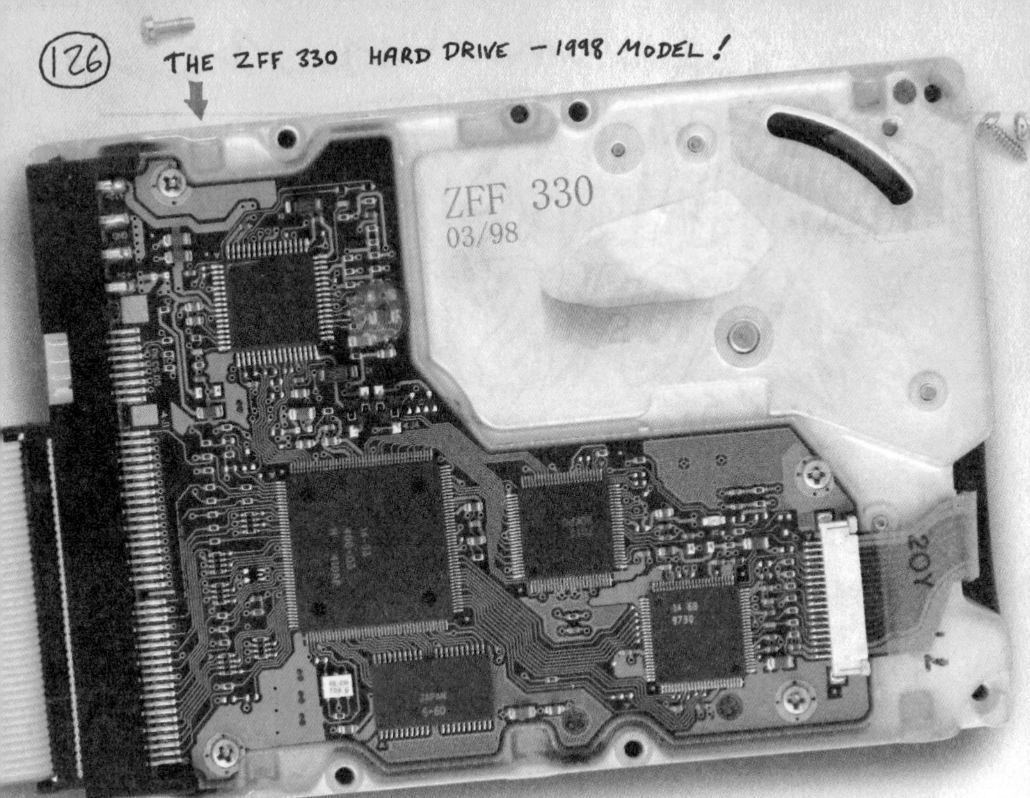

beyond the Prof's temporary lab, where Dad's computer set-up lived. The Quads had been busy getting everything ready. They'd set up a trestle table and rigged the old man's string of multicoloured light bulbs to brighten the place up, so the operating table looked a bit like a fairground sideshow. The plan was we could leg it upstairs to the practice room if we needed to clear out in a hurry. That was the theory, anyway.

"Where have you been?" Shufty asked with a good dollop of sisterly anger. "I thought you'd never get here. We've wasted, like, half an hour already, waiting for you. Did you get it?"

I pulled the drive out of my bag and handed it over. "ZFF 330, 1998 model. Second-hand, but working."

"What was the damage?" asked Frank.

"Three pounds." I handed back the mostly unused bundle of notes.

Shufty looked shocked at Jake's cut-price deal. "I thought it was going to be £450?"

"Dad was way out on the price. It was so cheap because nobody uses this old-fashioned rubbish any more."

"Let's get started," said Shufty. "Quads. Shut the doors. There are loads of press types milling about. We don't want them seeing any of this." The Quads carried out the order as she pulled the tarpaulin off Dad's computer set-up.

ANOTHER ONE OF DAD'S FAVOURITE SCREWDRIVERS

Frank was shocked by what he saw: "Wow. You know how this works, Shufty? You think you can plug Barry in to this pile of junk?"

"Errr ... yep. Sort of," she replied, unwilling to fill out the detail of how and why, or admit that she'd once quite liked Dad. When Shufty was much younger, she and Dad had been the very best of friends. During this long-forgotten era of tranquil peace, Eve and Barry had been created. She'd helped the old man to build both the prototypes. She'd been there when he'd programmed the software. Shufty, therefore, had always known a lot more about how Barry worked than she let on.

We needed to work fast. I plugged the drive into Barry's brain. It was covered in dust, but it fitted perfectly. Then I connected Barry up to the USB port on Dad's crazy old computer set-up, set him down on the table, and nodded to Shufty that we were ready.

The Quads crowded in to see if their old friend would come back to life. There was fear in their faces. The possibility that Barry might not have been quite as dead as we'd thought had been a difficult subject to bring up. How would they take it if this experiment went wrong? I tried not to think about it.

Now it was time to try to reprogramme his brain. Shufty typed in the password, and the green screen monitor came alive. "This is the most delicate point in the proceedings," explained Shufty in her serious voice. "Now I want you to know, Quads, that this operation has only a very, very small chance of success. We have to face facts. Barry might never be the same again."

The four of them nodded.

"OK," she said. "The software is running." Shufty's eyes flicked over the screen. "I am now meddling with the deepest recesses of your mind, Bazza, old son."

Wednesday mopped a bead of sweat from Shufty's brow with the washing-up cloth stuck on the end of a broom handle.

Shufty navigated her way through Dad's system until she found what she was looking for. "This is it. *Rebuild primary drive.*"

"Are you sure?" I asked.

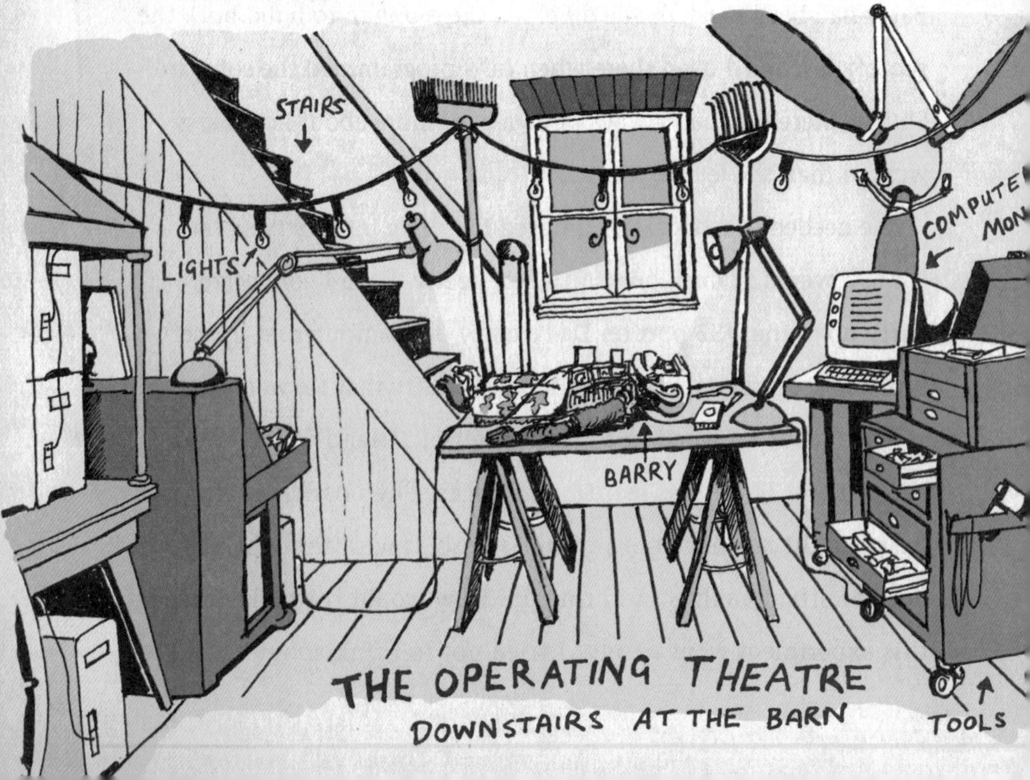
STAIRS
LIGHTS
BARRY
THE OPERATING THEATRE
DOWNSTAIRS AT THE BARN
TOOLS

"Yes. I've seen Dad do it before, so keep quiet," she said. "Do we want to restore and save original memories in the secondary drive?"

"Oh yeah!" nodded Frank. "You betcha."

Shufty clicked the relevant option box with the huge wooden hand-built mouse.

"Is it going to work?" I asked.

"Ace," smiled Shufty. "Hush, OK?"

She hit the return key and a progress bar appeared on her screen. Before our very eyes, Barry was being reborn as his old unreliable self. The computer made a pinging noise.

"Rebuild complete," said Shufty, disconnecting the lead. "He should be all set. Who wants to power him up?"

The Quads had gone very quiet, but Monday volunteered.

"Remember what I said," cautioned Shufty. "Even if he does come back to life, he may not be the same Barry you remember."

Monday pressed Barry's power button. He gave a little twitch, his eyes lit up, and his head turned towards the Quads as he slowly sat up. He turned his head back and forth, checked his arm, spun his ears around once, then finally seemed to recognize us. The Quads gave him a cheer. We all gave him a cheer. He gave us a "hoo-ho-ho" back.

"He's alive! And he's not going berserk," said Shufty.

Barry started to jump up and down, searching about frantically as if he was missing something.

"He's not right," I said, moving back and grabbing a hammer. "You've created a monster, Shufty. He *is* going berserk."

"You're right!" said Frank, arming himself with the soldering iron.

"No, Ace, he just wants his waistcoat," said Thursday.

I found his faded gunslinger's waistcoat on the desk behind me. As soon as he had it back on, Barry relaxed a bit. Then he shakily pulled a small black diamond-shaped plastic card a little bigger than a coin from the inside pocket, and handed it to Tuesday. He finally settled, giving us his usual blank stare.

"Let me see that," said Frank.

"What is it?" I asked.

Frank held it to the light, and turned it over a couple of times. "No idea. No markings ... wait, it has a Zircon Industries logo engraved on it."

At the word Zircon, Barry screeched. He pointed to the LED display on his stomach that was struggling to light up a very dim message.

BARRY'S DIAMOND-SHAPED PLASTIC CARD

"Dad's dodgy wiring," I said. I picked Barry up and squeezed his waist a bit. This usually brightened up the screen slightly. The dim letters glowed a little stronger. I read the words aloud to the others: "'FROM EVE: PROJECT X7X – INTELLIGENT PARASITIC COMPUTER VIRUS USING PROMETHEUS NETWORK'. So it *was* Eve I saw at the reception," I said. "It *was* her. Barry's sister. I was right."

"What does that mean?" said Shufty, inspecting the card again.

"I don't know, but Eve could have transmitted the message during the fight," I said.

"How?" asked Frank.

"Infrared data transfer," I said. "Barry and Eve were originally built to communicate with each other."

"Ace is right," said Tuesday, nodding.

"It doesn't mean much, does it?" said Shufty.

"There's one person who can tell us what the Prometheus network is," I said. "Jake. He knows stuff like that."

A car drew up outside. We could hear car doors banging and low, serious voices.

"Quick, they're back," said Shufty.

"But they've only been gone for, like, forty-five minutes," said Frank, a little annoyed.

Strange, I thought – they'd walked to the pub. I opened the door a fraction. I could see Dad and the Prof, but they had two other people with them too. It was the man and woman who'd been talking to Thumper, and who I'd nearly crashed into on my bike. They were back, briefcases swinging by their sides.

"Perhaps the date was a disaster?" I said.

"Everyone upstairs," said Shufty, switching off the computer and the fairground lights. She grabbed the diamond-shaped card from Frank and put it safely in her pocket. "Quick!"

I chucked the cover back over the computer, and followed the others up to the attic room. Something had gone wrong on the pub date, I just knew it. Who were the two people with the briefcases? If Thumper had let them through the cordon, then it was definitely a bad sign. Something wasn't right. I just knew it.

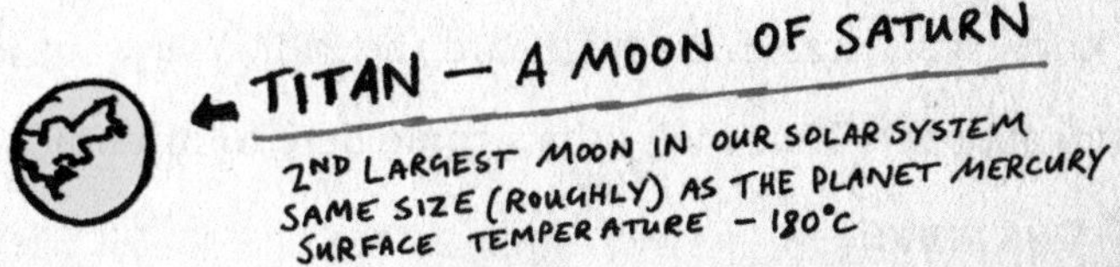

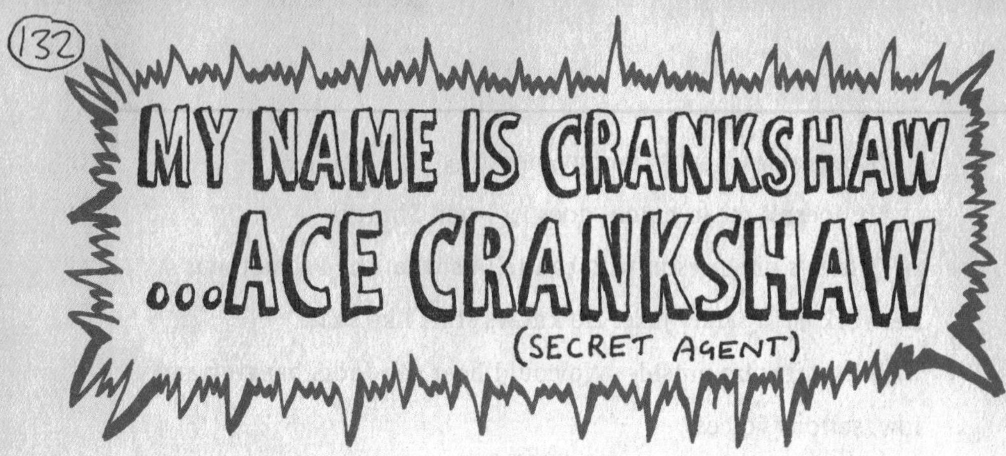

MY NAME IS CRANKSHAW ...ACE CRANKSHAW (SECRET AGENT)

By the time Dad, the Prof and their two mysterious new friends creaked up the stairs to join us in the attic room, it looked as if we'd been up there all night. We'd done a pretty good job in such a short time: the Quads were hard at work on Twister, Frank was coaxing life out of the stove for a brew, and I was texting on my mobile, all to a backing track being plinked out by Shufty on the piano.

Dad and the Prof both looked a bit edgy and worried. Had the date been a disaster?

"Kids, we've got guests. Meet Beverley and Clive. They work for the British government."

"What do you do for the government?" asked Tuesday straight out.

"We're agents."

"What, secret agents?" I asked.

Clive nodded. "Yes – something like that. We're very interested in Zack Zircon and the Great Space Race, so we've come here to talk to you about it."

Dad cleared his throat. "Kids – they want us to spy on Mr Zircon's Space Race, because they don't quite trust him."

"You've come to the right place, then," said Shufty. "We know it's a scam. We overheard the Prof. You want to ask her all about it. That's why she's come here to Britain, isn't it?"

"Is this true?" Dad asked his date.

The Prof said nothing. She crossed her arms and glowered angrily.

"Why didn't you tell me?" said Dad, looking first at us, then at the Prof, in utter confusion.

"I didn't know if you were in on the scam," replied the Prof. "You did invent the ZircoBot, after all."

Dad looked frustrated. "What is this scam you keep talking about?"

"That's precisely what we want you to find out," said Clive. "We want Team Crankshaw to be on the inside. We know Zircon's developed an extremely powerful computer virus. The X7X. We think a man named Jed Summers was working on the team who developed it."

"Jed Summers is my brother," said the Prof anxiously. "He doesn't design viruses. He was working on a top-secret satellite project for Zircon ... until he disappeared, that is. The reason I'm here is to look for him. Find some answers. The Space Race is an ideal way to get access to Zircon and his operation. Do you know where Jed is?"

"I'm afraid not," said Clive.

"X7X was mentioned in a message picked up by our ZircoBot prototype, Barry, over in New York," I said.

"But Barry is dead," explained Dad.

Shufty looked at Frank, who shrugged and said, "Yeah, go ahead, Shufty. Tell them about Barry. Why not?"

"Barry's not dead any more," said Shufty. "We got the message from him."

The old man's face lit up in wonder at this unexpected news. "But we buried him, didn't we?"

Beverley butted in before we could give an answer. "The monkey's alive?" she asked, taking out a notebook and pen from her bag. "What other information was in this message?"

"Something about a Prometheus network," I added. "That's all we've found out."

Beverley noted the name down, then smiled. "Excellent. We'll look into this Prometheus business straight away."

"Why would Zircon be designing a computer virus?" asked Shufty. "He's, like, totally rich. It doesn't make any sense."

"Well, that's what we need to find out," said Beverley.

"Why don't you just arrest him?" asked Dad.

"Mr Zircon has worked on some of the US government's top-secret satellite projects," explained Beverley. "He has connections in very, very high places. We need more evidence to be taken seriously."

"She's right – I got nowhere with the CIA when I contacted them," said the Prof. "Nobody was interested. They thought I was a nut."

"We're short on time," said Beverley. "The race is less than a week away, and you will be ideally positioned at the ZircoSpaceParc to find out more."

"We need evidence," explained Clive. "At the moment we don't have any. We think the X7X virus is somehow connected to the Space Race, but we don't know exactly how. If we can find the evidence, we'll stop the race."

"If we stop the race, we can't win the money," said Dad, clearly still in denial that the race was a scam. "We'll be broke."

"If you undertake this mission, rest assured, Mr Crankshaw, Her Majesty's government will reward you financially," said Beverley, slowly and clearly. "We can clear your debts. All we ask is that anything you discover you will pass on to us and absolutely nobody else. The deal is dependent on total and utter secrecy. Hopefully, Professor, we can find out what happened to your brother along the way. We have our best people working on it right now."

"If we find out any information, how do we contact you?" asked Dad.

"With this," said Clive, handing him a mobile phone. "It's pre-loaded with our numbers."

I didn't know if total and utter secrecy included Jake. I hoped so, because that was who I'd been texting about Barry's message when they'd all rocked up. I decided to keep quiet.

Hmmhhh ... Ace Crankshaw, rocketeer, guitarist and now international secret agent. Sweet.

Our preparations for blast-off carried on just as they had before, but with a sort of tasty "secret agent" edge to them. As if firing a rocket wasn't enough, we were now trying to find out

what our old enemy Zircon was really up to, and – this was the best bit – with the government's help. This felt good. Very good.

Weird stuff happened in those last couple of days before we left for America. The press kept trespassing. Climbing over the hedges. Snapping pictures of us and the rocket. Hovering overhead in helicopters. The media interest was massive, and the siege situation with all their satellite trucks and camera crews was so intense we couldn't leave The Mill. The police were operating a one-way system around the village, and the pub was now open twenty-four hours a day to serve the journalists, who "had quite a thirst on them", according to Sheila, the landlady.

Our last official visitors were Ki-Ki Sapphire and Billy Nansen. They arrived in a fat Roller the day before we were due to leave. Ki-Ki's camera crew followed behind in her people carrier crammed with masses of equipment like lights and tripods.

Nansen looked whacked out by the journey. He was sucking on an oxygen mask, while his nurse gave him a shot of medicine in his withered arm to wake him up a

$10m Space Race prize could be wo by £5 rocket

ALL SYSTEMS GO FO GINGER STREAK TEA

Space Race family say rocket is se for blast-off

by Vincent Salmon

One giant leap for backyard Moon sh as family rocket is shipped to USA

POLICE NOTICE

TEMPORARY TRAFFIC MANAGEMENT AND PARKING ALLOCATION

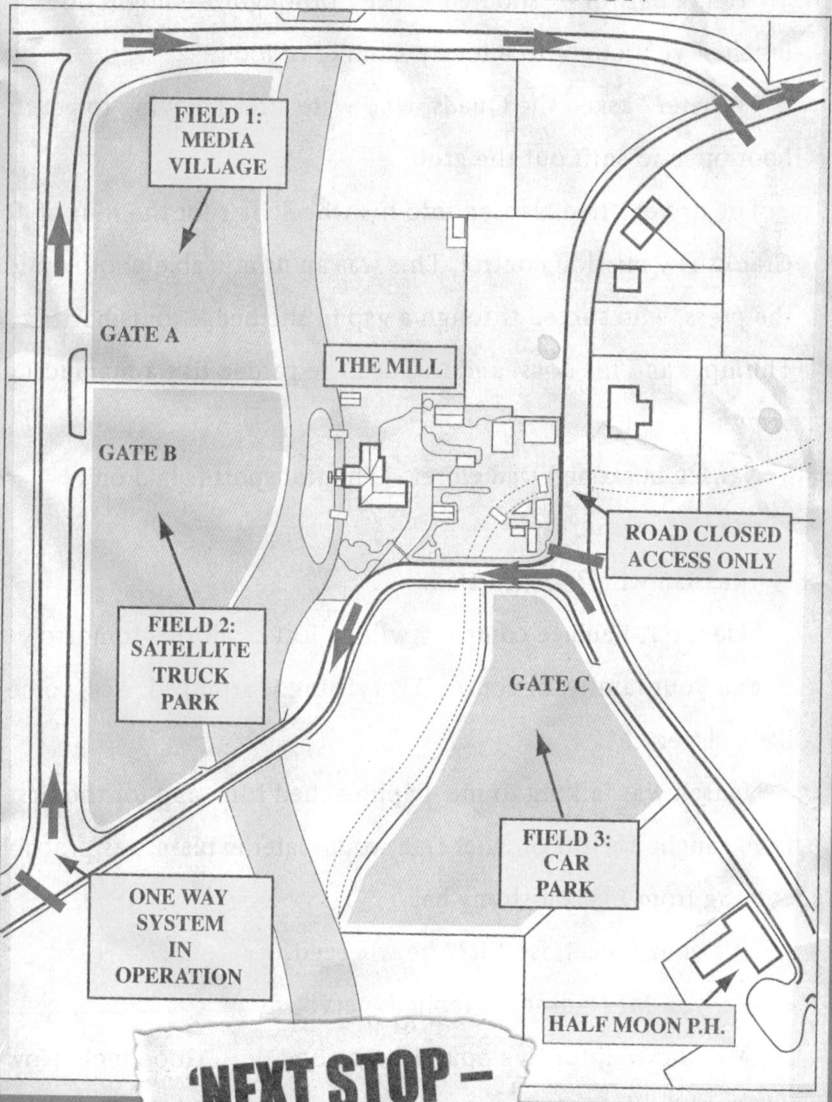

'NEXT STOP – THE MOON!' CLAIMS SPACE-RACE DAD

bit. The driver jumped out, then opened the passenger door. The great man peered wearily at the six trailers carrying the rockets. He seemed more dead than alive. A bit like the rocket, really.

"Hello, darlings!" shouted Ki-Ki. "I thought we might do lunch? I've brought us a lovely hamper of food."

"Where?" asked the Quads, who were already trying to get the boot open to sniff out the grub.

The driver lifted Nansen into his wheelchair for the tour of Crankshaw mission control. This was an unmissable photo op for the press, who surged through a gap in the hedge (outsmarting Thumper and his dogs) and invaded the garden like a marauding army.

Nansen beckoned Dad closer. "The transport is laid on ... Russian..."

"Russian what?" asked Dad.

"Planes. A haulage company will collect ... all this tomorrow ... and your family, of course. Everything is arranged. Ace, come a little closer..."

Nansen was talking to me. I approached him, and for the first time caught a whiff of what Dad would later explain was probably coming from his colostomy bag.

"It's your rocket, isn't it?" he wheezed.

"Er, yes, Mr Nansen," I replied, nervously.

"You did well for five pounds ... a good deal. Good luck. Now tell the nurse to get me home before that bunch of hooligans..." he gasped, "...spoils your vegetable patch. Tell 'em ... I'm only giving interviews to Ki-Ki."

Thumper had regained the initiative and unleashed the dogs.

Love and Hate darted back and forth, herding the press pack like sheep towards the mill pond. As quickly as he'd arrived, it seemed Nansen wanted to be off. The driver wheeled the great man at top speed back to the Roller, delivered him to the back seat, and within thirty seconds was tearing away at top speed down the drive in a cloud of dust.

However the Quads had managed to capture the hamper and were moving at an equally fast pace towards the kitchen with it, dragging it behind them with a rope like Arctic explorers man-hauling a sledge ... hungry Arctic explorers.

Shufty stood, her arms crossed, a detatched look on her face as she watched the scene unfold, shaking her head slowly from side to side in total disbelief. "Why me?" she said.

"Because you're a Crankshaw," I explained. "And weird stuff like this always happens to us."

"Do you think, Ace, that when we grow up we'll all be like Dad? You, me, the Quads? Is it possible?"

"I'm kinda hoping not, but from a strictly scientific point of view, it's all probably genetic. Look at Grandpa Crankshaw. He's barking mad. So, yeah, probably. You'd better get used to it, Shufts. It definitely runs in the family."

"Great," she said, stropping off in the direction of the kitchen. "Thanks, Ace. Thank you very much."

GOODBYE GRAVESEND HELLO CHICAGO

The next day, and by some sort of miracle, we were ready to go. The Prof had even worked out the whole launch routine, giving us a sort of Crankshaw-proof guide to launching the rocket.

There was nothing left to do.

Nansen was true to his word and had laid on transport for us to the States, so we packed everything up and prepared to leave. Our next destination was the ZircoSpaceParc and then, for Ginger Streak, the Moon.

Jake, seated on his bike, waved to the Prof and Frank as they drove the mothership down the drive and through Thumper's roadblock. Frank was in the front passenger seat, feet up on the dash, sipping a fruit smoothie and reading a business magazine.

"Not going with you?" asked Jake.

"No," I said. "They've got to take the mothership back to its owners. Nansen is flying them out on a later flight."

"Next time you see them will be in the States, then," said Jake. He nodded at the last Ginger Streak trailer being hitched up to the HGV. "Team Crankshaw all ready for blast-off?"

"Yep," I said. "We fly tonight. Nansen has chartered some massive Russian cargo planes to shift the rocket. Right up your street."

I could almost see Jake's geeky aircraft brain cells kicking into gear. "Antonov 124? Or the 225?"

"Not sure. I'll check."

"Get some pictures of it for me, man," he said, with more than a hint of envy. "What about Ginger Streak? Guidance software written? Fuse panel fixed? Laser weapons powered up?"

"All set. It's now or never. Shame your mum won't let you come with us," I added.

Jake pushed his bike backwards and forwards a few times, testing the brakes. "The new drum kit arrives next Thursday. Can't miss that, can I?"

"Nah – and when I get back we'll take the world of rock 'n' roll by storm. I've already got some songs worked out."

"Long guitar solos?" he asked.

"Massive. Massive drums solos as well. Together we can set about reinventing the entire language of rock."

"I'll get practising, then," he said with a grin. The final HGV truck's engine fired up with a harsh grunt.

"Reckon Ginger Streak'll be able to make the Kessel Run in less than twelve parsecs?" he joked.

"There shouldn't be any imperial battlecruisers between here and the Moon, so I've decided not to make the jump to light speed on our first trip."

"Very wise, man. Very wise," replied Jake.

"Anyway, it's a Crankshaw rocket," I said in a more realistic tone. "It's bound to blow up on take-off."

"Exactly what I was thinking."

"Cheers, mate. Thanks for the vote of confidence."

"No problem." He dug out a folded A4 printout from his back pocket. "I searched the internet for you, man. Put the word out,

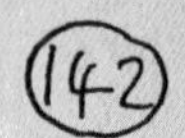

you know. The Prometheus network is a bunch of top-secret US satellites. Here's a section of their blueprints. Don't show anyone. It's not for civilians."

The top-secret printout showed a diagram of the satellite in full technical detail.

"Where do you get this stuff, Jake? The Bothan spies or something?" I asked.

"I've got my contacts. Reliable. This is the real deal. Straight up."

I inspected the printout, but it didn't mean much to me. "So what has Prometheus got to do with the Great Space Race?" I asked.

"No idea, man. That's for you to work out. Look, Mum's cooking tea for six. I'd better go or I'll be late." The last thing he wanted to do was go home to eat fish fingers and oven chips. Really what he wanted to do was come to America with the Crankshaw space programme. It was written all over his face.

"See you in a couple of weeks?" I said.

"May the force be with you, Ace, my young Padawan learner," he said, reluctantly. "The Gravesend branch of the rebel alliance is counting on you ... and I'll be watching you on TV."

I kicked at a stone on the drive. "I couldn't have done this without you, Jake. Buying the rocket and stuff."

"Yep. I know."

"If you'd bought Ginger Streak yourself, you could have entered the race," I suggested.

He thought about this for a moment, then chuckled. "Only the Crankshaws would be crazy enough to shoot a second-hand rocket at the Moon, man. It was always a mad idea. Win that money, Ace."

"See you around, Jake."

JAKE GETS THE GOODS EVERY TIME

I watched him wheelie down the drive, swerve past Thumper's barrier, and steer on to the track lined with TV satellite vans, which led off across the field. At the brow of the hill he turned to watch the last truck pulling out of our drive. He gave me a Vulcan V salute, then was gone.

I looked at the Prometheus diagram once more. What were we, the Crankshaws, involved in? Really? Suddenly a whole bunch of people had got in on my Secret Plan with secret plans of their own. The simple idea of winning a race to the Moon had somehow become very, very, very complicated. Spy satellites, Beverley and Clive the briefcase spies, Nansen the half-dead billionaire, the Prof and Frank, Zircon. I needed to find some answers – and fast. And those answers were across the Atlantic.

A minibus pulled up the drive and stopped by our pile of luggage. The Quads were sitting there quietly munching on the remains of Ki-Ki's food hamper. Dad and Shufty were locking the kitchen door. The moment had arrived. It was time to get our lunar mission started. If by some bit of luck we won the $10 million, it would be one small step for man, and one giant leap into profit for the Crankshaws.

Next stop Chicago.

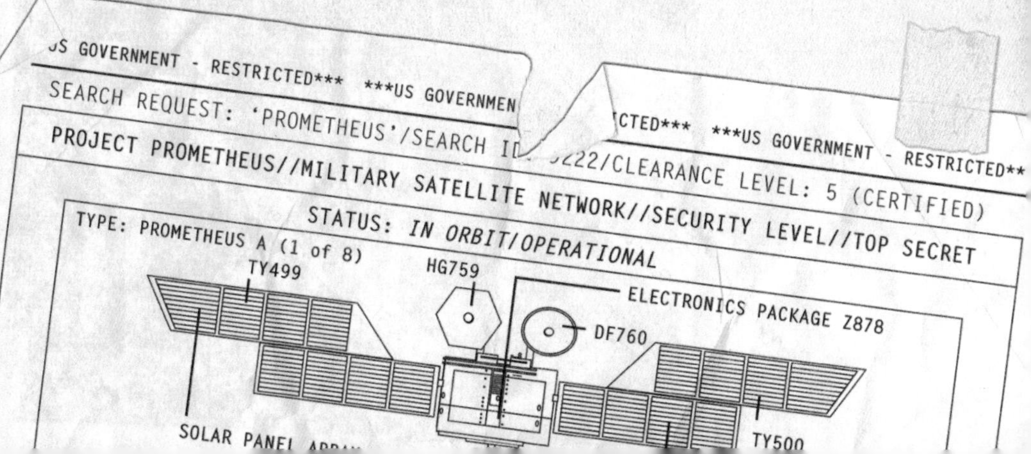

ZIRCO SPACEPARC

ROCKET ASSEMBLY FACILITY

'MARS' – MUSEUM OF SPACE EXPLORATION

ROCKET

ROCKET

THE HUB

ROCKET

ROCKET

ROCKET

ROLLER COASTER

MONO RAIL STATION

MISSION CONTROL, OR MISSION-CONTROLLED?

Once we'd landed at Chicago O'Hare Airport, we were driven straight to the ZircoSpaceParc. I'd read about this place. I'd seen the TV advert and glossy brochure in New York. It promised more space-themed entertainment within its ten-mile circumference than all of the rest of the theme parks in the country put together.

For years I'd dreamt of going somewhere like this. It was like nothing else we'd done before. We'd been on holiday twice in five years, camping in Wales. This was totally different.

We drove through the iron entrance gates and I was awestruck by the sight. The ZircoSpaceParc was radical. It was impressive. Very impressive. I had to admit our arch enemy Zircon had done a good job on the place. Tangles of rollercoaster tracks snaked over the place like spaghetti. There were rides that made you feel sick just to look at them. Yes – this was a destination you could show off to your mates about. This was a place people would be envious of your just visiting. "ZircoSpaceParc? Yeah ... I've been there," I'd be able to say. "Have you been on the ZircoCoaster? No? Yeah, well, you should try it, mate. Accelerates to 457mph and pulls 6G on the corners. It's like being strapped into a fighter plane."

GINGER STREAK →

+00:00:00:00

FLICK-BOOK SEQUENCE STARTS HERE!

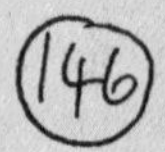

And what was better, the place wasn't open yet! And we were going to be among the very first people through the doors. Even if the race wasn't a race, at least we could say we'd been.

We drove through some more gates – heavily guarded this time – and into the private rocket launch area of the site. The driver dropped us at a huge lobby area. Inside, the place felt a bit like an airport. Everything was either round or curved and there was a whiff of new carpets and fresh paint. There was aluminium everywhere – the doors, the ceilings, the circular window frames. There were cool announcements over the intercom system like "Will Professor Theodore please report to launch coordinator at subsection K5, thank you". Long tube-like corridors branched off in all directions, while Zircon scientists wearing white uniforms marched about with clipboards.

TVs built into the wall showed the action from around the space park, all without exception having a countdown clock running along the bottom of the screen displaying how long was left until blast-off. When I saw the seconds ticking away my stomach gave a lurch, like the feeling you get when you're in a car going over a small bridge too fast. This place was the centre of the world, the epicentre of a great adventure, and we jokers had somehow stumbled into it.

Zircon was there to greet us. He was flanked by six of those creepy Mark 5 ZircoBots. "Welcome, Team Crankshaw," he said slowly. "You've made it. I hope your flight was comfortable?"

"Very," Dad said coldly.

"And your prototype ZircoBot?"

Dad had told the Quads to keep Barry hidden at all times, in case of a repeat performance with the Mark 5s. He was concealed in Tuesday's backpack with the power switched off to keep him quiet.

"Barry wasn't so good after he was mugged by your ZircoBots," said Dad with a tight-lipped smile. "They're meant to be toys, not robot-monkey soldiers with the power to electrocute."

Zircon smiled weakly, his eyes betraying that strange menace of his. "I've had my computer experts tinker with your software, Mr Crankshaw. I've never really understood computer technology, but they tell me they've made a few tweaks. My newer ZircoBots still have some glitches."

"Glitches? They destroyed Barry," said Dad. "We had to bury him."

"You don't seem very relaxed, Mr Crankshaw. No problems with the rocket, I hope. Is it complete?"

"We're ready to have a shot at the $10 million," snapped Dad. "How's the race coming on? No hitches? Nothing going to go wrong? Nothing we should know about? Nothing you want to tell us?"

"Rest assured." Zircon coughed. "Everything is perfectly set. Now, I wonder ... have you by any chance brought your musical instruments?"

"Oh, yes. We left nothing behind in Britain ... of any value," replied Dad truthfully.

"That is marvellous. It would be a great honour if you could play at the pre-launch dinner and countdown ceremony."

Monday piped up. "Ace ... Ace ... we're not playing for free again, are we? Coz we never got paid for the Mermaid gig – and Shufty says Zircon is completely loaded with cash, so I bet his pockets are stuffed with diamonds and pirate treasure and he sleeps on a bed with a mattress stuffed full of wads and wads of all that lovely money he owes us."

Yeah, you can always rely on Monday to tell it like it is.

"I will pay you six thousand pounds," said Zircon, a little angrily. "There will be a global audience, after all."

For six thousand pounds, we could hardly refuse.

"Six thousand pounds?" checked Dad. "That's ten times what you paid for my robot-monkey design."

Zircon laughed, and swivelled his wheelchair round. "Correct, Mr Crankshaw. Win the race, and you can add another $10 million to your takings."

"That's what Team Crankshaw is here for," said Dad.

Zircon stopped, but did not turn. "One last thing, Mr Crankshaw. The other members of your team, Professor Lavisham and her son, have been delayed. There's been a death in the family. They have to fly to Los Angeles to make funeral arrangements."

Dad called out after him, "Do you know who passed away?"

"An uncle. Ahhh ... Jed Summers. I don't have any further details, I'm afraid."

We'd been there less than five minutes and stuff was going wrong. Delayed? We needed the Prof if we were to have any chance of launching Ginger Streak. She was our trump card. The ace up our sleeve. We'd be completely sunk without her.

Shufty tried to text Frank to check what was going on, and find out when they were planning to show up.

"I'm afraid cell phones don't work here," said a woman who'd sneaked up behind us. We all nearly jumped out of our skins. "I'm Nikki." Nikki looked like someone in charge of something. That something turned out to be us. She wore a ZircoSpaceParc uniform and hat, and far too much make-up. When she spoke, it sounded as if she'd learnt her lines from a script. "I'm here to show you to your rocket assembly and accommodation areas."

"Why won't our phones work?" asked Shufty bluntly.

Nikki unleashed her dazzling smile. I'd never seen teeth as white as hers. "Oh, the electronic equipment of the various rocket programmes means we do not allow cell-phone networks to operate in the launch area of the ZircoSpaceParc."

That was going to throw a spanner in the works with our hotline to Clive and Beverley. We'd been there for less than two minutes and everything was already falling apart, in typical Crankshaw style.

"Well, when will they work?" asked Shufty.

"After the race has started," Nikki answered, her voice going up at the end of the sentence. There was that smile again. The subject was closed.

"Oh, great," said Dad, under his breath.

Nikki ushered Team Crankshaw aboard a monorail.

We zoomed off at high speed towards the Ginger Streak assembly area, passing over the massive complex at top speed. The Quads gasped in total wonder at what they saw. Nikki pointed out the press centre, the entrance to the theme park, the ballroom where they wanted us to play. It was like being shot through a James Bond movie set at high speed ... only it wasn't a movie set, it was real.

Slap in the middle of the site was the central Zircon complex called the Hub, from which the rocket-assembly halls stuck out like the spokes of a bike wheel. From the outside, the whole futuristic structure seemed poised to blast off into space and follow the competition rockets to the Moon. The launch areas were set in concrete bowls at the end of the spokes about half a mile apart for safety. The place was as busy as an ants' nest.

"There's our rocket," said Monday, seeing the trucks pulling up on the tarmac below us. Ginger Streak loomed under the tarpaulin – a menacing lump of untested 1970s technology.

The train glided into our own little monorail station. I could see two ten-storey-high cylindrical towers. A sign said: *Ginger Streak Consortium*.

This launch area looked different from the others, which were set further away in the middle of the complex. In fact, they looked as if they must have taken years to build.

"This is Mr Zircon's engine test area," said Nikki as we approached the entrance. "Of course, we weren't expecting you until a few weeks ago. It's very comfortable, and should suit your rocket just fine."

I tried to take everything in. What was it that Zircon was trying to cover up, if this race really was all for show?

ZIRCON'S PERSONAL ROCKET →

The doors of the monorail swooshed open. Nikki pointed to a round reinforced-glass roof ten floors up. "This is your mission-control and accommodation tower. The second tower will be your rocket-assembly tower. You can use the elevator over here to reach the floors above or any of the rocket stages once your rocket is in one piece."

It was an incredible place, I had to admit. It even had a small koi-carp pond.

"Cor, Dad, look," said Thursday. "That pond is just like the one you totally and utterly destroyed at the Mermaid when you flooded everything and made the electrics go bang in that massive explosion. I bet you could do loads of really expensive damage in here if you tried your hardest. You could wreck this place easily."

"Aaahh, yes," said Dad with embarrassment. "Well, I was being chased by wild dogs then, of

course, son, and it was an accident."

Nikki, undaunted by Thursday's terrifying story, pushed on with the guided tour. "I hope you'll all be comfortable. On the floors above us you'll find a gym, media room, office and private cinema. You can order food any time of the day using this computer monitor. Your bedrooms are on the sixth and seventh floors, and your workshops and assembly area are through these doors over here. Oh, and of course, your Ginger Streak mission-control room is below. So you're pretty much self-contained."

I thought of The Mill and its empty interior restyled by Thumper. Whatever happened, for the next three days we were going to live like kings.

"The rules of the competition state you have three days to complete your rocket," continued Nikki. "You must not speak to any of the competing teams, or contact them, or enter their assembly areas."

"Can't we have a go on the theme-park rides?" asked Wednesday.

"No," said Nikki very firmly.

"Not even the rollercoaster?" asked Wednesday.

"I'm sorry," said Nikki, with a hint of menace. "They won't be running until after the launch."

Hmmhhh. Just like the phones. I had that worry again. Something just wasn't right here.

"OK," said Nikki, "I'm going to leave you guys to settle in. If you need anything, just call me on this green phone over here."

"But that phone doesn't have any buttons," I said. "How do we call out if it doesn't have a keypad?"

"Just lift the receiver. It will connect straight through to me. Your luggage will be delivered a little later. Good luck." Nikki hopped back aboard the monorail and shot off back towards the central hub.

"It's a bit sinister, us being locked in here for three days," I said. "No Lavishams. No phone, either."

"Exactly," said Dad. "They don't want us poking about – so here's the plan. We try to get out of here through a fire exit or something, and find out what Zircon is really up to."

Shufty sighed loudly. "Fire exits? Is that the best plan you can come up with?" The General clearly wasn't interested in Dad's idea. "First things first. You lot need to start bolting Ginger Streak together. Make it look as if we're actually doing something here, while I try to find some answers."

"So what are you going to be doing while we're building Ginger Streak?" asked Monday.

"I need to find a way of contacting the Lavishams. They had plenty of time to send us a text to tell us about Jed before we arrived here. It just doesn't add up."

She was right. Nothing added up. I had a creepy feeling we were being sucked into a deadly dangerous and very expensive trap. What was Zircon up to, and what did he want us – the hopeless, poverty-stricken Crankshaw family – *for*, exactly?

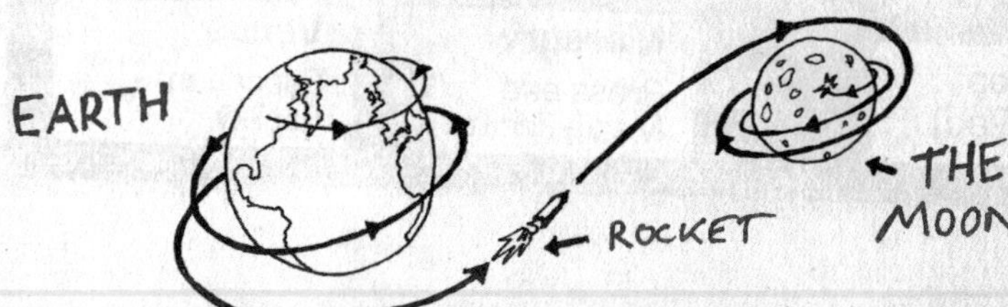

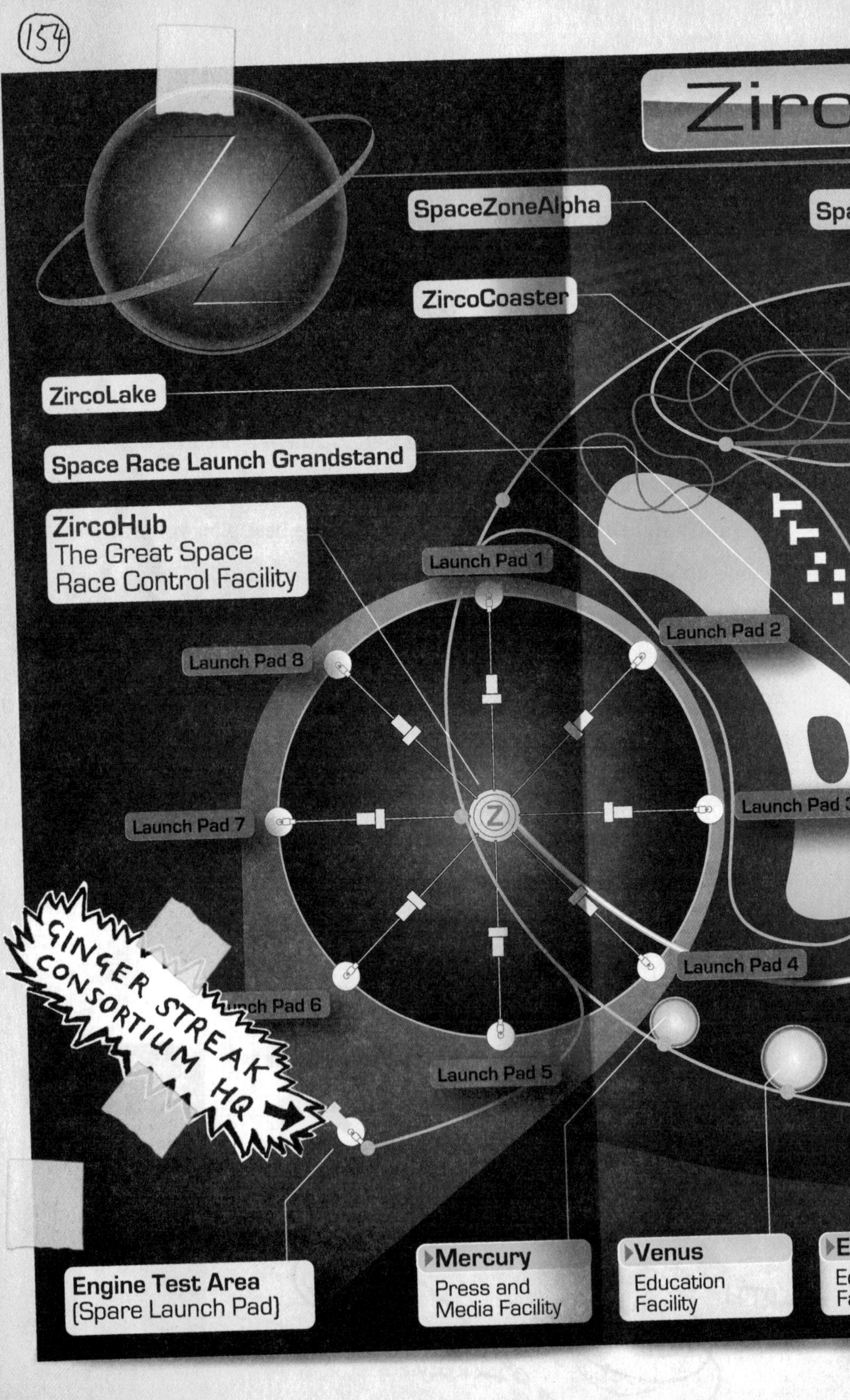
154
SpaceZoneAlpha
ZircoCoaster
ZircoLake
Space Race Launch Grandstand
ZircoHub
The Great Space
Race Control Facility
Launch Pad 1
Launch Pad 2
Launch Pad 8
Launch Pad 7
Launch Pad 3
Launch Pad 4
unch Pad 6
Launch Pad 5
GINGER STREAK
CONSORTIUM HQ
Engine Test Area
(Spare Launch Pad)
Mercury
Press and
Media Facility
Venus
Education
Facility

SpaceParc MAP

eta

Pluto
Entrance

Neptune
Holographic World

Golf Course

Uranus
3D Planetarium Complex

ZircoFlume
Water Ride

Saturn
Cinema & Hotel Complex

Mars
Museum of Space Exploration

Jupiter
Hotel and Spa Facility

D

C

B

A

Key:

Station	**Monorail**
	The Great Space Race launch zone (Access forbidden)
A	**Hotel**

+00:00:05:00

YEAH BABY!
MAIN ENGINES TO
FULL POWER

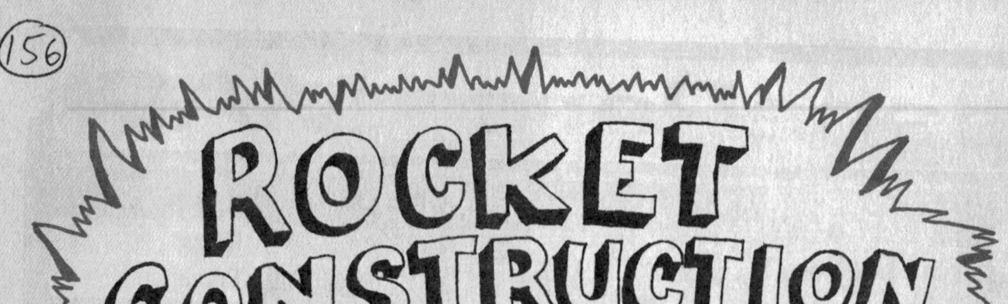

So, I can hear you asking, how easy is it to actually build a rocket? Well, I, Ace Crankshaw, rocketeer, can tell you from first-hand experience, that it is quite difficult – but not impossible.

When Ginger Streak was mothballed all those years ago, she was ready to fire. They had just disconnected each of the three rocket stages and boxed them up. All we had to do now was slot them back together again. And there wasn't anyone better suited to the job than my old man.

Now I don't want you to think I, the Quads or even Dad knew what all the wires we connected together actually did, because I can tell you for certain we hadn't got a clue, but each was numbered and each was shown in the manual in a neat drawing.

Our first job was to join up the three stages while the whole rocket was still horizontal. We borrowed the ZircoSpaceParc's hydraulic crane to shift the three sections off the back of the trailers. They were mounted in support frames on wheels, so once they were on the ground they were easy to position in a line. We wheeled the second stage in to meet the huge first stage. They were superbly engineered, and fitted together totally smoothly. There were four electrical connectors which slotted together as easily as a USB cable plugs into a computer (they were larger, obviously, and old-skool-looking). Dad tightened the ten

bolts around the circumference, and joined the first two stages together. Next we connected the two side boosters.

"Explosive bolts," explained Dad, tapping them with his spanner. "When the boosters have used all their fuel, these bolts fire. The boosters separate and fall back to Earth, leaving the rest of the rocket to push on into space a bit further until the first stage runs out of fuel, then it falls away..."

"Yep, OK. I get the idea, Dad," I said. I doubted he really knew much more about it than me.

We wheeled the third section in and attached it with surprisingly little fuss, connected the wires and tightened the bolts. The Quads weren't a whole heap of help, but they did pass Dad tools when he needed them. Construction was almost too easy. We lowered Zircon's brand-new moon probe into the cargo bay and adjusted the retaining straps. This turned out to be the most difficult job of the day, but with a bit of welding, Dad managed to bodge it in.

"Bolt-together technology," he said, taking a slurp of tea. "One finished rocket. All we need to do now is point her to the sky."

"I tried to get through to spy HQ, but the phone still doesn't work," said Shufty, approaching from the direction of the accommodation block with a look of thunder.

"Any word from the Lavishams?" I asked.

"That Nikki followed me around every second I was over there – but yes." Shufty pulled out an email printout and read aloud, "Eric and Siobhan. Sorry we can't make it to the launch. Our uncle Jed has died, so we are going to the funeral instead."

"Eric and Siobhan. No one ever calls us by our real names," I said. "Frank didn't write this."

"Oh, you don't say?" said Shufty. "Of course it's a warning. We have to assume Zircon's got them."

"And Zircon's a crazy old madman," said Tuesday. "He could've kidnapped them and be holding them for an enormous ransom to make himself even richer, or could have sold them to a pirate ship to be keelhauled."

"Now steady on, Tuesday. I'm sure they'll turn up," said Dad, optimistically. He'd made a study of looking on the upside of terrible situations. "Perhaps they really have been called away to the funeral."

"Yeah, and perhaps Tuesday's right," sighed Shufty.

If we were relying on the Quads to explain what was going on, then we really were in deep trouble. We had to find out where the Lavishams had got to. I doubted they were being keelhauled (Tuesday's grasp of what was history and what wasn't could throw up a few surprising theories). The clock was ticking and we were no nearer to finding out what the Great Space Race was really all about. None of the pieces fitted together. We were as far from discovering the truth as we had ever been, but now we'd lost the Lavishams into the bargain. Our new job as spies was hardly proving a great success. So far we'd discovered double-0 nothing at all.

EXPLOSIVE COUPLING – SIDE BOOSTER TO MAIN BODY

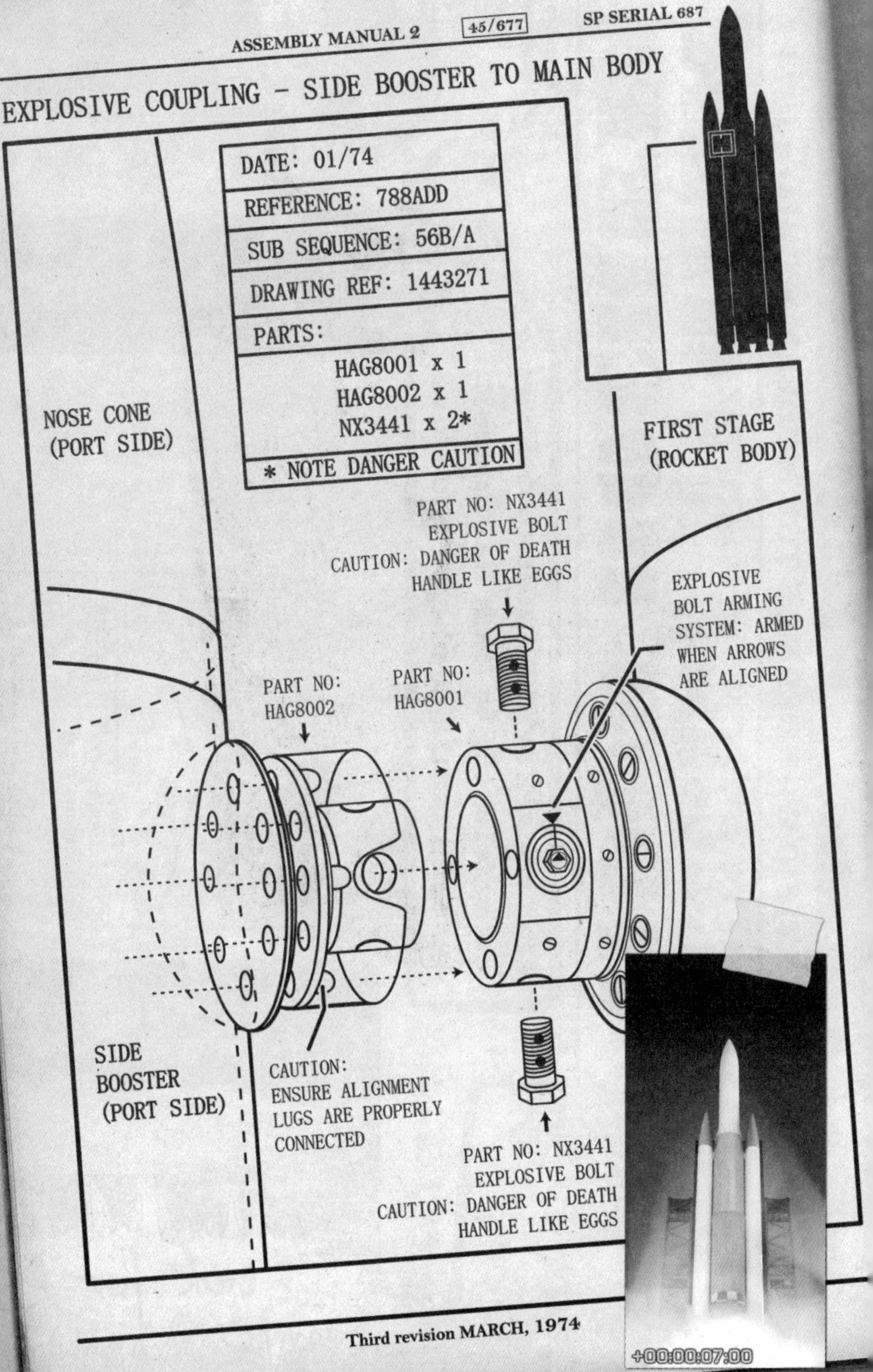

DATE: 01/74
REFERENCE: 788ADD
SUB SEQUENCE: 56B/A
DRAWING REF: 1443271
PARTS:
HAG8001 x 1 HAG8002 x 1 NX3441 x 2*
* NOTE DANGER CAUTION

NOSE CONE
(PORT SIDE)

FIRST STAGE
(ROCKET BODY)

PART NO: NX3441
EXPLOSIVE BOLT
CAUTION: DANGER OF DEATH
HANDLE LIKE EGGS

EXPLOSIVE
BOLT ARMING
SYSTEM: ARMED
WHEN ARROWS
ARE ALIGNED

PART NO:
HAG8002

PART NO:
HAG8001

SIDE
BOOSTER
(PORT SIDE)

CAUTION:
ENSURE ALIGNMENT
LUGS ARE PROPERLY
CONNECTED

PART NO: NX3441
EXPLOSIVE BOLT
CAUTION: DANGER OF DEATH
HANDLE LIKE EGGS

+00:00:07:00

SCIENTIFIC WONDERS OF THE MODERN WORLD – 1974

'GINGER STREAK' MOON ROCKET

3..2..1... Blastoff! How Ginger Streak could look

This rocket will be able to deliver a satellite into high Earth orbit, or even land a probe on the Moon

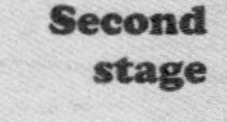

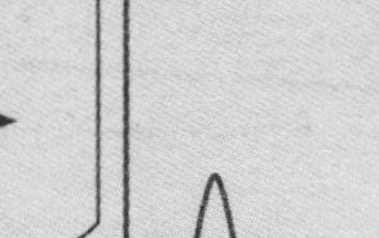

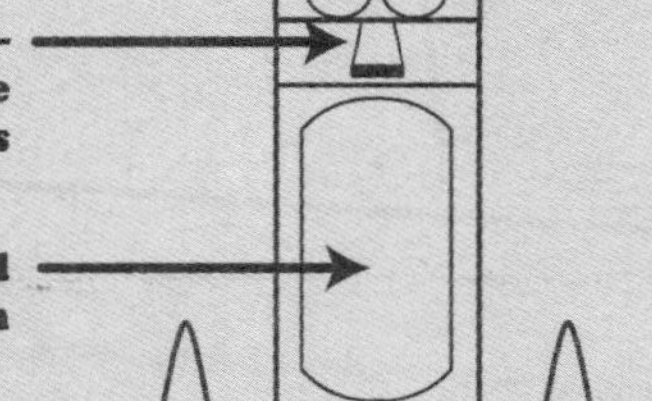

Not bad for £5

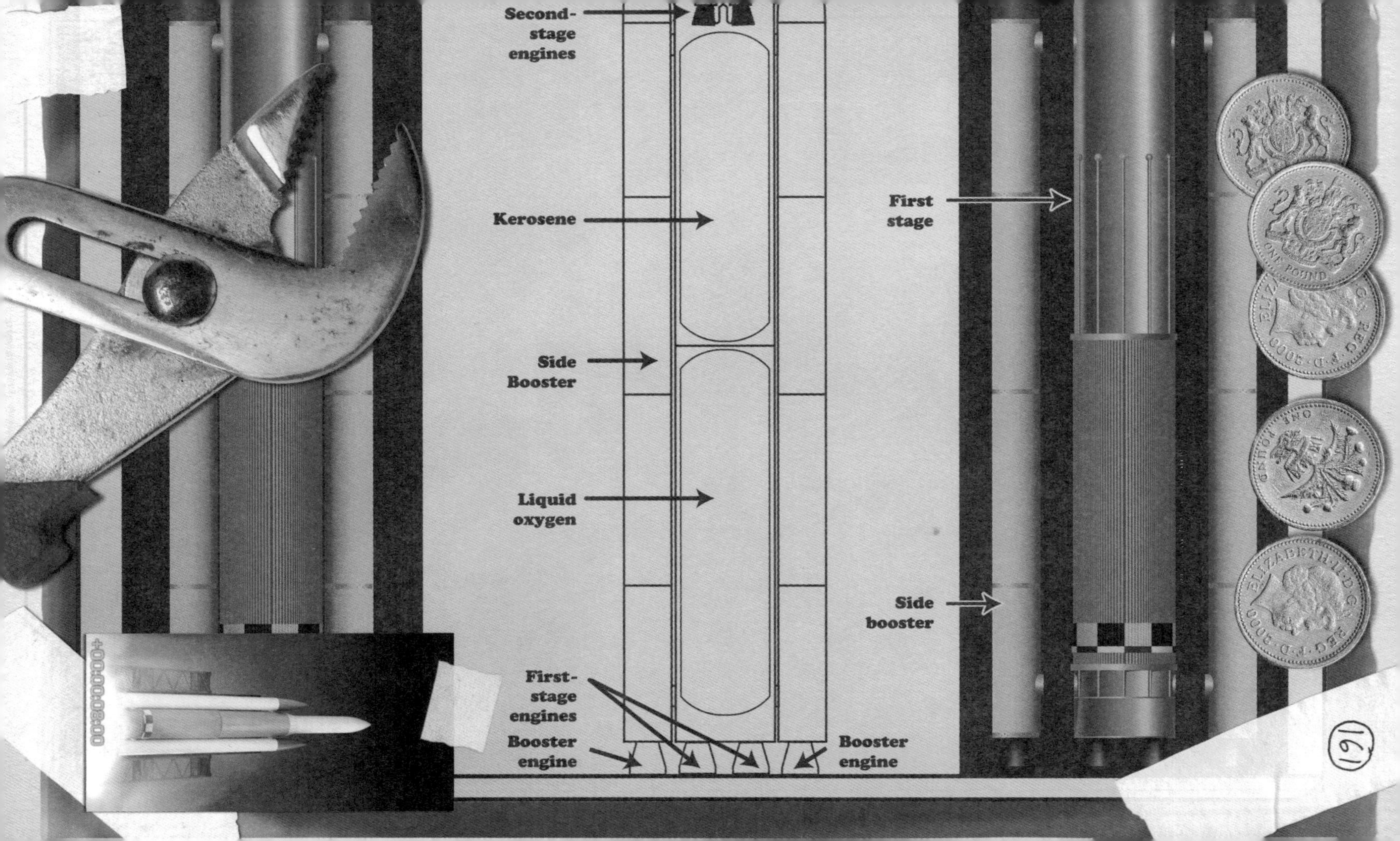

Second-stage engines
Kerosene
Side Booster
Liquid oxygen
First-stage engines
Booster engine
Booster engine
First stage
Side booster
161

Sir George Ginger (1910-1974)

BRILLIANT ROCKET DESIGN FACES UNCERTAIN FUTURE

THE END OF A DREAM: LAUNCH CANCELLED AS 'GINGER STREAK' ROCKET PROGRAMME CLOSES

BY JAMES TOOT, Chief Science Correspondent

The British aviation entrepreneur and business tycoon, Sir George Ginger, has died suddenly of a heart attack leaving his personal space programme in jeopardy. His tragic death was announced only two days after rumours surfaced that his space rocket, nicknamed by the press *Ginger Streak*,* was undergoing final assembly in Australia, and was ready for launch.

The story has elements of high drama; Last month political pressure from the Russians was being applied via the United Nations to try to stop Sir George's rocket building activities. The idea of a non-governmental space programme has alarmed many politicians worldwide suspicious of Sir George's ultimate plans for private rocketry and satellite launches. The consensus amongst many politicians in Britain is that satellites have no useful future in the commercial marketplace of the 20th and 21st century.

Sir George's plan to run the first privately owned rocket company operating a viable space vehicle have undoubtedly come very close to success – but at a considerable cost. Financial experts believe his scheme has placed an almost impossible debt burden on his other various aerospace businesses.

Since Sir George's death, fears that his rocket technology could fall into the wrong hands and be used as some sort of intercontinental ballistic missile have resulted in a rapidly concocted Australian and British Government initiative; a compulsory purchase order has been placed on the rocket 'to safeguard its future'. With the Australian Prime Minister's blessing, the project will be placed in the hands of the Royal Air Force for further evaluation in the UK.

The lack of any fight by the management of Sir George's space and aviation company against this high level purchase order indicates to some commentators that the project had virtually bankrupted Sir George, and his death could well have been a result of stress. An unconfirmed report quotes the chief scientist of his Australian operation explaining: "We had the rocket ready to launch, but the boss couldn't afford to fuel her up. We haven't been paid for months, either".

But don't expect to see any launch in the near future. A spokesman for the RAF said yesterday that they had no plans to attempt to fire the rocket. It will be boxed and shipped to Britain.

Many scientific questions are posed by this private rocket programme: what is *Ginger Streak*; what is she capable of; and why ever did Sir George build her?

The rocket has been designed to fire satellites into orbit, or launch a much smaller probe capable of landing on the Moon - by any measure a spectacular achievement with private funding.

Astronomy and lunar studies were a lifelong passion for the millionaire Sir George. He took nightly observations of the heavens whenever the weather conditions allowed. His driving ambition was to walk on the surface of the Moon before he was 75.

The multistage rocket complete with side boosters performed consistently well in tests. These were carried out on Sir George's vast tract of Australian outback bought especially for the purpose. His three sheep stations measured over 400 square miles, giving him a superb rocket proving ground.

Initial engine development began six years ago, with the creation of the GG-100A rocket engine. This was rapidly developed into the GG-500 production engine generating enough theoretical performance to lift his proposed rocket into orbit. Test proved it to be a robust and reliable design not prone to combustion instability or excessive vibration.

The side boosters and other stages were designed in parallel with the engines. SP SERIAL 685 was the first of two successful test vehicles. 685 and 686 both launched in the summer of 1973 carrying dummy payloads to prove guidance systems and gather data. The third and final rocket, 687, was to be the first attempt to land a probe on the Moon. It is this rocket that has been purchased.

The team of scientists running the programme are all expert in their fields,

MOTHBALL rocket SP Serial 687 will be transported to Britain for assessment by the RAF. A future launch remains possible, although further development is unlikely.

* 'BLUE STREAK' (1955 – 1972) WAS A BRITISH ROCKET. ORIGINALLY A BALLISTIC MISSILE – LATER USED AS THE FIRST STAGE OF 'EUROPA'. A SATELLITE-LAUNCHER

THE BEST FIVE QUID I EVER SPENT

£5 £5

The next morning Dad bounded up into the crane's cab and started up the engine. We were about to manoeuvre the rocket into position. As ever, the old man showed no fear. "Ready, Ace?" he asked. I checked Shufty had the Quads positioned well away from the action. I gave him the thumbs-up. Here we go, I thought. If the cable breaks, this whole rocket business could be over before we start.

Dad elevated the massive crane arm up into the sky to its full height. He double-checked the hoisting cable, then, using the controls, he gently began to lift the rocket. It inched off the ground, the nose rising towards the cloudless blue sky. The crane began to struggle as the engines responded to the weight. Up, past forty-five degrees ... up and up. The tail of the first stage's cradle scraped on the concrete, as Ginger Streak notched higher, pointing straight up to the stars. Then suddenly the rocket was vertical! He'd done it!

The old man, chin jutting out with his "I'm concentrating" face on, edged the

GINGER STREAK ON THE LAUNCH PAD THE NIGHT AFTER WE REBUILT HER!

rocket towards the launching platform, shifting it into place with unusual care and attention. He eased the rocket down on to the launch base, and with a slight kerrr-thump, it landed.

"It's there, Dad!" shouted the Quads, whooping and running about.

"Wow," said Dad, shielding his eyes against the sun and jumping down from the cab. "Not bad for a fiver, hey, Ace? Not bad at all." Dad wiped the grease off his hands. "No time to waste. Let's get started on the ground-control computer set-up."

I was still gazing up at my rocket. MY rocket. There in front of me.

After days of our piecing back together the intricate parts of Ginger Streak, our rocket now stood glinting in the sunshine. The British space programme was back on track. I wished that Jake could have been there to see it.

Ki-Ki strolled into view, carrying an aluminium flight case.

"I thought we'd shaken her off?" muttered Dad.

Nikki followed along behind with a worried look on her face.

"Hello, darlings," said Ki-Ki cheerfully. "I've brought you a camera. My techie guys say it will work from space. Means we can watch your rocket all the way to the Moon. It's only little. Just wondering if you could pop aboard so we can get some exclusive pictures? How does that sound?"

"There's not much room," said Dad.

"Oh, we'll pay you, of course," said Ki-Ki. "Exclusive worldwide TV rights. Worth a few quid.

I've brought a contract with me. Nikki says it is fine."

Dad's scowl turned into a false smile. "I expect we can find room for it somewhere, can't we, Ace?"

If there's the promise of hard cash, then there was never any doubt in my mind we'd find it some room.

"Ki-Ki," I said. "I was wondering if you could call this number. It's the Lavishams'—"

Nikki grabbed the piece of paper off me. "Now I've told you, nobody is allowed to contact the outside without clearance. It's against Space Race rules. Ki-Ki, I must ask you to leave the Ginger Streak assembly area, immediately."

"Temper, temper, darling," said Ki-Ki. "Now what about this interview with Mr Zircon?"

"It was worth a try," Shufty said to me, with a smile.

"We're stuck here until the launch," I replied, as we watched Ki-Ki stroll off with jailer Nikki. "There's no way out of this place. Zircon's trapped us."

"Your rocket looks good, though, I'll give you that," Shufty said with a rare smile. "Not bad at all, Ace."

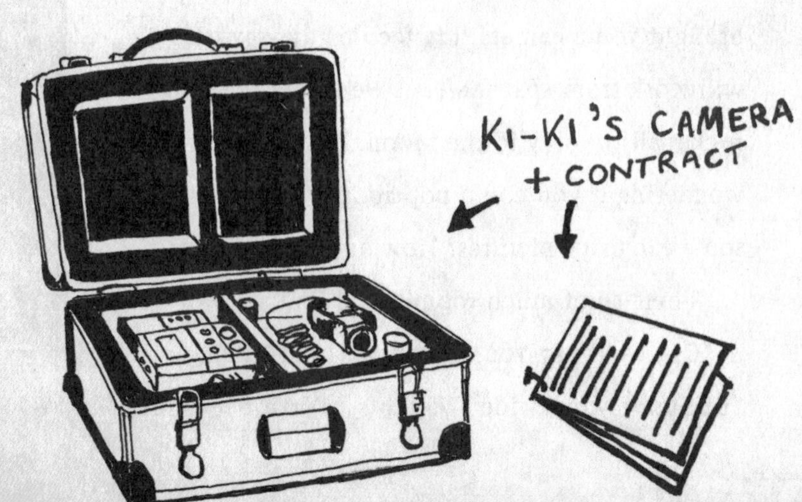

THE TEA BREAK OF DESTINY

The Great Space Race launch day had arrived. This was it! I'd hardly slept all night for thinking about it. The rocket was ready, fuelled up, and sitting on the launch pad, and we just had that £6,000 gig to play live on TV to the entire world before the race began. Quite a busy day then, all in all.

The grand ballroom at the ZircoSpaceParc was the biggest venue we'd ever played and, let's face it, were likely ever to play again: six hundred guests stuffing their faces at a party as big and glamorous as the Oscars. Circular tables were arranged around the room, with waiters and waitresses weaving between them with trays of food and bottles of champagne. When the moment came to climb the neon-lit stairs to the stage, I was shaking in my boots. For once Dad wasn't excited – no, for the first time in his life he actually looked worried.

I felt a whole heap better once I was reunited with my guitar. We took our seats and kicked off with "Fly Me to the Moon". We did OK, and I felt less nervous once I was playing. Dad adjusted the height of the microphone stand with a twist, then launched into his stage act, one joke wandering aimlessly into another. The audience were laughing as he got into his stride. I kept looking into the crowd, the faces a blur in the darkness as we were blinded by the lights. I eventually found Zircon seated at a table with the seven billionaire competitors. But during our second number I was surprised to see them all stand up and file out, Zircon leading the way in his wheelchair.

"Shufty! Ace!" Someone was calling me from stage right. "Guys!" My heart jumped into my mouth. It was Frank! He was on all fours, his face covered with dust and muck, beckoning us crazily to get off stage.

Shufty saw him.

"Oh my God! What's Frank doing here?" she whispered, casting a quick glance at the old man. She made a snap decision. "Dad's hardly got started. Quads, tea break."

We filed out just at the moment Dad got a huge round of applause. The Quads brought Barry with them, of course; he was still stuffed inside the rucksack. Backstage, Frank hustled us towards one of the dressing rooms. "Lock the door," he ordered, slumping into the chair. He had the wild-eyed look of a hunted animal, while his hands were scuffed with bloody scrapes.

"What's going on? You were meant to be here days ago," said Shufty. "We heard you were at Jed's funeral."

"Yeah, well, our plans changed after we said goodbye." Frank dropped his shades down to cover his eyes. "We never went to no funeral, that's for sure. Boy, am I glad to see you guys."

THE SECOND EVER INVITATION THE CRANKSHAWS HAVE EVER HAD

You are cordially invited to
The Great Space Race
Night Gala Charity Dinner
at the
SpaceParc Grand Ballroom

"So where have you been, then?" I asked. "We thought you'd never show up."

"Oh, you know. Kinda being kidnapped."

"I told you," said Tuesday. "And keelhauled as well, I bet."

"Who kidnapped you? When?" I asked.

"About ten minutes after we'd left The Mill," Frank told us, "Clive and Beverley pulled us over and grabbed us. They're not British agents. Those jokers work for Zircon. They flew us over here in a private jet, then locked us up!"

"Oh, we've been so badly duped by Zircon," groaned Shufty. I was thinking exactly the same thing. "We've fallen into his trap. Like Frank and the Prof. But why? What does he want from us?"

I ran through the situation in my mind. There was only one reason that made any sense. "He needs us here in America for some reason, like he needed to fry Barry's brain to stop that Prometheus message getting out."

"He wanted to know exactly what the Prof had told us about the race," said Shufty. "Zircon must have known your mum was on to him. His security guards chased her out of the reception in New York."

I began to see what had been going on. "By using Clive and Beverley he could find out what we knew, and make sure we turned up here in America by making us think we were spying for the British government."

"He must really want us to be here, then," piped up Monday. "And there must be a really, really, really good reason – it can't be to let Ace's ropy old rocket into his race because Zircon hates our guts

and he would no way give us all those millions of dollars even if we did get to the Moon first."

True, I thought.

"Where's your mum, Frank?" I asked.

"They took her away about an hour ago. Split us up. They moved me to another room. I kicked out a vent and started to crawl."

"How did you find us?" I said.

He nodded to the stage. "I heard that violin thing your dad plays through the air-con." Enough said. "Mom's still down there someplace, I don't know where."

"We've got to find her," I said. "We'll leave Dad on stage, rescue your mum, then all clear out of here fast and find the cops."

Shufty was thinking through the plan. "What about the race?"

"The race is a scam, remember?" I said. "There's no point launching the rocket if it's a scam."

"But Ace, that $10 million is our only hope of saving the family," she said, with her serious face, "no matter how slim the possibility. If we pull out of the race we could lose everything."

I thought about what Monday had said. I realized with a jolt that there was no way Zircon would ever give us, the Crankshaws, $10 million. He was a swindling crook up to no good. He hadn't brought us over here to fire Ginger Streak to the Moon. That much was obvious. He had other plans, and we had to find out what they were and stop him before it was too late.

I shook my head at Shufty. "We're officially pulling out of the Great Space Race. I've decided. Now let's find the Prof."

UNCLE JED'S PHONE CALL

We had to help Frank find his mum, but there wasn't much time. It wouldn't be long before the audience noticed we weren't on stage. Dad could crack a fair few jokes and keep the audience entertained for a while, but for how long? Five ... ten ... fifteen minutes max?

Frank led us into the maze of air-conditioning ducts which threaded through the building like veins. I was last in so I could make sure the Quads didn't stray off. It was pretty dark in there, so I handed my mobile phone up the line, and Frank used the display to light the way, its dim bluish glow reflecting off the aluminium walls. It was also pretty cramped in there, so most of the time we crawled along on all fours. We twisted and turned, dropping ever downwards into the heart of the complex.

Frank must have taken a wrong turn somewhere. After about five minutes, I could hear ummmings and errrings echoing back from him. We were lost.

"Frank, do you know where we're going?" I asked, my voice echoey.

"Yeah – kinda," he replied in a harsh whisper.

We pushed on until we reached a dead end, blocked off by a wire-mesh grille. Frank opened it and swung down. We followed one after

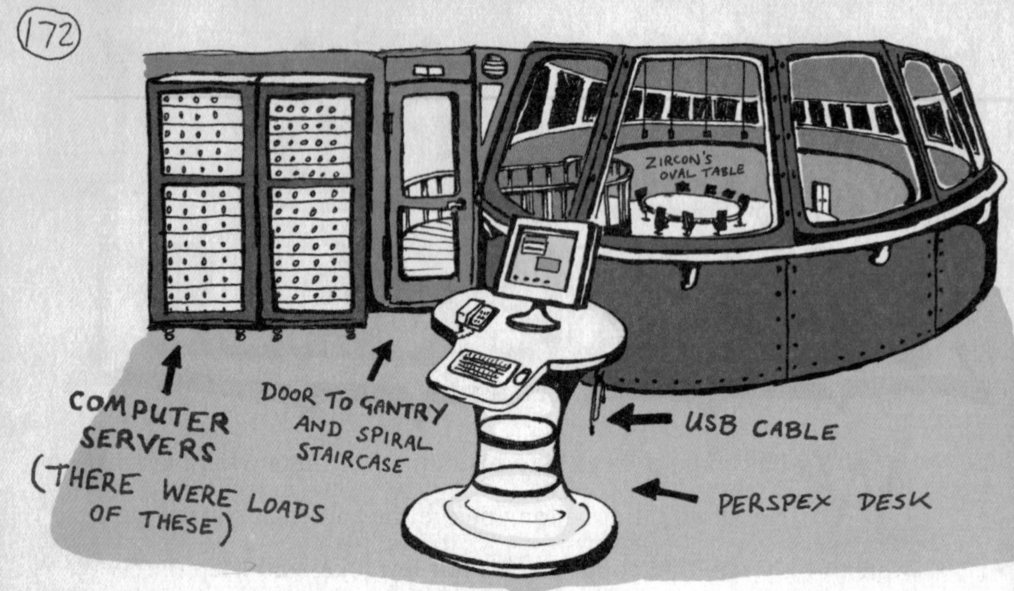

another, dropping like paratroopers jumping from a plane. "Mom's gotta be around here someplace," he said.

The room was filled with computer servers, their fans humming noisily. The walls curved around on one side. It looked as if we'd landed ourselves slap-bang in the middle of Zircon's central computer room. A thick reinforced-glass window looked down on a massive circular room below, containing an oval table with bulky chairs arranged around it. Everything was painted black and lit from above by small state-of-the-art spotlights hanging from the ceiling on long wires.

"We're trapped," said Shufty, trying the exit door – which had a thumping great electronic lock on it.

"There's got to be a plan of this place somewhere," said Frank, eyeing a keyboard, monitor and mouse sitting on a central Perspex desk.

"You can't just start using Zircon's computer," hissed Shufty.

"Watch me," said Frank, and without hesitation he began to do a search for Professor Maxine Lavisham.

Then the phone rang. It made us all jump. And before Shufty could stop him, Monday grabbed the receiver. "Hello?"

"What are you doing?" yelled Shufty.

"It's Jed Summers," said Monday.

Shufty grabbed the receiver and switched to speaker phone.

"Uncle Jed?" gulped Frank. "You're alive? How did you know we were here?"

"Frank," said a low, hoarse voice. "I'm trapped. Zircon downloaded me. I'm on the server to your right. When you ran that computer search on my name just now I launched myself and hacked into the phone system. I need your help. I need to escape from here. And fast!"

It dawned on me what was going on. "Wait. Jed, are you actually inside the computer system?" I asked.

"Yep, you got it. I was downloaded using an invention called the Brain-o-Matic 3000. It downloads—"

"—and replicates brain function," I finished.

"You know about it?" asked Jed.

"Know about it?" I replied. "My dad invented it."

Frank winced, his face filling with a mixture of chilled horror and pained astonishment. "I knew the Brain-o-Matic 3000 worked on a monkey, but *people*? Is Zircon mad?"

"I was downloaded – against my will," said Jed. "I discovered some of Zircon's plans for the Space Race, and they ain't pretty. He decided to test the machine on me to keep me quiet. My brain is now just a computer program. My body is cryogenically frozen and stashed away in a vault in the basement."

"Oh, man," groaned Frank.

"Yeah. I tried to escape, but I was trapped by firewalls. I managed to download myself on to that prototype ZircoBot Eve, then tried to make a run for it during the New York party you were at. Of course I was being chased by those Mark 5s and, in the end, my only chance was to hand your robot monkey a security card and transmit a message. But Zircon must have instructed the Mark 5s to destroy your robot, and the message."

"We got the message, but it didn't make much sense," I said. "What is Zircon up to, Jed? What's he going to do with this X7X virus?"

"He plans to take control of the world's data flow with it. Cause a technological meltdown."

"Why?" asked Shufty.

"Not sure. Zircon's going to use eight top-secret US government spy satellites launched last year in order to do it. The satellites' code name is Prometheus."

"Eight rockets, eight satellites, eight billionaires," said Shufty. "It makes sense."

It was all beginning to tie together. Jake had been spot on with his printout. I pulled the diagram out of my back pocket and checked it again. There it was. One of the satellites that Jake had given us co-ordinates for.

"Ace," whispered Tuesday. "Look." He pointed down to the spot-lit room below.

A dose of cold fear shot through my system. It was Zircon.

SUPERHEROES?

Zircon wheeled himself into the room we could see below, followed by all the other competitors. With a hiss from its electric motors, Zircon circled his wheelchair to a stop at the head of the table. As we peered through the windows above them, the billionaires' muffled voices suddenly came through some kind of microphone that had been linked up between the two rooms. The sound made us duck down, nervous they might see us. What could they be up to now?

Once they'd all settled, Zircon raised his hand and began to speak. "The Space Race cover story has served its purpose. It has allowed me to build this rocket facility in plain sight without fear of interruption or suspicion from the authorities. That stage of my plan is over. The next is about to begin."

The British billionaire Neemis, seated next to Zircon, began to pick at his face, pulling off large chunks of what looked like skin. But it was a latex disguise – and the face underneath looked curiously familiar. I couldn't believe what I was seeing. "It's Nansen!" I whispered.

"So *he's* in on the scam as well," said Shufty, entirely stunned. "We've been well and truly had."

"Our situation is quite simple." Zircon's words echoed round the

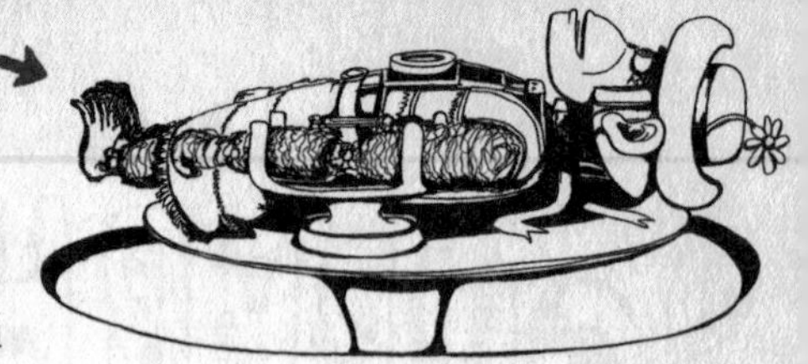

room. "We may be the richest people on the planet – but we're all so old, we're nearly dead! And when we die, our fortunes will become entirely useless to us. Think! All your carefully hoarded money going to waste... The challenge I set myself was to beat this confounded ageing process."

Robert Shredder, the American, banged his fist on the table. He spoke with the menace of a bank robber. "What, then, have you done with all our cash, other than build some dumb rockets and a theme park? How does all that save us – and our fortunes – just like you promised?"

"Mr Shredder," Zircon wheezed through a half-smile. "I have found a permanent solution to the age-old ... *ageing* problem – and for that we need rockets. Big ... powerful ... rockets!" Zircon's dim eyes seemed to roll about in their deep sockets as he then took a moment to cast them over the others sat round the table. I could feel the tension building in the room. Zircon began to speak again. "I offer you all ... nothing less than ... IMMORTALITY. Yes," he gasped, "I have found a way for us all TO LIVE FOR EVER!"

The billionaires looked amazed, but they were clearly still unsure of Zircon. I was pretty amazed myself. *Immortality*? Zircon had clearly flipped and lost it. Immortality was for superheroes, wasn't it? This bunch of old codgers didn't look like superheroes to me. Nope. They looked as if they were about ready for a doze in front of a TV quiz show. Meanwhile, Zircon was grinning as if he'd just taken top prize in the World's Most Dangerous Villain Competition.

Nansen turned to Zircon, some dribble on his chin. "But how? It's just not possible – no matter how much money we have."

Zircon's face snapped back to his usual ice-cold stare. He extended his withered finger and slowly pressed a red button on the arm of his wheelchair. Of all the things that could have popped up from the centre of the oval table, I wasn't really expecting to see our old friend Eve – Barry's sister.

"Let me introduce the first ZircoBot – the intriguing toy on which our survival now rests."

"What? *Eve*?" said Tuesday, as confused as the rest of us.

Zircon relished the moment: "The inventor of this robot is, without doubt, a genius. He is one of the most brilliant scientists on the planet! But, fortunately, neither he, nor the rest of the world, realizes it."

"I wish that judge could hear this," whispered Shufty.

"We shall use the very same procedure the inventor used to create this monkey toy."

Anton Petrov, the Russian billionaire, continued to look very puzzled.

Zircon's face lit up once more. "We shall become digital entities freed from the inconvenience of death. Your brains will be copied onto the computers installed in the moon probes on each of your rockets. When we launch, the probes – and your brains – will reach orbit and attach to the eight satellites already in position."

"It seems impossible! How can you be sure this is going to work?" asked Shredder.

"How? Because Zircon Industries built these very same satellites for the US government last year."

There was a gasp from the billionaires. There was a gasp from us lot, too.

"Cor ... Zircon's got the whole thing worked out, hasn't he?" said Tuesday.

"We shall live as gods," continued Zircon, gesturing skywards with outstretched fingers. "*Digital* gods. An orbiting pantheon!" Zircon paused, again savouring the moment before carrying on. "Then phase two of my plan will activate. The most powerful computer virus ever invented – the X7X virus – will begin to infect the whole world. In

ZIRCON
SCIENCE INDUSTRIES

INTERNAL MEMORANDUM: CODE NAME X7X

OUTLINE:

- X7X is an artificially intelligent parasitic computer application controlled by 8 overlord service hubs.
- X7X is capable of infecting, then controlling, all terrestrial digital data traffic within 53 minutes* of activation.

Computer modelled infection rates (averaged):

10 minutes: 4% global infection
15 minutes: 16% global infection
20 minutes: 45% global infection
25 minutes: 68% global infection
30 minutes: 78% global infection
35 minutes: 86% global infection
40 minutes: 94% global infection
45 minutes: 98% global infection
53 minutes: 100% totality

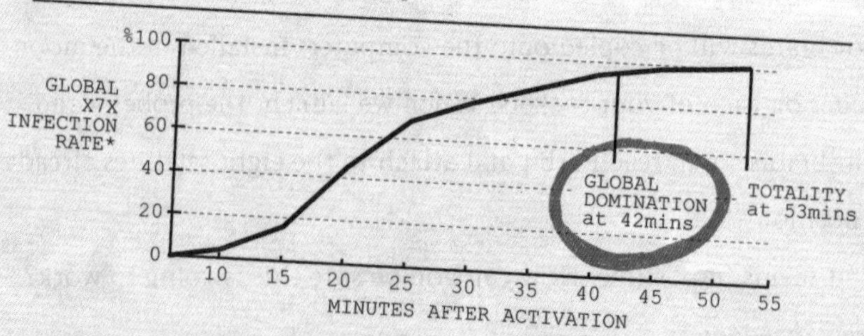

(*ESTIMATED +1/-1min)

- All governmental and secure military computer systems will be under X7X control within 42 minutes (estimated +1/-1 minute). These will include all nuclear missile assets, without exception.
- Once activated, X7X will lockdown all global data flow. Internet, GPS and communications traffic will be denied.
- 42 minutes after activation, X7X will be world dominant.
- Totality will be achieved 53 minutes after activation.
- At totality, control will

six hours' time, my friends, we will take control of the Earth's entire digital data flow by hacking into all of the key satellites – military and civil – orbiting the planet. The X7X virus will also infect the main data hubs here on Earth, with almost 100 per cent efficiency. We will be invincible. We will also be ... invisible."

Zircon backed up his wheelchair, turned and then began to circle the table. "While the world watches our probes racing to the Moon, we will be but moments away from controlling the Earth."

Zircon stopped, took a couple of sucks of oxygen, then hit the joystick and continued his lap. "We will cause total technological chaos. From chaos we will begin the process of moulding a world fit for our return – pencilled in for two centuries' time. By then, our investments in cryogenic research and anti-ageing genetics will have paid off, and we will be able to return to our own regenerated bodies."

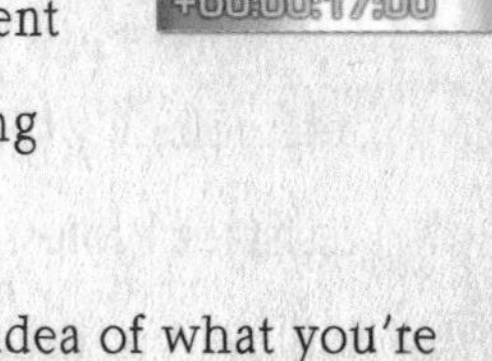

"This is outrageous! It's brilliant," said Neemis.

"The X7X virus is so powerful it will be dependent on all eight of us controlling it," said Zircon, parking himself back at the head of the table.

"And you're sure the authorities don't have any idea of what you're planning?" asked Petrov.

"There have only ever been two weak links in my project," said Zircon, carefully. "The first was a computer programmer here at the ZircoSpaceParc, a certain Jed Summers, who became suspicious of the X7X project. He was caught and has been ... contained."

"The second?" asked the woman in a thin, high, questioning voice.

"Arthur Crankshaw. The inventor of the Brain-o-Matic 3000 and the operating software upon which this whole enterprise depends." Zircon licked his dry lips and swivelled to his right. "Nansen, you and your two agents – codenamed Beverley and Clive – have done an excellent job in ensuring Mr Crankshaw and his family are here at the space port and under our control. Crankshaw's knowledge of his own software makes him ... uniquely dangerous to our enterprise."

"Will you let him launch his rocket?" asked Petrov.

"Never! Within the last hour, a small bomb with an altitude fuse has been installed inside Ginger Streak's payload compartment. This is a fail-safe. Should his rocket, by some accident, successfully launch then it will blow up at 500 feet. Ginger Streak's so-called moon probe is nothing more than a dummy. Besides, I have other plans for Crankshaw and his miserable family of musical urchins."

"Yeah, we'd guessed that," I whispered.

"Can Crankshaw's Brain-o-Matic 3000 really be trusted, Zircon?" questioned Northrup, the German. "You said you would offer us proof."

"Indeed ... I shall now demonstrate the entire procedure using the technology's very own inventor. Meet Arthur Crankshaw and his assistant Professor Lavisham! Crankshaw's children were also due to join us, but they have temporarily gone astray..."

We all watched, horrified, as Dad and the Prof were shoved into the room by a platoon of Mark 5s. Both had their hands tied, and their mouths had been gagged. They looked dishevelled and utterly terrified, and were struggling to break free. My stomach lurched.

Zircon was deadly serious about his crazy plan.

"No way!" said Frank. "Let me get those metal monkeys."

"Frank," I said. "If you go down there, we'll all be caught."

"But we've got to help them, haven't we, Ace?" said Monday, wide-eyed with terror.

"Look, Ace is right," whispered the General. "If they catch us we'll be downloaded, too. They want the whole family."

"We should find help, then," said Thursday. "Tell the police or something."

"OK, OK," I said, thinking hard, but not coming up with many answers. We were trapped down here. I didn't fancy taking on those Mark 5s in a fight and getting mugged like Barry.

Anyway, it was already too late. The backpacks on Dad's and the Prof's chairs were now opening up, to reveal a strangely familiar piece of apparatus rising out of each one. It looked like a large motorcycle helmet with wires threading out of it – and it was identical to a piece of junk that had cluttered up our barn for years: the Brain-o-Matic 3000.

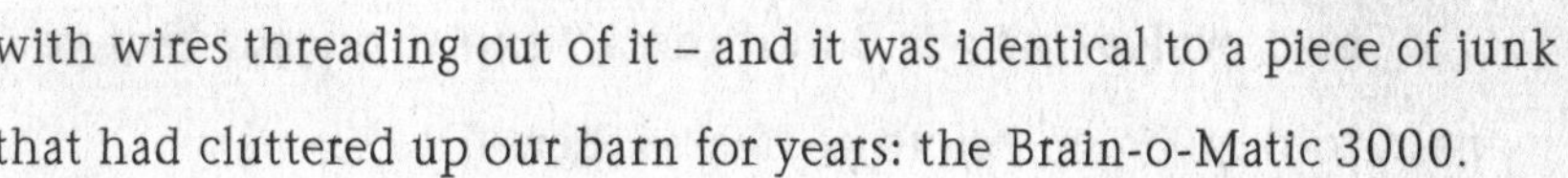

"Dad said we should never play about with the Brain-o-Matic," whispered Tuesday.

I froze with fear. Nothing in my life so far had prepared me for this. It seemed Zircon was about to do more than play with Dad's crazy invention. He and his bunch of ageing billionaires were planning to take over the world with it. The curse of the Crankshaws had struck again.

"OK," I said. "This has gone far enough. Let's find a way out of here and call the cops."

"They've switched on the Brain-o-Matics!" exploded Frank. "We can't just leave! That's my mom down there."

Dad and the Prof began thrashing about in their chairs like fish on a line, trying to escape. The computer screens around us began displaying huge quantities of tumbling data as the Brain-o-Matics copied and processed the entire contents of their minds. The information was being dumped into computer servers all around us, their thoughts converted to digital files.

"Can you stop the downloads, Jed?" I asked, frantically.

"The downloading won't hurt them," explained Jed. "But you need to stop Zircon before he freezes them."

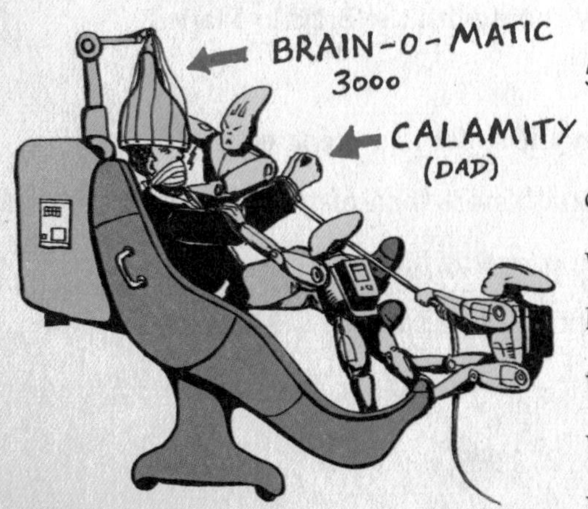

"We'll never get past the Mark 5s," said Shufty. "It's useless."

Shufty was right. What could we do? It was all very well Jed saying we needed to rescue them, but how? If we rushed down there and tried to storm the room somehow, we'd all be caught, so what good would it do?

The Brain-o-Matics suddenly eased back, their job done. Dad and the Prof were still trying to escape, but half-egg-shaped pieces of glass dropped from the ceiling on long cables, sealing them completely. They were still conscious for a couple of seconds, trying to escape, as cold vapour frosted the glass from the inside.

"They're being frozen, just like I was," explained Jed. With a hiss of ice-cold vapour, the cryogenic egg units sealed shut. The billionaires watched in amazement. We lot upstairs watched in amazed terror. In less than fifteen seconds the entire process was complete.

The large screen above Zircon flickered into life. A spooky digital version of Dad's face appeared. He looked terrible and sounded pretty angry, his voice fading in and out. "What are you playing at, Zircon?"

"Mr Crankshaw. You evidently survived the digital transfer?"

"Reverse the freezing process, Zircon. I demand you let me contact the authorities."

"Yeah, right, Dad," breathed Shufty. "Like that's going to happen."

"You wanted proof. Go ahead, ask them a question," Zircon challenged his cronies. "Mr Crankshaw," Zircon went on. "What has happened to your children? Where did they go during the concert?"

"I don't know. We were playing along, then I turned round and found they'd all just shoved off somewhere. It's not—"

Zircon turned down Dad's volume with his remote control just as the Prof completed her digital conversion and shimmered into view on the screen. She was speaking, but with the volume down we couldn't hear what she was saying.

Frank was totally shaken by what he was seeing. "Well, I guess she's still kinda alive."

"And Professor Lavisham ... I'm impressed, Zircon," Nansen said, nodding in approval.

"They have both become computer programs," grinned Zircon with satisfaction. "Exact replicas. They have both been contained. The demonstration is complete. Are you ready for your own digital conversion, now – and immortality?"

The coffin-dodging billionaires nodded like crazy. They were all keen to ditch their ageing bodies and get a new lease of life as digital data.

"Then let us not delay. We have little time before the race begins. We must let the world think the race is real until the X7X virus can be activated."

"Jed. Can you get us out of here?" I asked. "We've got to stop Zircon."

Jed thought for a moment. "Your ZircoBot – Barry. I put a Zircon Industries card in his pocket. That should allow us access to the rest of the building."

"We can't leave Dad here," said Monday. "Zircon might delete him, or the freezing might not work – like that lasagne we ate that had been in the freezer too long and had gone off."

"The kid's right," said Frank. "Your dad is Zircon's greatest threat. He's the only person in the world who knows how the Brain-o-Matic 3000 and the ZircoBots actually work. We need him."

"Jed, how do we get Dad and the Prof out of here?" asked Shufty.

"Those cryogenic eggs are guarded," said Jed. "You won't get close."

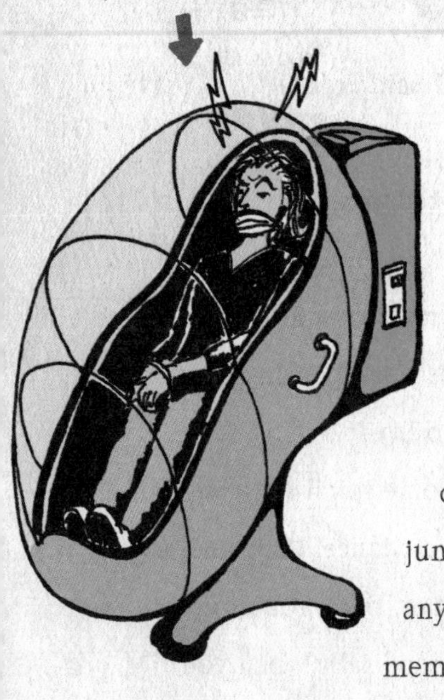
THE PROF ABOUT TO BE FROZEN

A genius idea suddenly struck me. "But we could take a copy of the digital versions," I suggested. "They're right here on these servers. Make pirate copies."

"What? A pirate of Dad?" asked Shufty.

"We could save them on a host computer," Jed jumped in snappily. "A laptop … anything with enough computer memory to save the files."

Tuesday bounced up and down. "But we haven't got a computer, Mr Jed, so we can't, can we?"

That wasn't quite true. There was an obvious solution, and he was tucked away in Monday's rucksack. "We've got Barry," I said slowly, as a superb idea formed in my mind. "We could download them into Barry's hard drive. The way you did, Jed, with Eve in New York."

"Barry won't have enough memory for both." Jed shook his head. "You'll need another ZircoBot at least."

"Look!" interrupted Monday. Things were happening around the oval table. "Look – the billionaires are downloading themselves now."

Zircon and his cronies were all leaning back on their chairs, bracing themselves as their individual Brain-o-Matic headgear fired into life. The computer screens went crazy again as the mass of data began to transfer and Zircon's dangerous world-domination plan started to take shape.

"We've got to work hard, my friends," said Frank. "We'll save your dad across to Barry."

"What about your mum, Frank?" I asked anxiously. "We can't leave her here."

Frank stumbled back to the window and pointed down to the table. He'd had an idea of his own. It was staring us in the face. "Eve. Oh yeah ... we can download Mom on to Eve."

Frank eyed the door leading to the chrome spiral staircase that descended to the room below. There was a chance. We could, in theory, save both his mum and the old man. Dad's robot prototypes were not the ideal place to save them to, especially when you considered their bodged innards, but they were at least all running the same operating system – Crankshaw Works version 1.0. Hmmhhh ... a pair of robot-monkey parents. It didn't bear thinking about.

"We haven't got a choice, Ace," thundered Shufty.

"There are about twenty Mark 5s milling around down there," I said.

FRANK ON THE GANTRY WALKWAY

"You leave them to me," said Frank. He carefully opened the door and crept at a stoop on to the gantry.

"Watch yourself down there," whispered Shufty, her face fixed with grim determination.

Frank gave us a thumbs-up and flattened himself against the gantry walkway, waiting for his moment when the Mark 5s left the room.

"Ace – we'll need a USB cable," said Shufty.

There were several coiled up beneath the computer terminal. I connected Barry to the computer and hoped the upcoming identity change wouldn't fry his brain. Thursday pressed Barry's power button and fired him up.

I glanced through the reinforced-glass window. The billionaires had finished their digital conversion. Their half-egg-shaped glass lids dropped down and sealed their cryogenic chairs tight shut. With a hiss of vapour they were frozen instantly, just like the old man and the Prof had been. Phase one of Zircon's crazy plan was well under way.

But our luck was finally changing. The Mark 5s began wheeling the cryogenic coffins off to storage one by one. The room below was emptying. As the final billionaire was manoeuvred out of sight through the doorway, Frank edged towards the stairs, tense with concentration. He turned and whispered, "If they catch me, run. Get some help."

I felt a bit guilty I couldn't offer him something more useful such as covering fire from a laser-blaster. "Good luck!"

Frank zipped down the spiral staircase in double-quick time, paused, then ran at a stoop towards the oval table and his prize. So far so good.

Zircon's large screen suddenly flashed up a complicated graphic. It almost made me jump out of my skin. It showed that the digital billionaires were now being saved across to the waiting satellites in preparation for launch. The screen divided, showing the competition rockets sitting on their launch pads, each hissing with condensing vapour. A crisp voice said over the speaker, "Space Race launch in T minus two minutes."

As the words echoed and died, three Mark 5s rounded the corner at the very moment Frank was grabbing Eve from the table.

"Run, Frank, run!" I yelled.

"They've seen you!" bellowed the Quads.

"Ace!" shouted Shufty. "It's working. Dad is downloading into Barry's hard drive."

I was caught – happy the old man was being saved, but now terrified for Frank. He saw the Mark 5s suddenly, his mouth opening in a moment of uncertainty.

"Run, Frank!" I yelled.

In a fraction of a second, he doubled back, gripping hold of Eve as tight as he could. He glanced up at me in total terror, mouth open. The Mark 5s picked up speed, scampering after him, their hands already sparking, their shifty eyes turning a bright crimson red, their metallic feet clattering on the concrete floor. Four more entered the room from a doorway to his left. Frank reached the spiral stairs, taking the steps two, sometimes three, at a time, all the while gasping for breath. The monkeys were right behind him, jumping and climbing the outside banister.

I held the door open as he stumbled through, crashing to the floor and sliding to a stop in a heap with Eve.

"Shut the door!" yelled Shufty. I banged it closed, hitting the lock just as the first of the Mark 5s slammed into the glass.

"That was close," said Frank, catching his breath. "Will the door hold?"

"It won't be long before they find another way in, so hurry," urged Jed.

Frank gently set Eve down next to Barry. The Quads greeted her like the long-lost friend she was. She'd suffered pretty badly at the hands of Zircon. Wires hung out of her neck and it looked as if she needed some repairs to her right arm. Thursday set about straightening up what was left of her cowgirl outfit and wiped the smudges off her webcam eyes.

"Cor, that Zircon doesn't look after his toys, does he," pointed out Wednesday.

"OK," said Shufty. "The transfer is complete. Barry's ready. Now plug Eve in."

"Hurry," urged Frank. Shufty swopped the cable over, and hit return.

"Transferring the data now," said Jed.

"What about Jed?" I asked. "We can't leave him here."

Shufty dug about in her trouser pocket and pulled out her keyring memory stick. She glanced at the Mark 5s and then jabbed it into the keyboard. "Jed, can you detect the memory stick?" she asked.

"I'm already downloading myself on to it now," said Jed.

A deep American voice boomed out of the speaker on the wall, making us all flinch. "'Space Race launch in T minus 10, 9, 8..."

"The countdown to blast-off has already started!" I shouted. "This is it!"

The TV monitor showed images of the guests from the gala dinner gazing at massive screens flashing up pictures of the launch pads.

"7 ... 6 ... 5..."

"We're too late!" screamed the Quads.

"4 ... 3 ... 2 ... 1 ... BLAST-OFF OF THE GREAT SPACE RACE!"

SHUFTY'S MEMORY STICK

THE GREAT SPACE RACE GETS UNDERWAY –
THE BILLIONAIRES LAUNCH THEIR ROCKETS

The floor trembled beneath us. I watched the screen split into eight, each segment showing a different rocket. We could feel the power of their engines rumbling through the building. Ginger Streak, of course, showed no sign of movement.

The building shook more and more violently, pulsing with the energy that was released from the engines pushing the eight rockets skyward. They all lifted off perfectly, their engines searing the air with white-hot flame tails.

The Mark 5s were hammering so hard at the door that the glass was beginning to craze with fine cracks. The noise was incredible.

"We don't have much time," I said, my mouth dry now as a result of the fear that was surging through me.

Monday pressed the power button on Barry's back. He sparked into life, reincarnated with Dad in control. He looked about and gave a little "hoo-ho-ho", then stared at his reflection in the Perspex desk. He put his hand over his face and sank down in horror.

"Dad?" said Shufty, peering at him.

Barry, or should I say, Barry-Dad, nodded. His conversion to a robot monkey was complete.

Eve-Prof fired into life seconds later. She sat up. The two prototype toys, both now with the brains of adults, looked utterly confused. Barry-Dad stood up first, lurched over and offered his hand to Eve-Prof. She took it, and stood up shakily, testing her limbs with a few cautious steps as if she was walking on ice. She stumbled on her third step forwards, and Barry-Dad caught her.

For a moment they looked at each other, then hugged.

"No time for mushy stuff," said Tuesday. "We've got to clear out of here."

The printer burst into life, and spat out an A4 page filled with complex data and diagrams.

"Here are the coordinates of the Prometheus satellites," Jed explained. "Take them to the police. It will be all the proof you need to show what Zircon's up to. Listen, in order for the X7X virus to spread successfully, Zircon needs all eight satellites to be working. Even if just one is knocked out, the others cannot function, and his plan will be ruined. This will be our best chance of stopping him from taking over the world. You must tell the police before it's too late."

The Mark 5s were smashing more holes in the glass with a sound like pneumatic road drills.

"We'd better get moving," said Shufty.

"There's a monorail station at the end of the corridor," replied Jed. "It's the quickest way out."

Once Jed had downloaded himself on to Shufty's memory stick, we started to run – Monday stuffing Barry-Dad in his rucksack and Frank with Eve-Prof under his arm, with all the panic of a bunch of bank robbers fleeing the scene of a crime. All we had to do now was persuade the rest of the world that Zircon had to be stopped ... with Jed's A4 printout and a pair of robot-monkey toys on to which we'd downloaded Dad and the Prof. How difficult could that be?

MARK 5s SMASHING THEIR WAY THROUGH THE GLASS!

ASTRO BAZZA

As we ran to escape the computer room, the first Mark 5s finally broke a hole through the toughened glass. They tumbled in after us, and I could hear the metallic snapping of their robotic hands and the scrabbling noise of their feet on the polished floor behind us.

+00:00:24:00

The diamond-shaped key card worked just as Jed had explained. Shufty swiped it through the lock, a green light flashed and it clicked open.

I was last out, checking to make sure we were all clear. I put my shoulder to the door behind me just to make sure the lock had caught and we were clear. It wasn't a second too soon, either. The Mark 5s slammed into the door two seconds after it closed.

The next door led to the small monorail station. Shufty swiped the card through the lock, and again it worked. There was no doubt about it. Jed had saved us from a long, chilly sleep in Zircon's deep-freeze.

The Quads crashed aboard the train, then Frank, Shufty and finally me. Frank hit the menu button on the control panel for the Ginger Streak assembly block, and we shot off up the tunnel. We were clear – but only just.

Rickenbacker

Shufty grabbed Barry-Dad. "Nod if you can hear me."

Barry-Dad nodded his head and spun his good ear for good measure. Blimey. What had we done?

Frank paced back and forth. "This is crazy. Nobody is going to believe us."

"We'll have to make them believe us," I said, with frustration.

"If we take Barry and Eve to the cops and tell them they are in fact your dad and my mom, they'll think we've cracked, especially if we give them the coordinates of a secret ring of spy satellites and tell them it's going to be taken over by Zack Zircon who is now a digital entity," said Frank, catching his breath. "It would take too long to explain. Even if they believed us, by the time they did anything about it Zircon would have all eight of his probes docked with the satellites and the X7X virus working and be halfway to plunging the world into chaos. The time to stop him is now."

He was right. There seemed to me to be only one obvious solution. "We're going to have to stop Zircon ourselves, aren't we?"

"Exactly, my friend," said Frank.

"But Zircon is already on his way to space," said Tuesday.

"Then we're going to have to go into space to stop him," I said. "And I think I know how..."

"What with? Oh, no ... not..." stumbled Shufty.

"Yep, with Ginger Streak," I said, grinning. Oh, yes.

"Ginger Streak is just a dumb rocket," said Shufty. "You'll need to send an astronaut to destroy Zircon. Someone needs to actually go to the Prometheus satellite to sabotage it. There's a bomb on board Ginger Streak, anyway."

"It's an altitude fuse," I said.

"Yeah, we could remove it," said Frank. "It should be safe, just so long as it doesn't go over 500 feet."

"Get real," replied Shufty. "Are you, like, planning to go into space yourself or something? You'd need a space suit, oxygen and some way to re-enter the Earth's atmosphere, none of which we have. It's a stupid idea."

"Barry," I said quietly. "Barry-Dad. He can be our astronaut. Barry could fit aboard Ginger Streak easily. We can blast Dad into orbit. He can destroy Zircon's satellite."

"Cor, yeah, Ace," said Wednesday. "That sounds really dangerous. And Dad would be great at destroying the satellite because breaking expensive stuff and ruining things is one thing we know he's really good at."

But for the rush of the monorail ... silence. Total and absolute silence.

Barry-Dad gave a little "hoo-ho-ho", his head tilting to one side. Had I really just suggested sending our dad into orbit to, er, save the world? I had – and what's more, nobody was laughing.

Barry's ears twirled. Or did I mean Dad's?

Eve "hoo-ho-ho"ed.

I continued to outline my dangerous plan. "Barry doesn't need oxygen. Dad can take out the Prometheus satellite. We only need to destroy one of them to stop the X7X virus. Eve-Prof can help us with the rocket launch here on the ground."

Eve-Prof gave a little squawk.

EVE (LEFT) + BARRY (RIGHT) WORLD-SAVING HEROES – OR BADLY-BUILT TOYS?

"OK, so how is Dad actually going to destroy Zircon up there?" asked Shufty.

"A space walk. A monkey space walk. Satellites are delicate pieces of electronics. He can disconnect the probe, smash the solar panels ... anything. Remember the Mermaid? He destroyed that easily."

The two prototypes looked at each other, then at us. They both nodded in agreement to the plan. Dad spun Barry's good ear, which fell out of its socket and dropped on to the carriage floor.

Shufty gave the faintest of smiles, then nodded too. "We're still in with a chance," she said. "Just as long as that rocket of yours actually fires, Ace."

"Ginger Streak will launch," I said, my fear suddenly dissolving. "It *has* to fire. I know it will."

BOMB DISPOSAL FOR BEGINNERS

Ginger Streak's forty-year-old engines were visible through the reinforced viewing window. I had a sinking feeling. Had we bolted all the pieces together correctly? If we'd known the world depended on it, we might have checked everything more carefully. Would that bomb go off accidentally?

Eve-Prof scampered straight to the launch control computers, and began to power up the ancient system.

Shufty took charge. "Ace and Frank. Disconnect the bomb and get Barry-Dad aboard the rocket. The Quads and I will help the Prof."

Frank jammed a chair under the front-door handle and barricaded us in. "That should hold off any intruders for a while."

I grabbed Barry-Dad, Dad's tool belt and a roll of silver duct tape for good measure. The rocket was standing clear from the assembly building, ready to fire. "Hit the launch-platform retraction button," I said.

Frank did as I asked. Outside, the rocket began to move towards the assembly building. He looked nervously at the massive rocket looming towards us. "Do you actually know what you're doing?"

"Not really," I said, getting into the lift. In an ideal world, the Crankshaw family wouldn't be the first choice to save the planet. The thought of blasting the old man into space made me quake in my boots. What if the digital version of Dad got stuck up in space, and we couldn't defrost the original? What then? We'd be Dad-less. What if the rocket blew up with him on board? I tried my best not to think about it.

Meanwhile Frank was coming up with some more worries of his own. "Does your dad know how to sabotage a satellite?"

I looked at Barry-Dad. He twisted his ear, then reached out and grabbed his favourite cordless drill from the tool belt. He gave the trigger a couple of squeezes and whizzed it up to speed, as if to say he was ready to give it a good try.

I took the long view. "Everything he touches generally goes wrong. It's like a reverse superhero power he has. We just need to aim him in the right direction and destruction usually follows."

"Like night follows day?"

"Yep. It's what he does best."

As we began our ascent to the nose-cone level of the rocket, I prayed the computer would fire up and Dad's repairs to the fuse panel wouldn't give out. The lift was an open design with no glass. I peered down to the ground floor to see the Quads and Shufty scurrying around the computer consoles powering everything up.

There were still no Mark 5s in sight, but for how long? Frank's face said it all – a mixture of 1) fear 2) bewilderment and 3) old-fashioned sweaty panic.

We reached level five just as Ginger Streak glided to a stop outside.

"We have to hurry," I said. "Those ZircoBots are bound to follow us here."

I opened the blast-proof door, and there was Ginger Streak. The night air rushed in and about me, cool and instantly refreshing. I glanced down, seeing the whole length of the rocket all the way to the engines far below. We'd fuelled the rocket before the gig, so even without

Zircon's extra help the whole thing was like a bomb ready to go off. My hands were trembling with the adrenalin and pure fear pumping around my system.

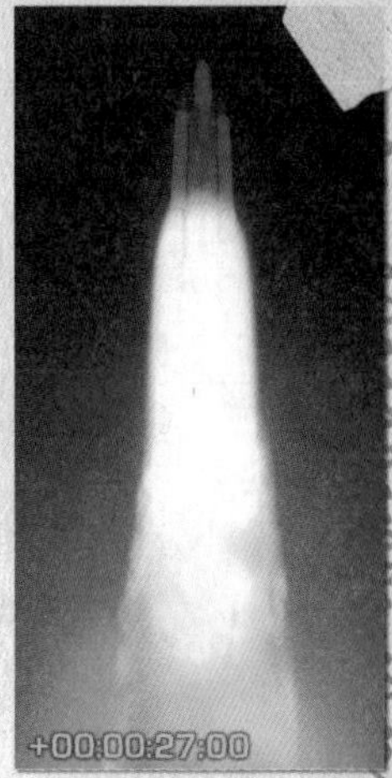

I opened the access hatch. Zircon's bomb wasn't exactly hard to find. It was stuck down with tape on one of the moon probe's retaining arms. It was about the size of a shoebox, but made of metal and painted matt black. A red digital display on the side told us it was armed, so Zircon had been telling the truth. We were now staring at an explosive device stuck to a highly flammable rocket.

+00:00:27:00

I hesitated.

I hesitated a bit more. Bomb disposal hadn't been on the school curriculum as far as I could remember.

Frank tapped me twice on the shoulder and nearly made me jump out of my skin. "How's it attached?" he whispered, as if a noise like speaking might set it off.

I examined the bomb more closely, my eyes adjusting to the gloom. "It's just tape, I think. Nothing more."

Frank carefully handed me Dad's multi-tool with the blade out, and nodded. I leant in, right in, and carefully cut the lower tape.

"I'll support it," said Frank, squeezing his arm in and taking the weight.

I cut the last two pieces of tape at the top, and the bomb was free. It was a lot heavier than either of us had expected, and for a second it dropped as Frank took the strain before lifting it clear.

"I'll set it down just here," he said, letting out a long breath. He placed it carefully down and patted it. "What next?" he grinned.

"We need to undo Ki-Ki's TV-camera pack and tape it to Barry-Dad. We should be able to receive live sound and pictures if the stuff works. We can keep a track of what Barry-Dad is up to once he's in orbit."

Two minutes later we had the camera and transmitter free. "Dad, you should be able to talk to us through the TV rocket-cam." Frank stuck the communications pack to his back with the tape.

The old man was wired for picture and sound. He gave it a test "hoo-ho-ho".

There was just enough room for Bazza, but it was going to be tight, especially with the cordless drill. I carefully positioned Barry-Dad where the bomb had been, and taped him in. "Good luck!" I said.

They were now sitting over a fully fuelled rocket. A single spark from Barry's innards could cause the whole thing to blow up in just the way the bomb might have. The old man "hoo-ho-ho"ed and spun his good ear. The first, and possibly last, robo-man-chimp-astronaut was all set for blast-off.

This was it. Everything was set. "I'm closing the access hatch now," I said.

It's difficult to have a meaningful conversation when your dad can only say "hoo-ho-ho". He nodded again, then braced himself. I caught a last glimpse of his ear twirling as I shut the hatch.

"All aboard," said Frank nervously. "Next stop – Earth's orbit."

"We've done all we can here." I carefully picked up the bomb. "Find somewhere safe to hide this, then get back to mission control downstairs."

"Ace!" I heard from far below. It was Tuesday yelling as hard as he could. "Ace! The Mark 5s. They're here!"

Zircon turned Dad's monkey-toy invention (Barry and Eve) into this – the chrome-plated Mark 5. Barry was always quite a laugh. Zircon's robot army of Mark 5s were just plain nasty (but a lot more reliable).

BLAST-ORF?

We were running out of time. The Mark 5s were pounding against the main door. At mission control Eve-Prof had Jed's printout of the Prometheus satellite coordinates. Shufty and the Quads were working through the launch checklist the Prof had put together back at The Mill. They were switching on panels, pressing buttons, and turning dials in the sequence she'd set out. The reel-to-reel tapes were spooling back and forth as the Prof adjusted Ginger Streak's trajectory and navigation for the vital interception.

Frank put the bomb in the shower cubicle of the bathroom on the first floor with five duvets and some cushions over it, then shut the door as gently as he could. "Hey, if you've got a better idea of what to do with it, you just let me know!" he'd said when Shufty had pulled a face at his plan.

Lights glimmered on the fridge-sized panels which controlled the rocket. Outside, Ginger Streak was rolling towards launch position with her new payload. Would her engines fire? Please let them fire, I thought. Please.

"Close the blast shields for launch, Ace!" shouted Shufty.

I pressed the button and instantly a siren hooter started up as the concrete blast shields began to close. The Mark 5s scraped, battered and rammed at the door, desperate to stop us before the heavy shields shut us off from the outside world.

"Faster!" I yelled, willing the slow-moving shields to shut us in and close off their attack.

The Quads took their places at their allotted console, putting on the old-skool headphones and digging out their checklists.

I ran to the main console and switched on the TV Ki-Ki had provided us with for the live camera feed from Ginger Streak. "I've got a picture!" I yelled as the picture flashed into life. "The camera is working!" On the screen I could make out a grainy image of the inside of the rocket illuminated by the camera's small light – Barry-Dad "hoo-ho-ho"ed to check it was working.

"The rocket has returned to launch position," said Frank. "We're ready to fire."

"OK," I said. I was ready to launch my ship. "Everyone take care, and do everything in order. Don't rush it. Just get it right. It is important we get this right."

Eve-Prof gave me the thumbs-up. Shufty nodded at me. I leant forward, lifted the Perspex cover covering the fire button, and pressed it down. It clicked. From a car speaker in one of the control panels, a clipped posh English voice said, "Ginger Streak launch initiated. Main engines start in T minus 30 seconds."

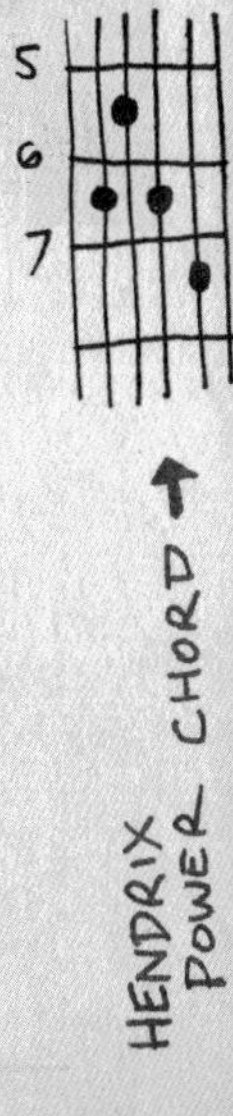

The electronics glimmered and flashed. What it all meant was anyone's guess. Eve-Prof scuttled back and forth along the console, checking dials and switches.

"T minus 15 seconds," said the posh voice.

Stuff glowed behind panels and there was a strong smell of 1970s dust burning as the archaic electronics built up to ramming speed.

The thick concrete blast doors ground to a stop with a clunk. The Mark 5s had been stopped, that was for sure. But I scanned

5
6
7
HENDRIX POWER CHORD

GINGER STREAK'S OLD-SKOOL LAUNCH CONSOLE

the ten closed-circuit TV pictures filming Ginger Streak from various angles, and the metal monkeys were now scampering towards the rocket, no doubt bent on its destruction.

The posh lady piped up again. "Ginger Streak will launch in 10, 9, 8, 7, 6 ... main engines start..."

Nothing seemed to be happening under the engine. Didn't sparks fly out or something to make the fuel catch alight? Yes, there should definitely be sparks.

"...3 ... 2 ... 1 ... blast-orf. Blast-orf ... blast-orf..."

I'd thought we'd hear a spectacularly loud roar as the engines caught. That's what was meant to happen. But there was nothing. Nothing at all.

My eyes scanned the closed-circuit TV screens hopefully. But Ginger Streak hadn't crept even a millimetre closer to space.

"It's a dud, Ace," said Monday. "Get your money back."

"I agree," said Shufty, crossing her arms. "I told you it was all a load of rubbish."

What had we missed? I looked along the panel. The lights had turned to red mostly, and there was a bleep, bleep, bleep sound coming from a button flashing *Fail-safe failure*. What did that mean?

"The cigarette-lighter," said Thursday. "Remember? We need to push the cigarette-lighter in. That's what fires the engines."

In all the excitement, I'd forgotten. That was the fail-safe.

Shufty lunged at the thing sticking out of the panel and punched it in. Still nothing happened. Ginger Streak stood rooted to the spot. So much for the Prof's explanation back at the barn that the starter button would be simple and foolproof. Seconds ticked by.

FAIL-SAFE SWITCH

PING

"Well?" said Shufty.

"Well what?" I said.

Eve-Prof "hoo-ho-ho"ed.

"Any ideas, Ace? It's your rocket."

The lighter pinged out of the panel. There was a puff of smoke from the engine, and the tiniest lick of flame. We stared at the TV screen, transfixed, but the glimmer flickered away to nothing and disappeared.

"Has it gone out?" asked Monday.

Nobody answered. What was it they said about fireworks – never return to them once they were lit? Did that apply to moon rockets? We gazed at the rocket, willing, praying for it to work, but one thing was for sure – the dormant giant wasn't waking up from its forty-year kip in any sort of a hurry.

"Was that a spark?" said Frank finally, lifting his sunglasses and moving even closer to the TV screen. "I'm sure I saw a spark, guys."

"You're just seeing things," said Shufty.

I wandered over to the panel in frustration and pushed the cigarette-lighter in for a second time. "Worth a shot," I muttered.

It pinged out almost immediately, and bang! The engines ignited and the lights on the panel turned from flashing red to steady green.

"It's working!" shouted Shufty. There was an incredible rumble. The engine caught, steadied, then began automatically to pile on the power. The rocket shimmered in the heat, the flame blasting out with incredible energy, until suddenly she began to lift off. My rocket was airborne. I had one thought – I really hoped Jake was watching. She gathered speed, flying higher and higher. The reel-to-reel tapes began spinning backwards and forwards faster than I'd ever seen before. The ancient electronics were steering my five-quid rocket towards the stars.

"Ginger Streak launch successful," said the posh woman. "Rocket on correct track. Course has stabilized."

We watched. The white-hot engine plume seemed as bright as the sun. It made a sort of tearing sound with an undercurrent of angry burble. It was like my guitar amp with the distortion set to ten. I walked forward and watched through the thickened glass in the roof above as the intense light curved skywards. The glare of the engines lit us like actors on a stage. The rocket, trailing a long plume of exhaust smoke, shot through the clouds, making them glow momentarily with incredible intensity. Higher and higher it flew, until I couldn't see the poorly painted body any more, only the fiery tail and the thread of exhaust smoke leading back to Earth.

"It's the most beautiful thing I've ever seen," said Monday, holding his hands up to shield his eyes.

Ginger Streak climbed until she was a pinprick of light. She was curving over now, but that seemed to be part of the Prof's plan. "T plus 30 seconds. Course and speed are good," said the posh voice. "Trajectory holding within limits."

It was easier to see what was happening on the automatic tracking camera now. The rocket was miles up, growing smaller and smaller. There was a slight puff of smoke, and Ginger Streak picked up speed as the second stage ignited.

Frank edged his sunglasses up. "You know, Ace, I never thought it would happen..."

"Yeah, well, nor did I, if I'm telling the truth," I said.

"Ginger Streak is leaving the Earth's atmosphere," said the recorded voice.

The glare of the rocket's engines faded. The smoke plume lit by the engine flare lost its neatness in the winds of the high atmosphere. Shufty turned to us with a smile. "I'm happy to report the Crankshaw Space Programme has reached space."

The Quads gave a cheer. We all gave a cheer.

Zircon's screen above the oval table showed that the first four probes had already docked with their respective Prometheus satellites. The fifth was nearly there. Zircon's plan was working.

"Payload separation in 5, 4, 3, 2, 1," said the posh voice. The probe, with Barry-Dad, was now free of the rocket and in orbit. Destination – Prometheus 1.

I picked up the microphone. "Dad, you're approaching the Prometheus satellite."

I heard a little "hoo-ho-ho" – the old man's first words from space.

Zircon's digitized face suddenly appeared on the giant screen. His eyes glowed red like the Mark 5s'. He was angry. Really, really angry. His face bulged and reddened so he looked almost like a gargoyle. To tell you the truth, he was quite terrifying. He was on to us, all right. It suddenly didn't look too good for us. We were trapped in his building, he was furious, and we were surrounded by his robot-monkey army. Great. Just great.

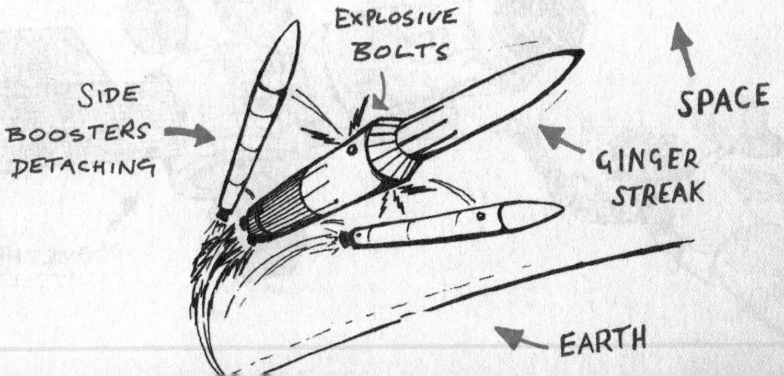

DAD, THE HUMAN MONKEY WRENCH

"Team Crankshaw," breathed Zircon, barely holding it together. "My control hub informs me Ginger Streak has launched. I congratulate you. However, you're off course for the Moon."

"We're on course for you!" I shouted angrily. "We've worked out what your race is actually all about. There never was $10 million, was there?"

"Yeah, we're after you, Zircon," said Wednesday. "You owe us big time."

His image cut to show grainy pictures taken by a camera aboard the Prometheus satellite. Zircon's probe was manoeuvring to dock. A faint glimmer behind was Ginger Streak.

"Before you try anything stupid, I'd like to show you all something," warned Zircon. The TV picture cut to show Dad and the Prof's cryogenic eggs. They were surrounded by four Mark 5s in white coats, their eyes glowing red. "I can boil people just as easily as freeze them, you know."

Zircon sounded as though he was ready to try it. Boiled Dad? That was never in the plan.

"No!" yelled the Quads. "You can't cook Dad."

"That's it, Ace!" said Shufty, watching the screen. "Ginger Streak has released the probe. Dad's approaching the Prometheus satellite."

I glanced at the live picture from Barry's camera. I could just make out Barry-Dad's hands undoing the tape and readying to tackle the Prometheus satellite, the curve of the Earth's surface and blue haze of the atmosphere behind them. The Prometheus satellite looked bigger and bigger in the frame, the detail of it coming into sharp focus.

Zircon's probe was clear to see. It was now attaching itself to the side of the satellite. Finally Dad pushed off and glided towards it across the emptiness of space, the cordless drill already spinning. He stretched his hand out and grabbed the edge of the satellite's right-hand solar panels and clung on tight, then set to work unplugging the left-hand panel.

"What was that?" said the digital Zircon, sensing he was no longer alone.

"A little surprise for you," answered Shufty. "Are you ready to receive your first space guests, Mr Zircon?"

"My ... my Prometheus is losing power," cried Zircon, in disbelief, his voice suddenly very uncertain. "You cannot stop me. Not the Crankshaws. Not after my years of planning."

"Oh, yes, we can," said Shufty. "Nobody makes a fool out of us and gets away with it. You've ruined us; now it's our turn. You're about to be Crankshawed, good and proper."

"Call off your ZircoBot, or you'll never see your dad alive again," commanded Zircon. His image faded in and out suddenly.

But Barry-Dad had set to work wrecking Prometheus I. He'd moved down and opened the side hatch, revealing the delicate electronics inside. In a frenzy of demolition, he started unscrewing everything he could with the cordless drill. He was unplugging stuff too. Handfuls of wires and cables came tumbling out. Circuit boards. Hardware. Disk drives. Expensive, delicate equipment vital for Zircon's X7X virus to work floated off into space. It was dangerous work.

He must've hit something crucial, because suddenly an enormous spark and flash lit up the TV screen. Barry-Dad was blown out and sent flying into the solar-panel wing. The Zircon probe went BANG and detached. It could be seen spinning off in the general direction of the Moon as its positional rockets fired haphazardly. Zircon was suddenly the clear favourite to win his own Space Race, while Barry-Dad was left clutching on to the solar panel of Prometheus 1.

KI-KI'S CAMERA WASN'T VERY GOOD, BUT HERE IS A PICTURE OF BARRY-DAD BESIDE THE PROMETHEUS

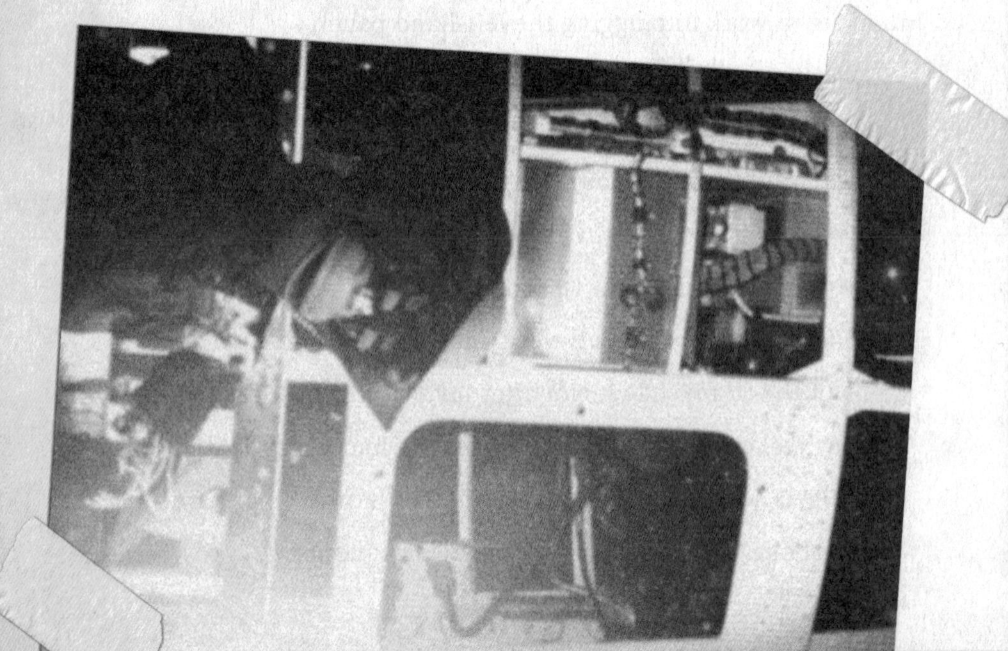

"Dad, are you OK?" I asked. All I could see was Barry-Dad's hand clinging on for dear life.

"Hoo-ho-ho!" came the answer, just as Zircon's tortured face faded to white noise with an ear-shattering yell. Our digital enemy was finished.

"That's it!" whooped Shufty. "Zircon has been disconnected!"

I felt numb suddenly – sick, almost. Zircon's world-domination plot had been foiled by us, Team Crankshaw. Could it really be true? I wasn't sure what was stranger – that we, the Crankshaws, had actually done something that had worked out, or that we'd just launched a 1970s rocket into orbit. I slumped down in the chair, trying to take it all in.

All this self-congratulation didn't last more than three seconds. The blast doors began to open automatically and a siren began to wail harshly. Despite being fried by Ginger Streak's engines, the Mark 5s were back. Burnt, smoking and singed, they were trying harder than ever to smash their way through the glass.

"Errrr..." I said, "does anyone have any idea what we do now?"

With an enormous crash, the door gave out and they began to pile in.

"The koi-carp pond!" screamed Shufty, turning back. "The Mark 5s can't stand water."

It was our only chance. Dad had programmed the prototypes to avoid water. There was a very slim chance Zircon hadn't reprogrammed the newer ones.

We sprinted towards the pond. The Quads were just ahead of me. Behind me I could see a blur of metal monkeys hell-bent on capturing us. I didn't hesitate, I dived in ... just as the first of the Mark 5s clutched my shoulder like a vice.

A second later the creature had me by the leg. I went under the water, thrashing about and trying to push the metallic body away with all my strength. Clearly these ZircoBots were not afraid of water! Soon I was aware of more Mark 5s swimming towards me. Another pair of hands had me around the waist and monkey-hugged me so tight I could hardly breathe, dragging me under water again.

I found the bottom and kicked my way to the surface, and managed to glance around as I caught my breath. Everyone else was in a similar battle.

The attack was relentless.

I lost my footing and went under again, struggling all the time to release the robots' fierce grip. They were dragging me down. I gasped for air and sucked in only water. With an adrenalin surge, I kicked and managed to surface again, but found myself staring into the red eyes of another Mark 5.

Then, with a colossal bang, the metallic head imploded. There, right in front of me. The pressure of the robot's bear hug suddenly eased and I could breathe more easily. There were more explosions all around me. The monkey robots were self-destructing.

"They must be connected to Zircon," said the General, disconnecting herself from two dead metallic monkeys.

"Pre-programmed to destroy themselves if Zircon went offline," I shouted.

"Without Zircon they don't know what to do," said Shufty, wading towards the Quads.

Frank whooped, "Yeah! If Zircon is dead, then..."

"So is his chimp army," I said.

FACE TO FACE WITH AN ANGRY MARK 5

AN ICE-COLD PROPOSAL

We found Dad and the Prof with the other frozen billionaires in a kind of creepy storeroom. Jed Summers and Ki-Ki, too. What she was doing in there was anyone's guess. They were still sitting in their egg-shaped coffins. Other than a slight pained look on his face, the old man looked quite peaceful. He had his Sunday-afternoon kipping face on – mouth slightly open, with a bead of frozen drool in the corner of his mouth.

For some reason I was given the task of hitting the defrost button. "You got us into this," said the General, "so it's your fault if this goes wrong. Five quid for a rocket. What were you thinking?"

Frank looked over at me, his finger hovering over his mum's defrost button. The Quads picked Ki-Ki and Jed.

"One, two, three ... go!" I said, pressing down.

Stuff whirred. Lights flashed. A beeping noise beeped. Lights came on inside and choir music echoed out of the speakers in the side. Vapour shot out of a pipe at the back and the egg-shaped dome lifted off.

"Is he alive?" asked the Quads, peering in.

Tuesday prodded his nose. "He feels ice-cold."

Ice-cold or not, he jerked a little, then rolled over and began to snore. Big Dad snores.

"Yep, he's alive, all right," said Shufty.

The Quads cheered and started to shake him awake. "Dad! Dad! You've just saved the world."

He was completely drowsy and not all there. Somehow he must have thought it was a Sunday afternoon and he'd fallen asleep on the sofa. He began to babble, "Has the *Antiques Roadshow* finished? Is *Time Team* on? I don't think the Prof's neck is all that long really, do you, Ace?"

"What?" I asked. He was back all right, just talking more rubbish than usual.

"What about the Prof?" asked Shufty.

The Prof blinked her eyes open dreamily and, like the old man, began talking gibberish. "I like your father, Shufty. Will you be our bridesmaid if we get married?"

"Did I hear someone say something about a lovely wedding?" asked Ki-Ki. "I can offer you a worldwide deal for the TV rights ... we could all make an absolute fortune."

"What?" said Frank. "Oh, man, no! What a mess."

"You can say that again," I said. "Where's the refreeze button?"

IF YOU DON'T ASK YOU DON'T GET

One week after defrosting Dad and the Prof, we were all summoned to the White House. We told the President the whole story as best we could, right up to the defrosting bit.

The President glanced over at Dad and the Prof, who'd been sitting quietly listening. "Quite a story – and your parents are back to normal?"

"Yep," said Shufty. "Worse luck."

The President sighed. "You saved the world from a bunch of insane billionaires, all with a 1970s rocket fired by a car cigarette-lighter? Outstanding. Quite outstanding. My military people say it would've been near impossible to shoot Zircon down from up there. His X7X virus would have caused complete technological chaos. He'd already cracked into both our ballistic-missile defence system and NASA's entire computer set-up. We wouldn't have been able to fire even a darned roman candle to knock him down. The Space Race was a very close call. Very close indeed."

"We didn't win the $10 million, though," said Monday. "We're still flat broke."

THE WHITE HOUSE – HOME OF THE AMERICAN PRESIDENT!

"We had the right rocket for the job," Dad said proudly, "and what's more, the right team to take on Zircon."

"Mr Crankshaw," asked the President, "how does it feel to be in two places at a time? This monkey toy has an exact replica of your brain installed on its hard drive. You too, Professor – the Eve prototype has a copy of you installed. That must be quite confusing."

"You can never have enough of a good thing," beamed Dad.

"I have some good news for you," said the President, leaning forward. "Barry was picked up by a NASA crew early this morning. He will be returned to you as soon as we have evaluated him."

"Perhaps the military would be interested in buying Barry – after I've wiped his hard drive, of course," tried Dad. "I don't want them getting their hands on my top-secret ideas for inventions."

"I like this guy," said the President. "I like his go-getting attitude. Do you play golf, Mr Crankshaw? We could play a round sometime? Chew over some of these ideas."

"I'm afraid I'm not a keen golfer – although I have been working on a very interesting golf-cart project," ventured Dad, putting on his salesman voice. "It's called the 19th Hole, and has an integrated bar and drinks refrigerator—"

THE 19TH HOLE – THIS IS WHAT DAD PLANNED BUT HE NEVER GOT VERY FAR WITH BUILDING IT

"Not that heap of rubbish," groaned Shufty.

The President was intrigued. "Really, really..."

"It promises to be a very fruitful venture for thirsty golfers. It has a mini-bar built in, you see? And an ice-making machine."

There was a sharp knock on the door. A slap-headed businessman in his fifties strolled into the room, carrying a briefcase. Frank was with him, also wearing a suit, but without his traditional dressing-gown.

They both greeted him formally. "Good morning, Mr President."

"Sorry we were late," said Frank coolly, pushing up his sunglasses. "A few last-minute legal issues, but we've got them ironed out to my satisfaction."

"Arthur, this is Bill Truebody," said the President, introducing the briefcase man. "I have some very good news for you, Mr Crankshaw. Frank here has just been working through the contract for your barbecue idea. You know who Mr Truebody is, of course."

"Errrr ... umhhhh..." stumbled Dad.

"Of Truebody, Truebody and Truebody? Better known as Triple-T BBQs. The largest barbecue-manufacturers on the planet."

Truebody stepped forward and shook Dad's hand warmly. "Yes, Mr Crankshaw, we want to buy your design. It's flaming brilliant! Totally revolutionary! Most of our products are badly made and rust to pieces after a single season. But, this jet design ... why, it's clearly the next step. A flagship product to make our cheap barbecues look world-beating! It's totally unique!"

I didn't need to look at Shufty to see what she was thinking. There was clearly no better place for the jet-powered barbecue than Triple-T BBQs.

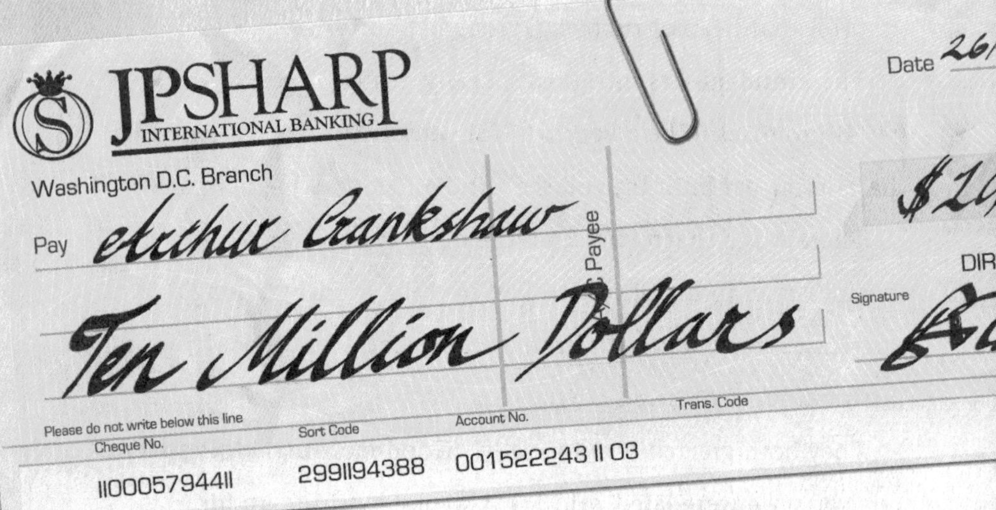

"A $10-million contract," beamed Frank. "Less my percentage."

The Prof gazed over to Dad with a huge smile. "Arthur, you're rich!"

"You see?" Dad smiled at me, Shufty and the Quads. "I told you everything would work out."

But the President wasn't finished. "We'd like to offer a token of gratitude to you and your family, Mr Crankshaw, but to tell you the truth ... how can I put this ... you're a very difficult man to buy presents for. Is there anything you'd particularly like? Any wish I could grant?"

"Well, I'm not sure," mumbled Dad. "What d'you reckon, Ace?"

"There was just one thing," I said.

"Well, ask the President, not me," Dad said.

I leant in and whispered in the President's ear.

"You've got to be joking!" exploded the President. "How do you know about that place anyhow, son? It's meant to be top secret."

"My mate Jake told me about it. Can he come too?"

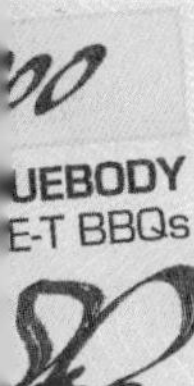

In return for our saving the world, I'd asked the President for a go on his space portal machine – the one Jake was always on about. He'd agreed ... just about. I mean, what else was I going to ask him for? I still wanted to go into space. I still wanted to play my guitar on a distant planet. The Crankshaw luck had finally changed for the better, so I'd taken my chance. That's how we found ourselves, one month later, at the top-secret US government Space Portal Research Facility, in the Nevada desert.

I want to point out that a) I was surprised the President had agreed to it and b) even more surprised that Jake had been right about the portal all along. One thing I've learnt is that Jake never lets me down. He might stink a bit when you're downwind of him, but he's my best mate. So we were all there – Shufty, Dad, the Quads, the Prof, Frank and Jake (who'd been flown over specially by the US government).

"Well, here it is," said the airforce colonel as he ushered us into an aircraft hangar, where a massive, complex and slightly scary-looking machine stood. It was the size of a house, and gave off a low humming noise. The smell was a strange mixture of electrical burning and engine oil. The whole thing looked like something Dad would have made. In fact, he was gazing at it with intense interest.

"It really exists," said the Prof, clearly impressed by what she saw. The Quads looked eagerly at one another, all clutching their musical instruments tight.

The colonel pulled a miserable smile and shrugged. "The problem we're discovering is that space is quite ... ahhh ... big. Finding alien life is proving to be more difficult than we thought. We keep on discovering planets, sure enough, but they're mostly about as interesting as the Arizona desert."

"Any life forms?" asked Jake. "Any advanced technology or weaponry?"

"Sorry. There just ain't much up there that's interesting or exciting. If you want entertainment, why not fly up to Vegas? It's a stack more fun than most places we've been to out there in the blue yonder."

I felt a bit cheated. "What, there's nothing out in space? No aliens? No space ports?"

"None that we've found," said the colonel, scratching his head with a look of total disappointment. "We did find a kinda six-legged rat creature a couple of months back on a planet in the Alpha Centauri system, but we've got plenty of rodents here on Earth, so we left it be."

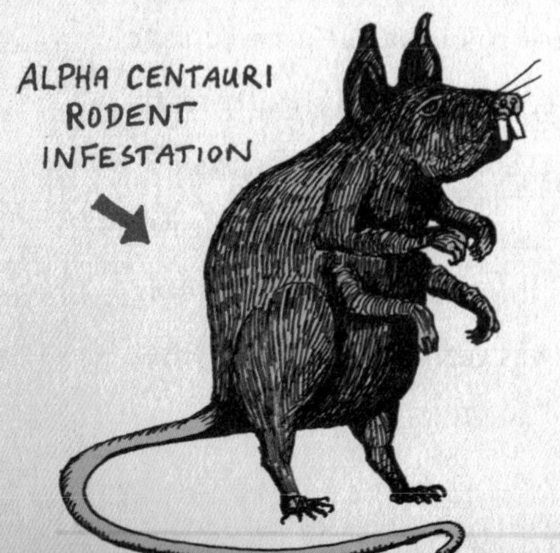

Jake didn't look convinced. It flew in the face of all his conspiracy theories. The colonel looked bored suddenly, as if we were interrupting his morning. "Where exactly do you all want to go, anyhow?"

I didn't like the sound of the rat planet very much. "Where would you recommend?" I asked.

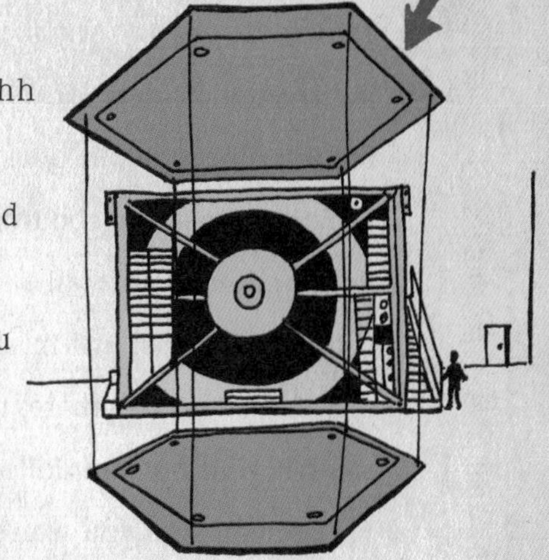

"OK, let me think ... well now, ahhh ... there's this planet off the Belt of Orion we've found, whose gravity and atmosphere are a lot like Earth's," he said, without much enthusiasm. "You could try there if you want, son."

"What's it called?" asked Jake, blowing his cheeks out. He was completely deflated by what he was hearing. Here, at the secret base – in the very hangar, in fact – that he'd studied for hours on Google Earth, he was discovering that space exploration was as dull as a wet Monday morning. The bloke in charge could have been running a fairground ride.

"Errr..." mumbled the airforce colonel. "Chuck? What's the name of that place you went to last week. Began with a B?"

A bloke wearing a boiler suit and wielding a spanner poked his head over the top of the machine. A cigarette dangled from his bottom lip. "Oh ... yeah. Uhhmm ... Bryte Zap 4 off the Belt of Orion. It's a dust bowl. Drier than a Thanksgiving turkey."

Dad grinned. Shufty looked worried.

"Bryte Zap 4, then, please," I said, my mouth drying in anticipation.

"Well, OK," said the colonel, tapping our destination into a computer terminal rigged up to the machine. "Sure you don't want to go to Vegas?"

I shook my head. "No way. It's space or nothing."

Frank stood beside me and slapped me on the back. "Inspired choice, my friend. Any planet that sounds like a cheap floor polish sounds ideal for the first music concert ever given by mankind outside our own solar system. Hit the button, colonel."

The colonel dug about in a beaten-up cardboard box on the floor and handed us all a small earphone device each. "You'd better take these. Just in case. Universal translators. If you bump into any aliens out there, they probably won't speak English. You can bet your bottom dollar on that."

"Are you sure you won't come too, Shufts?" said Dad, tucking the Stroh under his arm.

"It'll be fun," said the Prof. "Come on, live a little."

"I'm not going," she said, slumping into a chair. "This is a stupid idea, and Ace shouldn't have suggested it to the President in the first place. And don't call me Shufts, either."

"We'll be back in ten minutes," I added. "We're only going to have a look about, play a quick Chili Peppers number, then come straight back."

Barry and Eve jumped up and down. "Even these two look excited," I said.

"Are you certain this will work?" Shufty asked the colonel for about the thousandth time.

"Sure! We've had nearly a 100 per cent success rate. All they have to do is press the button on the controller when they want to return. It works a treat."

"I'm not going," said Shufty. "That's final."

We strode out nervously towards the hexagonal area marked out on the floor. I slung my guitar on my back and stood legs apart, arms folded, as we'd been shown. The machine started to make a low rumbling, griping noise like a car with a flat tyre. So far, so good. The room began to vibrate and oscillate. This was it. We were about to travel across space and time. This was the portal I'd always dreamed existed, and here we were – the first family band ever to try it out.

"Ready for the ride of your life, Arthur?" asked the Prof.

Dad took her hand and held it tight. "You bet, Professor!"

My vision became suddenly hazy under the influence of the immense machine. But then the door by which we'd entered the hangar banged open, and a man dressed in a military uniform burst in. I saw Shufty jump up like a cat. He had two dogs, which looked very, very familiar – it was Thumper, in disguise! He was still after the old man's cash. Shufty tried to escape, but there was no way past him. Her only option was to jump towards us – just as the machine fired into life and shot us across the galaxy...

She made it at the very moment everything went suddenly very, very dark. But echoing through the space-time continuum I clearly heard the bellowed words:

"Crankshaaaaaaaaaaw! Get back here!!!"

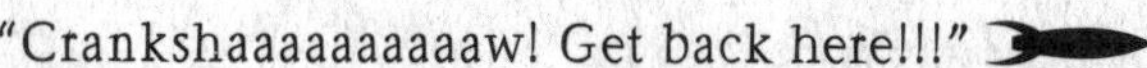

Captain Ace and the Stargazers is my band. It's mainly Jake and me reinventing rock music for the 21st Century.

Our new album is called 'ROBOT • MONKEY • COWBOY • HERO'* It's a sort of CONCEPT ALBUM featuring very loud guitars and drums. Check out some sample tracks at – www.thegreatspacerace.co.uk

(*recorded in Jake's dad's shed)

KI-KI'S AFTERNOON CUPPA

GUEST'S NAME

CAPT. ACE CRANKSHAW

GUITARIST / STAR PILOT (1st CLASS)

NEPTUNE CHORUS:

"WE'VE GOT A FULL TANK OF GAS IN THE SAUCER" (+ HARMONICA?)